W9-CKE-957

The Love Letter

Cathleen Schine

The Love Letter

Houghton Mifflin Company

BOSTON   NEW YORK

ISBN 0-7394-0364-8

Printed in the United States of America

Book design by Melodie Wertelet

To David, Max and Tommy

For the room of my own (which I borrowed from her),
I thank Betsy Frankenberger; for their patience and
good-humored instruction in the bookseller's art,
I will always be grateful to Jenny Feder and Jill Dunbar,
Hilary Sio, Tracy O'Dwyer and everyone else at
Three Lives & Co.; and I especially want
to thank Penny House.

O love is the crooked thing . . .

— W. B. YEATS, *Brown Penny*

The Love Letter

1

THE HONEYSUCKLE WAS EVERYWHERE THE DAY THE
letter arrived, like heat. Wild roses bloomed in hedges of
tendrils and perfume. There were fat bees, dirigible bees,
plump and miniature. It was a sweet, tangled morning, and
the sun rose, leisurely, in a spectacular blush. Helen sat on
the porch and she saw the day, right from the beginning,
ripening like an apple. June was the month that couldn't
last, the breezes so scented with blossoms that the flowers themselves trembled and swayed, intoxicated. An ant
crawled across the arm of Helen's chair, onto the table and
into her coffee. Ants were admirable, she recalled.

The letter came on a Wednesday late in June, the morning that had begun so well. The morning had continued
well, too. Bluebirds, a pair, had grazed on Helen's lawn, as
openly as fat Guernsey cows. Helen's coffee tasted particularly good, coming from a new, fragrant bag bought only the
day before. Steam rose from the mug. There was milk,
unspoiled, in the refrigerator, enough for not just one, but
two cups of coffee. A miracle, she thought. Like Chanukah.

As Helen drove to her store that morning, she felt that

her life was a good one, even with her daughter away at camp and her ex-husband making so much money. She loved her store, loved the books lined up neatly on their shelves, and loved, even more, to sell them. "I'm very good at selling," Helen liked to say, but what she meant was: I love to sell, to talk you into it, to make you my customer, to make you mine.

She drove beneath overhanging branches and new, summery leaves, and she was not only content, but pleased by her own contentment, as if happiness were an accomplishment, a good grade, an honor. She had never liked being dissatisfied. She found it so dissatisfying.

No one likes being dissatisfied, her ex-husband had said. One just is. And she had left him to it.

He's awfully rich now, she thought, turning the key in the door, walking across the sloping floor of the shop. She threw her keys into a drawer behind the counter. Awfully, awfully rich.

Her grandfather had been rich, too. He sold plumbing supplies and made millions. Helen barely met expenses in her store — books were not spigots. But sometimes she could convince her customers books were as necessary as indoor plumbing and, on a good day, as marvelous as running water.

Helen basked momentarily in what she had made for herself. Some things, like the tilted little house in which she'd opened the bookstore, she had to admit that she had not actually made. But I found it, she thought. I saw it for what it could be. And the town — she had grown up in Pequot. But I remembered it, Helen thought. I came back.

Horatio Street Books had four small rooms. Poetry took up the smallest, less than six feet long, five feet wide, a windowless closet really, slender volumes and stout collections side by side from floor to ceiling. The Death of Poetry

2

Room, Helen called it, privately, to herself, in honor of its vaultlike dimensions and its everlasting quiet. She stocked it stubbornly, a foolish believer bringing shiny trinkets, cow offal, marigolds, to a shrine.

Helen smiled at the shelves of poetry, at all the shelves of her store. The two main rooms were filled with fiction and general nonfiction. The fourth room, tucked away in the back of the store, was devoted to military history. This had been Helen's inspiration, a whim, really, that had panned out and so had been elevated in her personal mythology to an inspiration.

The shelves in this room contained more general histories, too, as well as a little sociology and anthropology, the theoretical studies favored at the college nearby, and a good-sized women's history section. But military history dominated. And military history sold — the Civil War and George Custer leading the ranks. It sold daily, to the same customers. They were voracious, insatiable, like mystery readers, only male. Helen had put the mystery shelves quite close to the military history shelves, hoping the two would somehow cross-pollinate, their fruit a new hybrid customer. Occasionally she took this task on herself, bullying someone to buy a mystery along with the new Civil War history he wanted; or to buy *Son of the Morning Star* in addition to the new Patricia Highsmith. But the seed never took, and Helen soon gave up. Each readership stuck to its own, inbred as Hapsburgs, as hillbillies.

—

The mail lay on the floor beneath the mail slot, splayed and exhausted after its long journey, its many, various journeys, a group of strangers with only one thing in common, and that one thing was Helen MacFarquhar. She got all her mail at the store, never giving out her home address. She liked to consolidate, liked the abundance that greeted her. And when she saw her name spelled out like this on all these envelopes, she liked that, too. Helen MacFarquhar. It looked beautiful to her. She loved her name and hadn't even considered changing it when she got married. It made her think of her father, whom she missed, who was always called Mac. Though whenever she herself wrote it, she was tempted to write: Helen MacFarquhar, Jewess. For the sake of full disclosure and, more important, chauvinism. Half Jewess, anyway.

She loved her mail when she saw it lying there, so promising, such bounty, a cornucopia of greetings and checks and invitations and information, fruit spilling from the bowl, the daily harvest of daily life — though most of it turned out to be nothing, flyers and come-ons for car washes or for credit cards she already had, bills and the payment of bills, urgent sweepstakes that beckoned to her misspelled name. But there were also early copies of new books sent by hopeful publishers or anxious friends from the world she had left behind. Letters and postcards came from former neighbors or a roommate from college or her mother, on one of her trips, or a customer seeking information.

On that Wednesday, there were many letters, a pile of large manila envelopes, white business envelopes, small square envelopes of eggshell or powder blue. "Dear Friend." But she was neither dear nor a friend to the correspondent. "Dear Member." But she did not belong and did not care to, no matter how many times she was selected and preapproved. "Dear Sir"? No. "Dear Resident." Yes. That would do. She liked the sound of that. She was a resident, after all. Who wasn't? Of someplace.

Helen went upstairs to the office and made herself more

coffee before moving on to "Dear Reader." Very nice. I *am* a reader, certainly, she thought, then tossed the letter, unread. A few "Dear Helens." Fine. And best of all — "Dear Mommy." How had this note from Emily come so soon? She'd driven her to camp only yesterday, and the card was postmarked two days ago. Helen grinned then. This letter was meant to be there, in the store, to greet her, to soothe the loneliness. Emily had sent it early, before she'd left home. Helen touched her cheek to it, as if the postcard were another cheek.

Dear Mommy,

I bet I miss you already! I bet I'm having a really good time at camp anyway. I probably made a good friend already. I wonder what her name is. I hope I don't have poison ivy yet. I love you. XXOO

Love,
Emily

(The one, the only, the greatest!!!
Soon to be a motion picture starring
Emily, the one, the only . . .)

She wondered if Emily had gotten her letter — the one Helen had sent early so that it would be there waiting for Emily when she woke up the first day, the letter sent to soothe Emily's loneliness. Was she sitting on the edge of her cot reading it now in the dim woody light of the bunk, as Helen read Emily's letter, again, and then once more?

⌒

It was altogether a rich harvest that Wednesday, a further fulfillment of a sunrise that had ripened like an apple and warmed the patch of earth on which Helen had chosen to escape dissatisfaction. She opened one letter, from her mother, then put it in her pocket, unread.

Helen sat on the old couch she kept in the front room of the store and picked through the remaining envelopes. One letter was from a psychiatrist friend who had enclosed an article he'd written on the difficulty of discriminating between manic behavior in the very rich and very rich behavior in the very rich ("'How,'" George had scribbled across the top of the Xerox, "as Dorothy Parker remarked when Coolidge died, 'can you tell?'"); there was another that invited her to cousin Judy's wedding; and a formal business letter from Dan the Ex which discussed Emily's camp fees. "Hi there! Read any good books lately?" he had scrawled at the end. "Yours, Dan." A textbook editor who had dropped out of publishing, gone to business school, and made a fortune as an investment banker, Dan had complicated feelings about Helen and her postmarital career.

She carefully filed the checks and bills and, tossing ever more junk mail into the wastebasket, watched the envelopes and flyers soar gaily to oblivion. As they thumped one by one into the can, she thought, That's why they call them flyers. Then, gazing idly down at the sofa, on which still more letters and envelopes lay waiting, Helen saw it: an oddly folded sheet of white paper, rising from the flat envelopes around it, bent up in the middle, uneven and asymmetrical, a tiny hump, an improper mound.

Helen reached for it, unthinking. She sipped coffee, the letter in her hand, crushed against the cup. Only later did she recall how wrong the letter had looked, the toadstool in the garden of her correspondence, how ill-fitted it had been, lurching up from the smooth surrounding layers. Now she unfolded it, almost mechanically, and began to read.

6

Dear Goat,

How does one fall in love? Do you trip? Do you stumble, lose your balance and drop to the sidewalk, graze your knee, graze your heart? Do you crash to the stony ground? Is there a precipice, from which you float, over the edge, forever?

I know I'm in love when I see you, I know when I long to see you. Not a muscle has moved. Leaves hang unruffled by any breeze. The air is still. I have fallen in love without taking a step. When did this happen? I haven't even blinked.

I'm on fire. Is that too banal for you? It's not, you know. You'll see. It's what happens. It's what matters. I'm on fire.

I no longer eat, I forget to eat. Food looks silly to me, irrelevant. If I even notice it. But I notice nothing. My thoughts are full and raging, a house full of brothers, related by blood, feuding blood feuds:

"I'm in love."

"Typically stupid choice."

"I am, though, I'm racked by love as if love were pain."

"Go ahead. Fuck up your life. It's all wrong and you know it. Wake up. Face it."

"There's only one face, it's all I see, awake or asleep."

I threw the book out the window last night. I tried to forget. You *are* all wrong for me, I know it, but I no longer care for my thoughts unless they're thoughts of you. When I'm close to you, in your presence, I feel your hair brush my cheek when it does not. I look away from you, sometimes. Then I look back.

When I tie my shoes, when I peel an orange, when I drive my car, when I lie down each night without you, I remain,

As ever,
Ram

7

Helen stared at the letter, at the diagonal creases where it had been folded, folded all wrong; at the neatly typed lines; at the signature, also typed. There was no date.

A sudden warmth pressed upon her, unfamiliar, a tenderness, someone else's tenderness. Why is this letter in my hands? I am a voyeur, she thought. This is not my letter. It was not sent to me. And yet, I hold it in my hands. I have read it and been touched by its sentiments. Someone has made love to me, someone I don't know. I've been letter-raped! I'm a peeping Tom, too. *Is* this my letter? Perhaps I'm having an affair and don't know it.

Helen had many admirers in Pequot, certainly. She cultivated them. They were a kind of hobby, better even than gardening, which she also enjoyed. Helen's customers came to chat, to sit for a while in the armchairs she kept in each room, to read beneath the lamps (which, always attentive to the details of bourgeois cultural comfort, she made sure were fitted with hundred-watt bulbs), and then, having chatted and read in the bright circles of light, to buy.

To buy what? Helen sometimes thought, amused. For first and foremost, she knew, they came for her. They walked through the door, expectant and hopeful, waiting to feel the words, the glances, the smiles Helen bestowed, sometimes just casually, even unconsciously — flung! — but always with unerring accuracy.

Helen was a flirt. She flirted in the spirit of good fellowship and because she loved to flirt. She loved the first moment when the other side was pierced by the arrow of her solicitude; loved the sudden, almost imperceptible retreat, loved the hesitant advance of the return glance, or a

smile or just a cough. When the customer came back —
and the customer always came back — the gentle, breath-
less volley would resume. Helen offered just the right volume of verse or a Tuscan cookbook or a novel from Black
Sparrow Press. Helen offered a light touch of her arm
against the customer's arm, or a joke, or a whispered fare-
well. To old customers, an embrace, a little too long, a little
too abruptly terminated; or a gentle, languid squeeze of the
hands. And always, the warm, intelligent beam of her attention, an exclusive circle of light surrounding each of them,
one hundred watts, pure Helen.

The first year she was back in Pequot, Helen did more
than flirt. She slept. Late. And with whomever she pleased.
Having opened the store, at one, one-thirty, Helen would
survey the few customers and think, I'm free, self-supporting. I have a child; my biological clock no longer
tolls the hours. My husband is gone; I can cook with
butter. I can sleep around, around the clock, around and
around.

And she did. Widowers looking for solace, divorced men
still reeling from court — short or tall, bald or ponytailed,
too old, too young, too sweet, too sad — they wandered
into the store looking for the latest novel by John Grisham
and came out with two by Julian Barnes and Helen's phone
number.

She slept with them with the intensity of a swimmer
in training doing laps. But she wasn't training for anything. This was it. She had already won. She was enjoying
her prizes. And eventually she tired of sleeping, as she
had expected she might. Some of her prizes didn't like
being prizes all that much, wanted to be partners or
husbands, or mistakenly thought she was the prize, or

9

turned out to be talking prizes with little of interest to say, or felt that, as prizes, they deserved the most prominent place on her mantelpiece. Helen began to get up early, very early, when no one else was about, when no one stirred.

I'm free, she thought. Self-supporting. And Helen had flirted.

—

She stood up and looked out the window, and the store felt dark and hollow, the air dead. Whose letter, Helen? A customer, perhaps. But which customer? Outside, a boundless blue sky, clean and cooled by its own innocent breezes, seemed far away, inaccessible. She folded the letter and . . . and what? Do I throw it away? Helen thought. With the letters from the American Cancer Society and the Nature Conservancy? This letter belongs to someone. It should be returned to its owner, like a stray. Returned to its owner. You know — Goat.

Helen stamped her foot. This letter had stumbled inadvertently upon her blooming fields of mail. It had tripped and fallen and floated uselessly, like a frog in a swimming pool. And she had discovered it the next morning, meaningless and bloated, where it did not belong.

She unfolded the letter, folded it, unfolded it. It must have fallen from an envelope. Which one? She pulled papers from the trash, tried to match the letter with other letters, tried to fit it comfortably in an envelope, any envelope, the one from George, from Dan, from the woman who had come to run the library, from the University of Chicago Press.

It's not mine, she thought, cramming it where it would

not go, like the feet of Cinderella's stepsisters. It's not mine, it's not mine.

"It's not mine," she said aloud.

Helen put the letter from Ram to Goat in a drawer behind the counter. And then, she could not think why, she locked it. You'll be safe there, she thought, as if the letter were a beast, easily angered, easily misunderstood.

2

JOHNNY WATCHED HELEN WHEN HE COULD GET away with it. If he had to have a boss — and who did not? — then at least he could study her behavior. For fun and profit. Knowledge was power, or so his Colonialism and the Novel professor had repeatedly maintained. It was only a summer job in a bookstore, not the cultural and economic oppression of entire continents of peoples, but surely the same basic rules applied. And he liked to watch her.

She was on the short side, and Johnny assumed that her voice, loud and commanding, was used to make up for that. She had told him once that she was not beautiful, except for her eyes, which she knew *were* beautiful, and she added that she accepted her figure as vigorous, a vision of good health rather than of fashion. He had not known how to respond, of course. But he had known that he wasn't really supposed to respond, that she had spoken just to embarrass him, to keep him in his place, which seemed to be the same as everyone's place — at her feet. Was she beautiful? Perhaps not. Yet when she stood in the doorway of her store, leaning her head absentmindedly, until it just touched the frame, when he saw her like that, she was lovely. He could hardly have said that to her, that she was lovely, not beautiful. So he said nothing. He often said nothing.

On this Wednesday late in June he watched her as she read a letter, then stuffed it in a drawer. Her face often had this intensely gentle look, but he had learned that it gave no clue to her state of mind. He was not surprised when she caught his eye, and said "Yes?" in a poisonous voice.

Johnny spun to face a bookcase of art criticism and wondered desperately if K came before or after N. The alphabet, a pillar, a solace and a certainty since kindergarten, had suddenly deserted him. He stood, bewildered and staring, as if he'd suffered a crisis of faith. Does the alphabet exist? If the alphabet exists, why is there so much suffering in the world? The alphabet is dead.

"All books a quarter inch from the edge," Helen said, kindly, now. She had come to stand beside him, and he faced her as she turned her head comically, almost upside down, trying to read the title of the oversized volume dangling from his hand. She straightened up, put her hand on his arm, and he felt the warmth of her wide palm. "Johnny?"

His father had arranged for the job with his friend Helen MacFarquhar when Johnny said he'd like to come home for the summer and save a little money. And Johnny was grateful. He liked his father, a large, distracted man who spoke in a magnificent rumble but had very little to say. He was a biologist and sometimes looked at his family with a sudden, avid interest, recognizing it as a complicated arrangement of highly developed organisms that might someday merit further study. Then the moment passed, he smiled, and went back to his proper research. Johnny was fond of him and grateful to him for convincing Helen to hire him sight unseen. He realized now, after three weeks of being under her employ, what a miraculous feat that had been. He did wish, though, that his father had called him John when speaking to her. He'd tried to correct Helen at first, telling her only his family called him Johnny. "John," he said, "John Howell," as if the last name might convince her of the first. But she replied simply, "Helen has no diminutive, Johnny."

"Johnny?" she said again, her hand closing on his arm. She shook him gently.

"Right!" he said, turning back to the shelves. What am I doing here? he wondered. What a stupid summer. What a mistake. There were two disconcertingly good-looking girls who were working at the store with him, which at first he found promising. But gradually he'd realized he wasn't that interested in what they promised. He'd just broken up with his girlfriend, and it had come as something of a relief to be on his own. For June and July, his parents were in Austin, where his father was conducting yet another fruit fly experiment at the University of Texas. Johnny was alone in a house he barely knew. He had never really lived in Pequot, for his parents had moved there when he'd already finished high school. After a lifetime in New York City, Professor Howell had been lured to teach at the elite little college in this picturesque seaside town.

For Johnny, the idea of a summer on his own in a comfortable, rent-free house was seductive. He could work at an undemanding job. He could go to the beach. He could pursue his hobby. It was quaint to have a hobby, he knew; he might just as well have been in the Boy Scouts. Could he have earned a badge for his hobby? Probably not. His hobby was poking through libraries in the local history section. It had started years ago, when he was nine or ten and his family still lived in New York. His father told him that the apartment building they lived in on Central Park West had originally been built for the architect's mistress a hundred years earlier. Something that was so clearly his, to which he belonged and which belonged to him, had an existence that predated him, a life to which he had not been necessary and of which he was not a part. This shocked him, and excited him, and he began reading about New York, about his block in particular. He found out whose farm it had been. He knew how many cows they kept. When he first came home from college to visit his parents in their new house in Pequot, Johnny immediately felt a familiar curiosity. The town had been there for so long, without him.

"What a funny hobby," his father had said.

"All hobbies are funny," said his mother. "Imagine collecting stamps." Her husband had examined fruit flies under a microscope for his entire adult life. She had grown tolerant.

"Make it pretty," Helen said to Johnny. She pointed to the shelves. She smiled, which she did extremely well, a slow, personal, suggestive communication.

When Johnny first met Helen, his first day of work, she had taken his hand, shaken it warmly, and smiled at him in the same way. Then she laughed. He later realized that this was it, this was how she did it. She held your hand in her own strong, smooth hands, smiled, looked into your eyes with her own eyes — they were rather small, a pale brown, in some light turning almost yellow — and then she laughed. It was an encouraging laugh. Perhaps there's hope, it said. Perhaps there's hope. But he was only twenty, and he hated to be laughed at, even if there were hope.

On that first day, three weeks ago, she led him around

the store, introducing him with exaggerated warmth to customers. "Look what I've got," she said, still holding him by
the hand, "a college student." And, angry and blushing, he
had prayed she would like him, would lead him around by
the hand to the ends of the earth, if the ends of the earth
were where she happened to be going. Helen drew people
to her with her insults, like a siren calling out "You fool!"
one minute, and then the next, "Come to me!" as if fools
were what she admired, what she wanted, what she craved
above all other things.

How can she know something? he wondered, for surely
she does know something, something about me. How can
she know it, whatever it is, so soon?

He watched her when a customer came in. She went up
to the man, who was nearly twice her size, took his hand
in both of hers, and said his name with almost startled
pleasure: "Adam." Adam broke into a self-conscious, contented grin.

Johnny was presented to him, then to an older man in
crisp Bermuda shorts, two women in exercise tights, the
two girls who worked in the store, and another woman,
Lucy, the store's manager, who made a little bow, then
vanished up the steps. Johnny said nothing. He wanted to
say things, intelligent observations about the range of sub-
jects represented in the store, the rich fiction section, the
unusually large poetry selection. Something to show he
noticed that the store was special, and that he was special
for noticing. Instead, he followed Helen around like an
animal on a leash: not a dog, he thought, but something
bent over or waddling, a turkey, perhaps, on a leash.

She had led him out to the sidewalk, and turned, the
solid proprietess, to face the store. It was in a bungalow on

the town's main street and was painted pink. "I felt that this was a town in which people would respond to a pink bookstore," Helen said. "I was right. I'm often right."

Johnny noticed that they were dressed identically, each in jeans and a white T-shirt. They both looked down at the other's feet. White canvas sneakers. Johnny felt himself blush again. Helen took his arm and ushered him back toward the door. "Horrible, isn't it?" she said proudly, stopping, holding her arms out toward the store, the pink paint bright and almost insanely out of context in the morning sun. All around it, the shops of the exclusive town glowed with demure wealth. The pink store, like an upstart, like the town tart, posed shamelessly among them.

She led him into the room in back devoted primarily to books about military history. Johnny glanced at the Civil War shelves. He had collected toy soldiers as a child and he still had his most valuable figures lined up in a glass case in his room at home along with some favorites worth next to nothing. Hundreds more were stored in shoe boxes in the closet. He noticed several volumes on the shelves which he'd read, and he experienced a boyish thrill. Guns! he thought. Sabers! (Senseless slaughter! he added, for he was a little ashamed of his passion for battles, for strategy and tactics.)

Helen dropped into a large armchair that took up much of the military room, and said, "I knew you'd like it."

"How?"

"I like it, too," she said, as if that were the answer to his question. "Now, why would anyone want to spend his summer here, Johnny?"

"Well, I don't know . . ."

As he spoke, Helen rose and headed for the front desk.

Helen is bored, Johnny thought as he watched her go, and he felt himself blushing again. Bored by me. Already. Day one. Sentence two. Blush three.

—

In the three weeks since, he had seen her turn on her charm, and turn it off, so many times, so arbitrarily, almost playfully, like a child flicking a light switch, that he began to enjoy the unpredictability and to admire Helen. In an essentially boring summer job of unpacking and shelving cartons of books, there was time to experience Helen's temperament in all its detail. Johnny tried to chart her moods, and they fluctuated, certainly, but followed no pattern. She devoted herself to customers, cutting pieces out of magazines if she thought someone might find them interesting, sending books on approval (they always approved), sharing her lunch, dispensing advice, Fiorinal, pens, peppermints from a tin box. Or she hid behind the counter, crouched on the floor sipping coffee, forcing him or whoever else was around to tend to the customer, the same one she herself had fussed over the week before.

"God, I can't bear it," she would say, seeing someone on the sidewalk, diving behind the counter.

Couldn't bear what? Johnny wondered. But he supposed he knew. Couldn't bear the responsibility of being Helen. It *was* a responsibility. If she seemed as alert as an animal to every movement, every sound, every thought around her, surely, Johnny thought, it was because she controlled every movement, every sound, every thought. She watched customers, she watched Kelly and Jennifer, the two girls who worked for her — she even watched her friend Lucy, the store's manager. She watched, listened, probably sniffed too. And then she spoke or refrained from speaking in a way that told you she was watching you, listening to you, paying attention to you, experiencing you, understanding you.

On Wednesday morning, though, Johnny thought, she seemed different. Rather than avid, she seemed almost hysterical. Instead of arranging the front table with different volumes of nature essays and gardening books as she had planned, she was jumping from shelf to table, piling up copies of Keats's letters, Joyce's letters, Violet Trefusis's letters to Vita Sackville-West, H. L. Mencken's, Philip Larkin's.

"What can you think of, Johnny? What letters? What letters have you read?"

He wondered if he had ever read a collection of letters in his life. "Why this sudden interest in letters? Is some collection coming out?"

"Oh, never mind. Is *archy and mehitabel* in print? That's brilliant, brilliant, Helen. Look it up, Johnny."

Yes, my captain, he thought. "But what are you doing, exactly?" he asked.

Helen, who had beat him to the counter and was already leafing through *Books in Print,* raised her head. She had instantly decided to like Johnny, but then she had barely noticed him. Johnny the college boy. What does a college boy look like these days? she wondered now. Young, she answered herself. His face was clear and smooth and his cheeks so fresh — it was the only word she could think of — so fresh she wanted to touch them. His eyes, large and blue to begin with, opened wider as she looked, nearly bulging. Did the color change? He wore an earring in one ear, a pimple above one silky brown eyebrow. His wide, full mouth turned down in a provocative curve. Why, he's got

Jeanne Moreau's mouth, she thought enviously. I like him, she decided again. I like having Jeanne Moreau's mouth around. He was scrubbed and scruffy in that summery, twenty-year-old way. His dark brown hair was long and hung, swinging like Carmen's skirts, in his clean, uncreased face. He was quiet with her, although she'd heard him with the girls who worked in the store, with the customers, his voice a confident mutter, joking, usually about himself. It's true she sometimes felt an urge to kick him — when he shuffled, or stared out the window as he sometimes did — to hurry him, to propel him into the world, the land of the living grown-ups, the glare of life.

Helen placed a copy of *The Letters of Ayn Rand* on the front table and congratulated herself on being expected to sell it rather than read it. She wondered if she should devote not just a table but a whole section of the store to letters. She had already been behind the counter twice to open the drawer and read the letter she'd gotten that morning. I am not a goat, she thought. Who is Ram? Who wrote my letter, Johnny? *I'm on fire,* said the letter. She looked at Johnny. He, at least, was not on fire, a boy slumped over the cash register. *And love's the burning boy.* A line from an Elizabeth Bishop poem. How did it go, the rest of it? She would have to look it up. She tried to picture Johnny, who obviously thought letters were something your parents received or you received from your parents, getting a love letter, *the* love letter. From some college girl, Ram the Girl. Could there really be a girl called Ram? Maybe it was a typo for Pam. *When I tie my shoes, when I peel an orange, when I drive my car . . .*

He stared back at her uncomfortably.

"What kind of car do you have?" she asked him.

"What?" He looked embarrassed. "Well, it's my grandfather's car. I mean, he died and then my grandmother gave it to me."

There was a pause as Helen waited for him to continue and he waited for her not to be interested anymore.

"A Lincoln Continental," he said finally. "Nineteen seventy-six. The biggest car ever made that wasn't a limousine. So he could fit his wheelchair in the trunk." He smiled. "Big trunk."

———

When eight o'clock finally came, Helen watched the last customer of the day depart through the white Dutch door, and she felt privacy descend lightly on her and her books. Wednesday was finished. They were halfway through the week. Johnny was in the back. Lucy was upstairs. She was alone. She unlocked the drawer and reread the letter, the fourth time that day. *I know I'm in love when I see you.*

My little mystery, she thought, and wondered again if it might, indeed, be hers. Surely there must be other, more likely suspects. In any mystery, you must examine the clues. Rule out the suspects, one by one, until you arrive at your man. Or woman. As the case may be.

Johnny could, of course, be ruled out. There had been no letter for him from the folds of which the love letter could have fallen. And he was simply too young. What book would he have thrown out a window, anyway? He was too respectful of books. What was he reading these days? She didn't know. She would have to ask him.

Johnny appeared, and Helen jumped, as if she'd been caught, found out. She turned away and folded the letter, careful to repeat the original, disorderly pattern, put it back in the drawer, and turned the little brass key.

———

When Helen went home that night, it was raining. She drove along the familiar road, past the curve where she had hurtled through a windshield twenty-five years before, past the stone wall into which her boyfriend had driven his car as she watched, from the passenger seat, watched the wall rise up before her, watched the glass shatter, watched the stars overhead and the faces of the men who carried her stretcher. She had recently seen the boy who'd been driving — now a man, a lawyer home to visit his parents. He paled when he saw her, as if she'd died in the crash and so shouldn't be there to remind him of it. The bend in the road was now marked by yellow signs, three diamonds, each bearing a bold black arrow, and by two yellow rectangles as well: 15 MPH and 15 MPH. Such was her influence on the little town, even before she came back to open her store. Those signs were her legacy.

Bailey, her cat, stood on the front porch screeching at the neighbors' monstrous orange tom. The peonies, confident that morning, lay flat, their gorgeous round blooms smashed like faces in the mud. Inside, she got herself a beer. *I'm on fire. It's what happens. It's what matters. I'm on fire.* It's what happens, what matters? Well, yes, Helen thought. Up to a point. Passion has its place.

She stroked Bailey and, wet fur stuck to her fingers, opened the letter from her mother. "I think I've been putting this off," Helen said. Sometimes when she spoke the cat answered her with a strangled mew, as if he felt sorry for her for having been reduced to speaking to an animal. But he ignored her now and stretched himself out on the kitchen table, and she had nothing left to do but read her mother's letter.

Dearest Helen:

I know you did not take me seriously today when we

spoke on the phone. Perhaps if you see this information written down, maybe then you will take my proposition seriously, even though it's written in pencil, since as usual I could not find a pen. Pencil has no authority, does it? But this is almost like writing in pen, since this pencil has no eraser. Very final. From my end, anyway. And I don't suppose you read armed with an eraser, do you? So we're all right. Are you sitting down comfortably at home or are you still at the store? It's ridiculous not to get mail at home. Very eccentric of you, Helen. I don't understand it. Now, as I said on the phone, I have a strong desire to come back to Pequot for a while. You may laugh, but there it is. Not for a long while, mind you, but for a while nevertheless. It's summer, after all. No one's in New York. I don't want to travel, not on a trip, you know. I thought of renting a place on the beach somewhere, and then I thought, Why rent a place on the beach? I own a place on the beach. If it weren't such a large place, of course I would leave you in peace. But fifteen rooms is fifteen rooms, even if I'm in one of them. And Grandma Eleanor is in another of them. Did I mention that part? She is coming also. I guess she needs a change. Bored with Santa Fe, as who would not be? All that landscape constantly demanding admiration. Very tiring. Grandma Eleanor thinks she might stay awhile with you. She could baby-sit, you know. Though she never did when you were a child. Well, I'm looking forward to spending some time with you and Emily. I bought you some things in Florence. Florence is very provincial socially, I think, but I met some lovely people. Reminded me a little of Pequot. Don't you agree?

Love,
Mom

Florence? Pequot? Helen tried to imagine her mother, now flourishing as a kind of globe-trotting free-lance dilettante, back in Pequot among the boat-shoe set.

Helen had always admired her mother, and loved her, too, in a remote sort of way. When Helen was little, they would drive in her mother's small yellow car, not quite a sports car but rather dashing for that time and place, and terribly unsafe it later turned out, and sitting beside her mother in her own bucket seat, Helen would be allowed, would be requested, to light Lilian's cigarette from the smoldering red coil of the dashboard lighter.

"Light my cigarette, cookie."

Helen could still feel the cigarette between her fingers, the weightless weight, like an empty robin's egg held with thumb and forefinger. Her mother smoked Pall Malls. The paper would pull on the skin of Helen's lip as she puffed gently. Tobacco crackled. Smoke sighed through the air. The lighter glowed in her other hand. When Helen saw *One Hundred and One Dalmatians,* she was fascinated by Cruella de Vil and thought her glamorous and fun, for she reminded her of her mother.

Helen thought it very odd that Lilian wanted to come back even for a visit. She hated Pequot. When Helen was a child and her father was alive, there were sometimes discussions of leaving Pequot, but they had the desultory quality of conversations about events long past — the snow storm of forty-one, remember? — not of some plan for the future, some course of action that might yet be put into effect. New York, remember? Helen's father loved Pequot, and Helen's mother loved Helen's father. And so they stayed in the large white house, and Helen buried her deceased pets beneath stone markers in the backyard and waited impatiently to be able to drive a car.

When Helen's father died, they moved almost immediately. Helen was twenty and away at college, her mother, Lilian, just forty. If it was hard to leave her ancestral home forever, as Helen put it to herself at the time, it was also hard to be around her ancestral home. All those dead pets beneath all those stones. Her father, beneath his stone. She remembered her father walking through the door after work, a scented cloud of pipe smoke chugging behind him, sweet exhaust, paternal motor; Daddy driving off each morning, waving from his car as she waved desperately from the window. Did he see? What if he never came back? But he always saw. He always came back. Until the year Helen turned twenty. Sometimes Helen imagined he was just on an extended business trip, that he would arrive one morning with a souvenir Eiffel Tower nesting among his wrinkled pin-striped shirts. She was reluctant to move, but she suspected her mother might be right, that it would be best to leave Pequot, to start anew.

Start a new what? she asked herself then. A new life? But there was only one of those per customer. Her father had apparently used his up. He was gone. There was no new life. A new career? She had no old career. A new accent, new political movement, new skirt length? A new bedtime! In this way she distracted herself, amused herself, and prepared herself.

For Lilian, there were none of these questions, there was no question at all. Pequot equaled marriage in her eyes — marriage to Helen's father. Without him, Pequot disappeared. She stepped out of the town as she would step out of a cab. And she never understood why, almost twenty years later, Helen moved back. "An artists' colony without the artists," Lilian said. "Not poor enough to be quaint, not rich enough to be charming. An upper-middle-class backwater."

It had not always been that way. Pequot began as an artists' colony in the twenties. But all its resident writers and painters had long died, and it was now affluent, full of New England liberals with IF A WOMAN'S PLACE IS IN THE HOME, WHY AM I ALWAYS IN THE CAR? bumper stickers, the home of professors from Kathleen Hollyhock, the nearby college, and the only place within fifty miles where the students could buy a cappuccino. Helen bought the cottage on Main Street next to the espresso bar, painted the little house pink, and she was in business. There were two other bookstores in town, one a chain offering discounted bestsellers, one an independent offering discounted bestsellers. Helen's more literary store existed precariously, teetering financially one year, on the verge of prosperity the next. It was able to continue at all because of the college on the one hand and an aging college-educated population on the other (they favored biography, she had discovered); also because Helen had capital and could see the store through the dry patches, and because of Helen herself. She knew her customers and stocked what they liked. She knew her customers and stocked what *she* liked and taught them to like it, too. When she read Wilkie Collins's *The Woman in White* for the first time, she sold twenty copies of the book the following week. She flirted with the town, and she seduced it.

The upper middle class reads books, Helen had explained to her mother. It has reading groups that meet each month. It buys the books it reads. Pequot was ideal, the perfect spot for a small independent bookstore to service not only the wonderful upper middle class, but the children of the upper middle class, as well, many of whom attended snooty Kathleen Hollyhock, at which they also read books.

"Children of the upper middle class," Helen said to her mother. "Just like me."

"Oh, you," Lilian said. "You're sinking fast."

—

Helen found the new journey of the wandering Lilian Lasch MacFarquhar, the return of this nephewless Auntie Mame to the town of Pequot, quite mysterious. She wondered if she minded that her mother and her mother's mother were coming for what sounded like an extended stay. It was hard to tell now, blurred by her pleasure at the thought of seeing them at all. Then she wondered what her mother had gotten her in Florence.

She went to bed in the quiet of early summer, a time before the bugs swarmed like tourists in the night heat. She reread the letter from her mother, thinking she'd missed the date they would be coming, but her mother had, typically, not mentioned it. Then she read Emily's letter again. Helen wished she had brought home the love letter so she could read that again, too. The cat lay at the foot of the bed, motionless. The dog came in, his toenails clicking on the floor. He settled down for the night on the rug by the bed. Even so, the house felt empty. When she turned off the light, she knew she missed her daughter. She enjoyed missing her, though. The solitude was almost sacred.

When Emily was born, Helen had stopped working: stopped teaching and stopped struggling with her dissertation. She had long ago realized that if she never finished her dissertation, she could continue teaching freshman English for years and never have to find a real job. That had appealed to her. And even better, if she didn't finish her dissertation, she would never have to finish her dissertation. That had appealed to her even more. Her dissertation was on the British novelist, fascist, and vorticist Wyndham Lewis. She had gradually come to realize she hated Wyndham Lewis.

Emily was far more work and far more interesting. When Emily was out in the park, with a babysitter or a visiting grandma, Helen would sit at her desk and write "Emily" in different scripts, like an adolescent writing "Ringo." The restaurants and stores and friends of New York seemed very far away. The prospect of them annoyed her. They were intruders, loud and vulgar. Helen and Dan lived near Central Park, and she went there and pushed her daughter on the swings until her shoulders ached and her mind went blank, and she was happy.

She had friends, she and Dan, and nursery school interviews for Emily. But more and more she ignored Dan, which was easy to do. He was never around. Still a textbook editor when they got married, he decided rather abruptly to start business school. Helen had been sure he would hate it and drop out, but instead he emerged, miraculously, like a butterfly from its cocoon, an investment banker.

One day Helen realized what she had been thinking for a year: that she would leave Dan, that her family was Emily, that Dan's family was Emily, that between them there was nothing else. Dan was a stranger. She hadn't seen him in three years, since he'd left publishing, and she hadn't missed him.

Dan had shrugged when she told him she wanted a divorce. He shrugged when he got emotional. Shrugged and looked away. She assured him about custody — they would have joint custody. They would work out the times. She assured him about money — she didn't want alimony. She would move, but just a few hours away. They would share their family, their Emily. It was an oddly cold discussion, and she wondered that they had ever married at all. But I was so in love with him, wasn't I? Swept away. Well, now I've been swept back, clean sweep, new broom.

Helen took her child and her furniture and moved back to Pequot, to the house her mother had kept for so long even though neither of them wanted to live in it. Now it was run-down, neglected, and shabby after years of being rented out. In Helen's family, "the Tenants" was a phrase for troublemakers, like "the Reds" or "the Blacks" or "the Jews" in other families.

With the insurance money from her car accident and various contributions from her mother, she began to fix up the house. She was handy and, before seeing the house, had thought she could work on it herself, make it livable, anyway. But when she stood on the doorstep with her little daughter, her dog, and her cat and looked in, she saw that she could not. It was a mess, wallpaper peeling, floor boards curling. The plumbing dripped or gushed. The boiler heaved and groaned. No wonder the tenants had complained. We're slumlords! she thought.

She immediately went out and hired the local contractor. Room by room, slowly, slowly, like sands through an hourglass, Ray Bean worked on Helen's house. He was also running for mayor and brought her newspaper clippings about his campaign speeches. He gave telephone interviews from her kitchen.

"Just do my room and Emily's and the kitchen," she told him. "We'll seal up the rest. Let it rot in peace."

But of course that was impossible. The roof loomed,

damp and disintegrating, above; the pipes wailed below. In between was a huge house, fifteen rooms, a ridiculous house. A crumbling, ridiculous house. Ray lost the election by just a few thousand votes. A few thousand out of a few thousand. In the years that followed, he scraped the walls and planned a comeback.

With her settlement from Dan — he had been strangely generous and accommodating and she realized gradually that he'd been having an affair for years and was relieved to dissolve the marriage — Helen had started Horatio Street Books. Emily was there from the beginning, a little girl drawing in little corners. Now she bicycled around town herself, dropping in to do her homework at the store sometimes, or for the company, or to beg for money, or just to give her mother a hello and a kiss on her way to a friend's.

Helen missed her and closed her eyes and tried to hear the surf pounding below the cliff at the edge of her property. She couldn't. The leaves rustled, though, and she thought of the letter, in which leaves hung unruffled by any breeze. And she saw the bent hump of the love letter. And she thought, Ram did not really throw Goat's book out the window. She's just saying that. And she thought, Why do I say "she"? Does Ram sound like a name for a she? And yet she knew somehow that Ram must be a woman. Unless she was a man. And that she did not really throw the book out the window, but was only saying that. Because, otherwise, what book was it? Where had it landed? Ram would have said where it had landed if she'd really thrown it out a window. She would have mentioned its title. And Helen wondered what book it was, and she wondered where it did land, just supposing it had been thrown. But that would depend on where Ram lived. And Helen wondered where Ram did live. But that would depend on who Ram was. And

Helen wondered who Ram was. And she thought that she knew someone's secret, but whose secret was still a secret. And the solitude of her room seemed like a joke, so populated with the romantic indiscretions of so many masked farm animals and mountain sheep, and she slept a long, uneasy sleep.

3

THE NEXT MORNING AT THE STORE, HELEN WENT straight for the drawer containing the letter. She read it, realized she had it practically memorized by now, told herself it had absolutely nothing to do with her, and put it carefully away. She leaned her elbows on the counter and waited. Helen had designed the counter as a kind of ark. Perhaps widow's walk was more accurate, Helen thought on slow days, as she stood and searched the horizon for customers. A dark green and polished oak structure, the counter jutted out from the left wall of the front room. The old oak planks she'd found in the basement now wrapped around her and her cash register like the prow of a ship. The floor within was raised five or six inches, so the captain of the ark (or the pacing widow) could stand surveying a glassy gray sea of shelves, books, and customers, could stand at once protected and elevated. At the opening that allowed one to enter, an oak board could be pulled down, like a hatch, extending the counter, closing it off entirely.

Good thinking, Helen, Helen often told herself. She liked her ark. She liked leaning on the polished counter, which smelled of beeswax and was smoothly grainy beneath her elbows. She sensed the order around her — the shelves for labels, for bags, the slot for credit card receipts. She had designed it and built much of it, too, and sometimes she ran her hand down a vertical support and marveled at its sturdy utility and its debt to her.

She watched Johnny slit open a large cardboard box, convinced he would slit the books, as well.

"Angle the knife," she said.

She heard him not reply, heard the effort it took to keep from telling her off.

"Just a reminder," she said.

Silence. Deep breath. "Okay, thank you," said poor Johnny.

Helen enjoyed tormenting him. She liked him. And she went back to thinking of the letter, for the anonymous, wayward love letter was, whatever she might tell herself, on her mind. It had become a nuisance overnight, a house-guest that would not leave, would never leave; but wouldn't come downstairs for breakfast either. The letter was a useless hanger-on. But it did hang on, disturbing her privacy. Go away, she thought. Get a job. Take a course at the New School.

She looked through a tiny, paperback volume of Rilke's *Letters to a Young Poet,* a gift item, really. Should she give it to someone, then? The letters all seemed to be about solitude and art, which was refreshing; when she'd looked up "Letters" in *Books in Print,* almost all the entries had been how-to books. Perhaps the Goat letter was included in one of them, an exemplum. But of what?

"Buy this," Helen said to the customer who'd just come in, one of her favorites. "Buy it, Janet. It's about solitude."

Janet was a customer whose husband had left her to

a life of hideous blind dates, which were a source of great amusement to both Helen and herself. Janet collected them now, like butterflies. There had already been a bejeweled Afrikaner carrying two wine glasses from his car to her front door, a man wearing crystals and never without a copy of M. Scott Peck's *The Road Less Traveled,* and a magnificently handsome Swede who suggested couples therapy on the first date. When Janet finally found someone she liked, a community activist she met on a business trip to Toronto, he turned out to be living under an assumed name, as he was on the lam from a marijuana bust twenty-five years before in Texas, and was led away from an Indian restaurant in handcuffs as Janet paid the bill.

"Maybe I should date Rilke." Janet looked at the little book. "Maybe I already have."

Helen left the counter to sit with Janet outside on the stoop and hear about date number twenty-three, a psychoanalyst Janet had met on the beach. Across the street, Miss Skattergoods, the librarian whose family had built and donated the library to Pequot, was dropping a letter into the blue mailbox on the sidewalk. Why hadn't she mailed it from her own mailbox at home? Was using a public letter box like using a pay phone? Did it mean your letter couldn't be traced? What was in the letter? Was it a letter that began "Dear Goat"?

Miss Skattergoods waved.

"Hi," Helen called.

"He said he liked the way I walked my dog," Janet was saying. "When I went to dinner at his house, he put on twelve hours of videotape of his dog's last days before her death from cancer, set to music."

"What —"

"I left him there, transfixed, after forty minutes. 'Look at her labored breathing,' he said."

"What —"

"Breed? Lab."

"No. What music?" Helen said.

"Oh." Janet sighed. "Pachelbel."

—

Apes may speak, Helen continued to herself when Janet left without the Rilke, buying instead a pile of Fay Weldon novels; apes may speak, as scientists claim, with signs and grunts; but they don't write love letters. They don't even write bread-and-butter notes. How very human were letters, how elevating. Only we write letters. Helen shook her head. Why not just phone? She hated writing letters. She hated writing anything. Why write when one could read? Her letters could not compete with Keats's letters. Let everyone read Keats's letters, then. If a letter happened to come her way from someone other than Keats, from a friend or an acquaintance, of course she would read it. She was democratic in that way. But she soon learned that her correspondents often expected more than a reading: they expected a response. Helen had therefore perfected the genre of the picture postcard, choosing carefully from the salesmen who came to the store hawking their collections every few months, and employing what she liked to think of as a style of elegant restraint and modesty. "Hello!" often did nicely. Sometimes she sent postcards when they were least expected. These were the most satisfying. "Sorry, *sorry* I had to hang up so abruptly," she would write after an innocent, impersonal call to remind a customer to pick up a special order. "Should've made the call from a more private phone. Do you forgive me? Do!" The postcard would be enclosed in an envelope and sent off to a man or woman who could barely remember the phone call but now felt the resurgence of a previously nonexistent longing, and wondered what exactly had been said, and what had been left unsaid.

Helen liked to distribute suggestive notes to Lucy and the other employees, as well. With a demand for someone to call the jobber the next morning and find out the reason for the delay of a delivery, there would be a quick personal coda: "You wore my favorite T-shirt today. I want it." She would leave a slip of legal paper for Lucy which said: "Look through new title catalogues, though you are a frivolous and insipid creature," and leave a lipstick impression of her mouth rather than a signature. Finding a list left for her that said the store needed toilet paper, Priority Mail envelopes, and coffee filters, she would respond: "Your handwriting is so friendly," and stuff it in the author's pocket like a dollar in a G-string. Were these notes letters? Helen wondered. Helen thought a lot about letters that Thursday. Only we write letters. But which one of us?

I'm on fire. Is that too banal for you? Yes, it is too banal for me, Helen thought. Love letters lack taste. No restraint: falling off cliffs, going up in flames.

She checked the mail carefully, hoping an answer to yesterday's letter might somehow show up, part of a correspondence independent of letter writers — a postmodern romance between the two letters themselves. There was no answer to the love letter, though, and Helen wondered, not for the first time, why she cared, because she did care. The letter was a noise from the next room, it was a glimpse through an imperfectly closed door, it was every accidental vision, the couple in the apartment across the street making love with the blinds up, the lights on, there's something confusing about them, their faces, both are facing down, they're both men, you realize as you pull your own blinds.

You'll see, said the letter.

Pull your blinds, thought Helen.

You'll see.

And it was not even an extraordinary letter, was it? Ram was on fire and said so. That was what a love letter was for, wasn't it? Wasn't every love letter essentially the same?

On fire, said the letter. *You'll see.*

How many love letters had she read in books? How many had she received? Why be unnerved by this one?

Because someone is on fire, Helen thought. And I'm watching someone burn.

I must take a more pragmatic approach to this romantic cryptogram, Helen told herself. Who had written the letter? And to whom had the letter been written? She read it once more. She made a list of people whose mail had arrived on Wednesday. Her ex-husband, Dan? Self-important enough, it was true, but he hated oranges. Anyway, he never would have taken the time to write someone a love letter. A love memo, maybe.

Could it have been written by George, her high school friend, now a psychiatrist? Certainly he hadn't written it to her. They had circled around each other for four years of high school, never quite getting together. Now he was happily married. Helen had run into him one morning after she'd just moved back to town. They stood and talked and Helen watched him, noticed how little he had changed, although his hair had gone completely gray, and she thought, I could do this if I wanted to, and I do want to, but I won't. She was sure he was thinking the same thing, and they both suddenly laughed, with relief. They'd been comfortable friends ever since. So George, happily married George, had not written a love letter to her. But then to whom *had* happily married George written a love letter? And how had it come to Helen? He had decided not to send it, perhaps, or it was an early draft that he'd left on his desk, then scooped up accidentally with the article he'd Xeroxed for Helen. Perhaps it had been sent *to* George. Who would do that? How dare she? Helen thought.

What about her mother? Could Lilian have written the letter? Not to George, though. Mommy? Mommy was having an affair! Or wanted to. No. If Lilian wanted to, she did. The idea of her mother having an affair was not difficult for Helen. But writing, or even receiving, a love letter so tender, so full of doubt — very unlike her.

Miss Skattergoods, arriving back in town after years and years in order to take over the family archives and library? Maybe. Hard to tell. She was an odd duck, keeping to herself and her library. She existed so centrally, yet so independently, of the rest of Pequot, like a statue on the town green.

There was Cousin Judy. But Cousin Judy was about to get married, and Helen hoped the letter was not hers. It would make the ceremony rather embarrassing to watch. Sordid, almost. Though such things did happen, she supposed. One just didn't know about them, which was how it should be. Who else? Could it have been the clerk who stuffed American Express bills into envelopes? No, computers did that. Perhaps the computer that stuffs American Express bills into envelopes had written the love letter.

Johnny was on the phone calling in special orders. "*Love and Marriage in the Middle Ages,* Georges Duby, University of Chicago . . ." Middle ages, Helen thought. I suppose I'm middle-aged myself. How odd. What if, Helen, the letter was not a mistake? What if it was really meant for me, middle-aged or not?

Helen was disturbed by this possibility. Anonymous love letters for Helen MacFarquhar? I am the maestro, the puppeteer, the dominatrix of suggestion and half-acknowledged desire. I am the flirt. I would know. I recognize my own creations. I am an artist. The clay does not form itself into a sculpture. The paint does not slap itself onto the canvas. Words do not write themselves. Lovers do not love of their own accord, not my lovers. If they did, they wouldn't be mine, would they?

"*Poets in Their Youth,*" Johnny said into the phone. "Eileen Simpson . . ." And Helen noticed a youthful, poetic cast to Johnny's complexion, a bloom of color, a stain of health and innocence visible on his cheek. Or were poets supposed to be pale? She would have to check her Rilke.

If you got a letter in the mail that did not belong to you, what would you do? Helen longed to ask Johnny. Or any of her friends, though how could she? They were all suspects.

But what *would* you do? she thought. Would you take it to the pound and hope someone came to claim it? Would you alert the police? Would you hang up a sign, saying, FOUND: ONE LETTER, WHITE WITH BLACK INK, ANSWERS TO THE NAME OF GOAT?

As she rearranged the piles of mass-market paperbacks on the two back tables (a task which she believed required considerable delicacy, commercial intuition, literary taste, and a fluid sense of design, and so always reserved for herself), Helen again ran over the list of suspects. George. Yeah, yeah, yeah. And Lucy? She could hear Lucy upstairs. The wheels of the desk chair made the floorboards creak. Helen heard her footsteps now and waited to see her at the top of the staircase. What ruled Lucy out? Not her marriage, certainly. If happily married George were having an affair, Lucy might as well have one, too, Helen thought. If I were married to her husband, I certainly would.

Helen watched Lucy leaving the store carrying packages for the post office. She was Helen's closest friend in Pequot, but that was not saying all that much about proximity. How close were they, really? They had grown up together, neighbors, Lucy three years older and the purveyor of much false information. They had always known each other, always liked each other. But if Helen was purposeful and busy, surrounding herself with protective activity, Lucy was simply aloof. She kept her distance gracefully, instinctively. She was genetically programmed to do so, all those years of high Wasp propriety. Propriety of form or propriety of substance? Helen wondered. What about Lucy? Lucy and the letter?

The letter might have predated Wednesday's mail. It might have been tossed away on Tuesday, rejected, then forgotten and left, crumpled and desperate, huddled miserably on the couch until Wednesday's mail had cascaded down around it. Or, on the other hand, Lucy, pining with love for Goat, might have written the letter herself.

Something had been going on with Lucy, that much was clear. Her husband was away for months at a time. And hadn't she gotten new shoes — shoes so expensive that she would not reveal the price to Helen for fear her salary would be cut? And that new haircut! Wasn't that a dead giveaway? Sprucing up for Mr. Wrong, Mr. Goat? Lucy reminded Helen of a goat sometimes, leaping up the steps with her demure little hooves. *My thoughts are full and raging, a house full of brothers, related by blood, feuding blood feuds.* Lucy had brothers. They feuded, too, didn't they? Something about the family firm.

What about the girls who worked at the store? Had one

of them dropped it? Kelly and Jennifer both attended Kathleen Hollyhock College, which catered to the richest and most bohemian of girls, and had for almost a hundred years. Boys had been admitted for the last twenty years, but the male presence somehow managed not to change the tone of the school at all. When she hired the girls, Helen had noticed their out-turned toes (too many years of ballet classes), their expensive boots and worn jeans, their sweet but gently whining voices, their slender bodies, nonchalant slouches, and she had felt a pleasant stirring of long-lost camaraderie. Had nothing changed? They even listened to the same music — Aretha Franklin, Bob Dylan, Billie Holiday. They read Kurt Vonnegut. Their long hair hung down the backs of their faded flannel shirts. And there, printed in pen on one girl's jeans, was a quote attributed to (who else appeared on nineteen-year-old girls' trousers?) R. D. Laing: "The statement is pointless. The finger is speechless."

They had been excellent customers, as were many students at the college, especially the girls. There was nothing better than a spoiled young woman with artistic tendencies. They were such good customers, in fact, that Helen knew they wouldn't do as well on the other side of the counter. They liked reading books, not selling them, and they were still too young to know the difference. Helen recognized the girls because she had been so like them, intelligent someday, pretentious at the moment, indulged, idealistic, selfish, liberal. They are comforting and familiar, she thought. They will amuse me — if I don't spend too much time with them.

But when the girls showed up for work the first day, Jennifer had shaved her head.

"For the summer," she said. She smiled and stroked her skull affectionately.

"And you?" Helen said to Kelly. She imagined two of them behind the counter, cone heads bobbing.

Kelly ran her fingers through her long hair. "I'm very ambivalent," she said.

"Good," said Helen.

Could you be *very* ambivalent, though? she wondered. The word did not work as well with an intensifier, did it? Can you be enormously neither one thing nor the other? She still looked with annoyance at Jennifer's bald head, but she felt a little better. Grammar was so soothing.

Maybe the letter had been sent to Kelly or Jennifer. But as Helen watched the girls striding through the store, she knew it had not, for if it had, she would have been told, it would have been displayed and discussed, fondled, ridiculed, and revered — not left casually on a couch. Why do girls gossip about themselves? Helen wondered. Because they still have nothing to lose.

Helen went upstairs, where Lucy worked on the books and orders. The windows were open, but the room was hot. She wondered how Lucy could stand it here and put on the fan, which blew against her face and rifled through Lucy's piles of papers. Helen made a fresh pot of coffee and listened to the drip as it brewed. It made such a small sound, a musical, aromatic promise of the beginning of the day, and yet it was the middle of the day and the sound was so very small, something far off, a muffled peep. The diminutive tone, the suggestion of distance, seemed, for a moment, important. She missed Emily suddenly and hard. Helen began to cry.

"Helen?" Lucy stood in the doorway.

Helen looked up. I really, really don't want Lucy here at this moment, and my face perhaps reveals this sentiment, she thought, for Lucy was holding her hands up, as if to protect herself. She was laughing, not unkindly, but she was laughing.

"What a face," she said.

"Oh, fuck you."

"Why not?" Lucy said, coming back in, patting Helen on the head. "The last frontier." She pushed past Helen to the coffee machine. "Hey, Helen, maybe you're losing your touch. Why *don't* I lust after you?"

"You do."

Lucy was the only person Helen really enjoyed having work for her. As the manager, she was very nearly an equal partner, although both understood that Helen could not bear true equality. Equality struck her as demeaning.

Helen recognized the utility of her other employees (though she admired it less than the utility of one of the vertical beams she herself had hammered into place, perhaps because she herself had not hammered the girls into place), but she also resented their claim on her time, their place in her vision — resented them not violently or heartily or even noticeably, just resented them, just a bit, just enough.

Helen would have liked to be alone in the store, alone with her books and her customers. But she couldn't, she needed a staff. She had known it right away and hired a young woman to help her. It had not worked out. Instead of making it easier, the young woman had required constant attention. Helen, explaining, pointing, reassuring, had wanted only, really, to be shaking — shaking the girl's shoulders until her head went back and forth, flip, flop, like a poorly stuffed rag doll's. Then the young woman conveniently married a corporate raider and moved to a duplex on Fifth Avenue.

For months Helen had not had the heart to replace her.

Instead she worked too hard and too long, dragging little Emily to the store after school to sit on the floor surrounded by muffin crumbs and crayons as Horatio Street Books grew in popularity and size until Helen could no longer pretend to have it under control. Helen did not like to lose control, as a general principle. She knew she had to find someone. She found Lucy Dodge Hall.

Since high school, when Lucy had gone off to Miss Porter's, she and Helen had seen each other less and less. But they picked up again immediately when Helen moved back to Pequot. Lucy was small, wiry. In her mid-forties, a few years older than Helen, she looked younger. Oddly formal at times, she moved with an almost cartoonish intensity, abruptly, leaning forward to shake hands like a Viennese general (she nearly clicked her heels): "How do you do! I'm Lucy Dodge Hall." I grew up privileged and Episcopalian, I'm attractive, intelligent, humane, and tolerant, and there's not a thing you can do about it, was the subtext.

She had been a regular customer, often lingering in an armchair like a pretty shell brought in by the tide, her glasses reflecting the lamplight — two yellow circles. "That man beats his dog," she would say when a customer left. Or, "They built a gazebo on their wetlands, and the zoning commission made them tear it down." There she sat, her legs slung over the arm of the worn plum-colored upholstery, chatting with Helen, reading a little. She colored with Emily. She interrogated other customers like a lawyer on TV. Lucy was, in fact, a lawyer, but she no longer practiced.

"My clients were all so guilty," she said.

She had stopped practicing to raise her children, but even now, with the children grown, she preferred to sit in Helen's store grilling innocent customers. "Why do you read mysteries? Are Italian cookbooks better designed than

French? I mean, in general? What *is* postmodernism?" On one evening, a Friday, when Helen's daughter went to her father's and Helen kept the store open until eight, Lucy slouched in her accustomed place watching a man in a bow tie and floppy fishing hat who had cornered Helen. Helen saw Lucy watching, and wondered why, now, when she needed her, Lucy was silent.

"Perhaps," the man said, "you have noticed the unconventional — no, no — the *foreign* attitude of the school system in this town."

Helen did not, as a rule, take to men in bow ties and floppy fishing hats. She tapped her fingers irritably on a shelf. The shelf needed dusting, she noticed. All the shelves needed dusting. She had no employees. She would be here all night, dusting shelves.

"Let me be frank," said the man. "*Their* Festivals of the Trumpet are *school holidays!*"

Festivals of the Trumpet? (She wondered if there was any Pledge upstairs. Or was it Endust she liked?) What were Festivals of the Trumpet?

"But *our* American holidays — Columbus Day, for example . . ."

Our? Their? *Whose?*

". . . not even a half day! Rosh Hashanah, Yom Kippur — the schools close down, get the day off, *two* days off, *whole* days. Do you understand me?"

Oh. *That* "their." But your their, sir, is my our. Helen opened her mouth to speak, stumbling mentally over possible replies.

"Oh," Lucy had already begun, her head to one side like a curious hound. "Oh," she said with sincere interest, "are you anti-" (she pronounced it *antee-*) "Semitic?" Then she waited courteously for an answer.

That night Helen thought to ask Lucy to work at the store. "You're here all the time anyway."

"You'll be very unpleasant to work with, though," Lucy said with her clear, innocent smile.

"Work *for*," Helen said. "Will I?"

———

At first, Helen and Lucy had worked side by side, placing orders, checking back orders, lugging overstock to the basement.

Then one day, as they sat on the couch in the store, a little break between customers, Lucy said, "You really *are* unpleasant to work with."

"I am not. Why am I? Who says so?"

"Why don't I work upstairs sometimes, do all the book-keeping and inventory, which you screw up anyway? I'll take some of the afternoons, you can spend more time with Emily —"

"You think I'm a bad mother."

"What?"

"You think I *had* a bad mother."

"You did?"

"Certainly not. How dare you?"

———

And so Lucy worked upstairs when Helen was there, only occasionally marching down to announce to anyone she saw, "How do you do! I'm Lucy Dodge Hall. May I help you?" and nearly click her heels.

Maybe it *was* Lucy's letter, left on the couch, not mailed to Helen at all. And maybe it wasn't, and Helen was projecting romantic fantasies on an innocent woman with new shoes. She looked at Lucy pouring herself a cup of coffee, so aggressively demure, so soft-spoken and outspoken at the same time, as alien to her, she realized, as she had been the day they met.

Lucy smiled brightly at her. "I got a tattoo," she said. "Want to see?" It was on her ankle: her monogram.

—

When, that afternoon, George came into the store, brushing back his gray hair, which was luxurious and rather pretentious in length, Helen looked up from the letter in her hands. *I no longer eat.* Well, George looked well enough fed. She examined him closely. Did his clothes seem more carefully chosen, more expensive? Why, he was positively well dressed. His tie, for example, was of a chic mauve-brown adorned with flowers. Flowers!

She waited behind the tall counter and watched him with suspicion and with secret pleasure. *I have dinner with you and your wife. Your daughter spends the night at my house with my daughter. We watch the fireworks together, all of us, every year. We go to the movies, grill fish wrapped in aluminum foil. And years ago, you and I shared a fraction of a moment of understanding, an admission, a stab of pleasure, and we shared a decision, a decision not to.*

"Hi," she said. She said it softly.

"Hello." George smiled. Because he smiled infrequently, although he always seemed in a perfectly pleasant mood, it was an almost radical act for him. Helen was caught off guard momentarily.

"You may approach the bench," she said.

"The altar," he said, and he did. He ran a finger across the back of her hand, which lay on the countertop.

She saw Johnny standing in the doorway watching. She raised an eyebrow at him, and he vanished. Poor thing. She would have to be nicer to him. Just twenty and alone in a town that managed to be both cold and stuffy, and with Helen as a boss.

"George," she said then, "these weeks without you hanging around have seemed like — weeks! I just got this little Czech novel in, and I put it aside for you . . ."

She watched him as he watched her, felt his hand tighten on hers. "Thank you for the piece you sent me," she said.

He often gave her articles he'd written in various journals. (In this one — "Manic or Merely Rich?" — he discussed a woman, a *principessa* from a town near Milan, whose family worried that she might be manic because she had just bought a chateau for several million dollars. "I often buy chateaus," she noted. "But I do usually look inside first.")

"My grandmother buys houses by phone," Helen said.

My grandmother, she thought. My au pair to be. George smiled again. Very unusual, two smiles. She grabbed his tie and checked the label.

"Barneys!" she said.

"A gift," he said.

And he seemed so happy, jaunty almost. Had he always been like that?

"George!" she said in her harshest voice. "What's going on?"

Instead of answering, he shrugged and kissed her on the lips, very delicate, very chaste. It was something he had learned from Helen, that kiss. A private public kiss. As he browsed through the shelves, she glared at his back. George? Perhaps. He was perusing an oversized gardening book. Yes, he gardened, didn't he? Well, good, tend to your garden, George. Your vineyards, your orchards, your flocks . . .

When George returned to the counter, he had a copy of *Anna Karenina*.

"You want this?" she said.

"I do."

"You do?" *Anna Karenina*? Surely he'd already read *Anna Karenina*? She looked at the fat Penguin paperback. She picked it up. Helen too liked to read books over and over. Maybe she should reread *Anna Karenina*. It had been years. Decades.

That's not the point, stupid. The point is George. Why is *George* reading *Anna Karenina*? She thought she knew why. Outraged, she nevertheless suggested the Norton Critical Edition, which she preferred.

"Would you like *Madame Bovary* as well?"

"Okay. What a good idea, Helen. Why not? I have a patient I could give it to. *Madame Bovary*. Helen, you read my mind even when there's nothing in it."

She had read his mind? How unfortunate. She was right? He *was* having an affair? With this patient. Goat the patient. The letter had fallen out of the envelope with his article in it, then. He'd written it. Or had she, Goat? But then, if she had written it, she would be Ram.

But I didn't really mean it, Helen thought. I didn't really mean what I read in your mind. I read your mind, and so you are having an extramarital affair with a patient. I am responsible.

And now, with her guidance, George would make a literary study of adultery, too. Oh well. Literature could be so therapeutic. Fuck your patient, then kiss her off with a copy of *Madame Bovary*, a copy of *Anna Karenina*. Keep her busy on those long, lonely nights ahead. A professional gesture. Responsible doctor provides hours of classic, bleak assessment of bourgeois adultery. Patient understands hopelessness of situation. George off the hook.

At that moment, Theresa, the Polish au pair, pushed

open the door, and Helen came out to help her maneuver the stroller, a double stroller containing two doughy babies, the Goldstein twins, Kevin and Ariel.

"Theresa! What would you like today?" she said, scanning the racks of periodicals for the newest issue of *Signs*, which, along with *The Star*, was Theresa's favorite publication. She read both with a Polish dictionary.

George was thumbing through *Madame Bovary*, humming.

Helen handed Theresa the periodical, and Theresa said, "I have!"

Helen waited. Theresa used English pronouns with stubborn creativity.

"I have!" Theresa was slim and strong, darkly beautiful, though of a rather tragic, cloudy demeanor. She sighed. "You are so happy."

"Am I? Good. Now, you *have* this issue?" Helen said.

Theresa looked confused. "I give to me."

Helen glanced sympathetically at the sleeping twins. So young, so many parts of speech.

"Anna Karenina, *c'est moi*," George said, and left.

—

Helen stayed late at the store that night, staring at the letter. With Emily away, she had no reason to hurry home, and she liked to work. She needed to. She was physically strong and temperamentally rambunctious. She ran to the beach almost every morning, and if it were warm enough, she swam a mile before running home. She worked out at a gym, too, run by Barry and Eliot, two of her customers. But it was never enough. The urge to do something pushed her to do *something*, to read books, sort books, order books, build shelves for the books she had ordered, read, and sorted. Sometimes, when she was alone, she simply jumped up and down, like a child. Had George written the letter? Maybe he had written it to her. It had come to her address, after all. Possession was nine tenths of love letters, surely.

A young, shy couple came in and asked if they could register at the store for their wedding. Helen couldn't think why not and they spent an hour browsing and making up a list. When they left, she looked at it and saw it was half poetry, half military history. She wondered if she should move the poetry section closer to the history section.

The only other customer that night was Miss Skattergoods. A New England dame of about sixty decked out in high-waisted trousers and a faded striped sailor jersey, Miss Skattergoods was from an old Pequot family, but she herself had moved away from the town long ago — years before Helen was even born. No one knew why. She'd come back last January after her old aunt died and a replacement was needed to look after the library and family archive. It was said she had lived in Greenwich Village. Greenwich Village — the name was spoken with a combination of disgust and awe.

What had she done there? Miss Skattergoods had the plain, private, weathered look of the New England gentry. Whether this suggested mild depravity or moral superiority or both, Helen couldn't make out. She was a little afraid of Miss Skattergoods. She tried to picture her in a brownstone, the ground-floor apartment. Was she a painter, a writer, a stand-up comic? A lesbian, a rich man's mistress, a poor man's meal ticket? A librarian by day, a jazz singer by night? Miss Skattergoods had sent her an announcement of a signing and tasting at the library by a local cookbook writer, a benefit. Helen had received it yesterday, the day she'd gotten the letter, the letter to Goat. Helen liked the idea of Miss Skattergoods as someone's goat, or ram, for that matter. Someone's love-beast.

"All alone?" Miss Skattergoods said. "That boy of yours gone?"

"Boy?" Did Miss Skattergoods think she had a son?

"He's in my library all the time. Reads old letters. Some college paper."

"Johnny?"

"Mmm. Scholars are snoops," Miss Skattergoods said. She lit a cigarette, looked blandly at the NO SMOKING sign, winked at Helen, paid for a volume of poetry by Christopher Logue — she was Helen's second best poetry customer, the first being Helen herself — and started to leave.

Helen reached for Miss Skattergoods's cigarette, held it between her own fingers, took a long drag, and handed it back.

"Miss Skattergoods," she said, "do you have a first name?"

"Certainly," said the woman. And she left.

4 ′ ′ ′ ′ ′ ′ ′ ′ ′ ′ ′ ′ ′ ′

IF THE LETTER WERE MEANT FOR HELEN, IT WOULD
not be the first time. She received ardent letters from
customers fairly regularly, although the ones she'd gotten
up till now had all been signed. What would be the point
otherwise?

> Helen,
>
> I hope two things. One, that I mail this, and two, that
> my writing it at all does not strike you as an intrusion. If it
> does, please disregard this letter at once.
>
> Who am I? In this instance suffice it to say that when I
> am in the store we usually say hello. Today when we said
> hello, I was wearing a khaki suit. Necktie. Hair combed
> back from a high forehead. Early in the day.
>
> Who are you? I write because I would like to know. I
> have said hello so many times and would like to say more.
>
> If you find yourself similarly inclined, perhaps you would
> ring. Or drop me a line in the post.
>
> Respectfully,
Will Winslow

More than signed, these letters, like servants sent as messengers, identified their masters with descriptions sometimes detailed — lists almost — of the letter writer's looks, his lands, his hopes and desires. The letters made no claim on Helen. They were polite. After all, said the letters, bowing their heads, we are relative strangers.

Yet somehow, the very existence of the letters changed that. Simply by arriving, Helen thought, by introducing themselves however graciously, the letters passed over the threshold into her life. When they spoke of their author's tender emotions, rather than expressing a bond between Helen and the besotted writer, the letters boldly created intimacy. Gentle and a little shy, the correspondents were sometimes modest, but the letters were not. How could they be?

Dear Helen,

I've been an off-and-on customer at Horatio Street Books over the years. Last week, you sold me a John Keegan book, and we talked about travel memoirs.

When I come to the store I've always been struck by how beautiful you are. Mental lists of books I wanted evaporate when you say, "Yes? Can I help you?"

I live on a farm a few hours north. There's an old white clapboard farmhouse, four or five barns, an old slate-roofed sugar house (where the maple syrup was cooked). There's a pond, fields of alfalfa, a herd of cows (50), 7 geese, 3 goslings, and 30 goose eggs being sat upon at this moment. There are 2 cats, 3 four-legged dogs, and 1 three-legged dog. I'm an anthropologist. I teach at Kathleen Hollyhock. I take trips to Central America, where the birds are surprising and the foliage aggressive and the indigenous peoples disappearing.

Your beauty struck me and made me feel wonderful.
Thank you.

Paul

Helen's features were small and regular, a legacy of the MacFarquhar side of the family. Her eyes, a light, gilded brown, were unpredictable, set deep between a wide forehead and high cheekbones that looked almost Asiatic, as if her Russian Jewish ancestors had mingled with their Siberian neighbors, which they probably had. But what people most noticed when they saw her was her skin, luminous and childlike. The first sight of Helen, which she instinctively prolonged with a slow introductory gaze, was experienced almost physically, as when one is in the presence of something gentle and heartbreakingly innocent, something just born.

Johnny saw how others saw her, and how she handled them, how careful she was, how delicate, the reins of other peoples' feelings lying lightly in her hands. But what was the point of such skill if it was used only to keep those who might love you just beyond touch? She was silly, Johnny thought. And old. In her forties, certainly, though vivacious and well preserved, he supposed. Johnny saw how she handled the others, and he saw what the others saw in her. She was in almost absurdly good shape, muscular, beneath a layer of soft, feminine flesh, and she moved with an abrupt, hearty ease. Her loud voice was husky and soft when she wanted it to be. Her eyes were hooded and sleepy unless she chose to aim them at you; then they opened, as alert as cat's eyes, but round, beckoning, with a hint of warning.

She aimed them at Johnny now and then, when she wasn't busy with a customer, and when she did he would feel a surge of confidence and gaiety. He would laugh at something she said. He would say something himself, something clever enough to make her laugh and regard him with curiosity. Then, abruptly, she would turn to other things, and Johnny would stand where he was, his hands and feet suddenly large and ungainly, his laugh uncouth, his voice, even his words, an awful gaffe, an unwelcome, uncontrollable noise overheard but politely overlooked by the hostess.

He tried very hard to please her. He arrived at Horatio Street Books early and left late. Sometimes, lulled by the quiet, by the sleepy building itself, he would stand absently looking out at the bright glare through one of the little windows and he would feel the comfort of the store, as if he were beneath the soft shade of a tree.

There were moments when Helen blurred, when a sense of vulnerability framed her like the blush of a sunrise, when she softened and sweetened and the customers left the store dizzy, their vision rosy, their nostrils drawing in only fragrance, the air itself no longer necessary. And there were other moments, far more numerous for Johnny, when she appeared with a sudden, slashing clarity.

Which will it be today? he wondered. In the corner of the store's front room, he cut the twine from a bale, unleashing a pile of brown bags printed with the bookstore's logo. Which will it be this time? He held up a bag, examined it, and brought it over to Helen.

There were no customers. The store was not open yet. Johnny could smell the coffee in Helen's mug, which sat on the counter between them. Helen took the bag and examined it. The ink was blurry.

"Send it back," she said in her shortest, most ill-tempered voice, a deep snarl of sound.

Johnny flinched, like a horse, his chin up.

"You're right about this guy," she said a minute later,

lifting up a new paperback, stories about disaffected New Jersey youth, not usually her cup of tea, but Johnny had been so enthusiastic about them she'd read the book and admired it. "Thank you." And she walked over to him softly and kissed his cheek.

———

The main street of Pequot bisected the little peninsula and led directly to the water. There was no beach right there, just some rocks, but the town had erected a few benches, and Johnny often ate his lunch there. That afternoon was bright and sunny, and Lucy appeared and sat next to him to drink a bottle of water that seemed to be her lunch.

"Surviving?" she said.

"Oh, yeah. It's great."

"Helen driving you crazy? Miss your parents? Good relationship with your parents? Any friends here?"

Before Johnny could answer one question, she would ask another. He was reduced to a series of quick nods.

"Lonely? What did you have for lunch? Sunny, isn't it? I hope you use sunscreen? Want some water?"

Johnny drank from her bottle of water. He liked Lucy. She did all the getting-acquainted work.

"When Helen and I were young, we used to sit out on the beach and fry. We meant to get tan, of course, but we usually ended up streaked with red, which hurt like hell and then peeled. But we did it anyway, every year. Are teenagers still so stupid? I'm sure they are. We used to iron our hair. Helen has dressed in exactly the same way since she was five years old. I have pictures of her."

"Really?" He wanted to see the pictures, a little Helen, no front teeth, jeans and a T-shirt, her little playmates awestruck and under her spell.

"Mmm-hmm. What did you wear when you were five? I wore dresses with little petticoats. Did you see the meteor shower last night? There were too many clouds, of course. Like meteor showers? Why do you drive that big, old car? Do you think I need a new car?"

Was you ever bit by a dead bee? Johnny thought comfortably, half dozing in the pleasant air and the gentle gust of Lucy's inquiries.

———

Even when he left the store, Johnny felt Helen's presence. "You work for Helen?" people said. The druggist, the lifeguard, the lawyer next door; the women walking their dogs at the beach; the butcher, the baker, the candlestick maker; all thought of Helen, spoke of Helen, whispered, dreamed, remembered, tried to forget, to forgo, Helen. Most of them seemed to have either slept with Helen or wished they had slept with Helen. Women, men — he half expected toddlers on their swings to sigh, "Helen, ah, I remember it well. The moon was high, the music low . . ."

Helen? he asked himself each time this happened. Helen, the yellow-eyed, snarling fiend? The feline, cruel and lovely, flicking her squealing prey playfully about, who didn't kill to eat, who didn't even kill, who blinked and licked her pretty chops hideously? That Helen?

One day, she kissed him on the lips. The customers had all gone, and Johnny stood beside her at the cash register. She had discovered she could not get hold of a collection of letters between George Bernard Shaw and Mrs. Patrick Campbell, and she was staring darkly at a roll of Scotch tape.

"Helen," he said softly. "Are you okay?"

Then she bent her face toward his and gave him the

lightest of kisses on his lips, a sigh of a kiss, a warm passing breeze, a petal fallen from a flowering branch.

"As ever," she had said.

—

Johnny worked hard, surprised at how physically draining the job was. A bookstore! he had thought. I'll read books all summer. But all those books he wanted to read had to be ordered, unpacked, checked in, shelved, and then sold. Helen did everything, moving on to the next task before the previous one was completed, leaving shreds and tatters for Johnny and his coworkers to pick up and sort out. She was like a bull stomping through her own china shop. On some days. Other days, she stood behind the counter looking radiant, attracting customers like the Statue of Liberty attracting immigrants. He gazed up at her lantern with the rest of them. Even the other two college students, Kelly and Jennifer, fell under her spell. They began to talk like her, use her intonations, her curses.

"*Please*," they would say. Or "That defeats its own purpose." Or, constantly, "Fuck you."

Johnny liked Jennifer and Kelly. They were a relief from Helen, first of all. They ate chocolate and discussed their poetry seminars. And he liked the way they looked, physically different. One, girlish and lithe, her head shaved so smooth he longed to run his hand over it; the other, robust, a living television beach body, flawless and self-conscious — I am a body! it cried out. See me move! The girls spoke almost identically, though. Johnny suspected they were cousins. He suspected all girls were cousins.

"Are you looking down my shirt?" Kelly, the beach girl, asked him one day.

"Absolutely," he said from his perch behind the counter.

"Jerk," she said with a good-natured laugh.

But one day he caught her looking down his.

"Jerk," he said.

He sensed this was some primitive form of flirtation.

Kelly and Jennifer were both beautiful, and Johnny appreciated that. Jennifer's shaved head gave her a vulnerable, delicate look. Kelly flung her long hair around like a horse swishing flies with its tail. Their daddies were rich, their mamas good-looking, and they were both. When they weren't quoting Woody Allen lines to each other, they discussed whether or not Kelly should shave her head, or at least get her nose pierced, and whether they should live with their boyfriends. Johnny liked the sound of their big boots, the sight of their long legs in little shorts, the drone of their indistinguishable voices.

—

All letters are acts of aggression, Helen decided, for they demanded an answer. Even this love letter was an act of aggression. Especially this letter, for how could she answer it?

Dear Goat and Ram,
　　I have my own problems. I am not a sheep-shagger.
　　　　　　　　　　　　　　Nevermind,
　　　　　　　　　　　　　　Helen

Helen remembered some lines from Auden. She often remembered lines from Auden, when they rhymed.

　　Letters of thanks, letters from banks,
　　Letters of joy from girl and boy . . .

Something, something, something, something.

And timid lovers' declarations
And gossip, gossip from all the nations . . .

Mm-hmm-hmm. Then,

Clever, stupid, short and long,
The typed and the printed and the spelt all wrong.

And, Helen thought, the fucking anonymous.

—

Helen listened to the crickets and felt the damp air and thought back to the last time she, her mother, and grand-mother had all been in the house together. She had just returned from the hospital, her face scarred, her neck in a brace. The two women, her father, too, had busied them-selves bringing her snacks. She remembered the oppressive, wet air and a constant supply of snacks, one after the other, a stalk of celery, a cookie, a glass of lemonade, a slice of cheese — each item brought in and dangled, like a worm before a baby bird. How kind they had been, how far away she'd felt from her new vantage point as a disfigured teen-ager. For that was how she thought of herself. Disfigured. And disenfranchised — cut off from the great cultural event of her life.

"*Why* can't I go to Woodstock?" she had asked the doctor. "Put me in a body cast and my friends will throw me in the back of a van."

"Helen, you have a broken neck."

"No, I don't. I have broken vertebrae."

"Helen, your vertebrae are your neck."

The whole thing had seemed preposterous to her. The accident itself, the recuperation — they were in her way.

Even the scars, which plastic surgery eventually reduced to thin, barely noticeable lines, upset her less because they changed the way she looked than because they had no business being there in the first place. When her boyfriend Tim, who had been driving, came to see her in the hospital, he turned pale and cold beads of sweat popped out on his forehead. He left the room and fainted, and she thought, Oh, come on, this whole thing is ridiculous. It's only me, Helen. Let me out of this hospital, out of this traction, out of these scars.

How horrible it must have been for her parents. She thought of that now that she was a parent. She didn't think of it then. She didn't think of anything then except getting to do what she wanted to do. But she had noted how gentle they were, how hard they tried to make her summer as enjoyable as possible. She remembered early mornings with her father, sitting on the terrace while he drank coffee and she drank orange juice that he had squeezed for her. They planted a vegetable garden together, or rather he planted and she pointed. Her grandmother gave her a wonderful panama hat. Her mother gave her *Memories of a Catholic Girlhood* to read. Now her father was gone for good, taking with him his pipe-tobacco smell and familiar, friendly pipe-tobacco cough. And her mother and grandmother were coming home.

⸺

Johnny noticed that customers always began by saying, "I need something to read."

"I need something to read," he heard someone say to Helen. It was one of the gay guys who owned a local gym, Barry or Eliot, he still wasn't sure which was which. He thought surely they had made up their names, anyway. They were on the lam, using aliases, bad aliases — so bad that no one would suspect they were aliases. Johnny judged them to be lovers by the tone of infinite, amiable contempt they saved for each other. They reminded him a little of his parents.

"Something just like *The Makioka Sisters.*"

"I hoped you'd like it," Helen said, and then, as if confiding something, "I *knew* you'd like it."

Johnny had never heard of *The Makioka Sisters,* and he quietly went to find it on the shelf. A fat postwar Japanese novel. Surely not for a man who probably waxed his chest. What had Helen been thinking of?

But Helen had told Barry or Eliot to read *The Makioka Sisters,* and so Barry or Eliot had read *The Makioka Sisters.* Helen had told him to enjoy, understand, and prosper by means of *The Makioka Sisters,* and so he had enjoyed, understood, and prospered.

Tell him to take out the trash, too, Johnny thought.

"It has the best last line ever written, don't you think? I'm not sure there *is* anything else just like *The Makioka Sisters,* though," Helen said. She gave a short, mischievous laugh. "How about *The Brothers Karamazov?*"

Johnny took the trash out himself.

—

After *The Makioka Sisters* episode, Johnny spent the next two weeks memorizing, very nearly, the titles in the store. He started with *The Woman in the Dunes* by Kobo Abe and ended with Zola's *Nana.* When he dusted, when he put books away, when there was no work for him to do, he scanned the shelves, pulled out each volume, read a few pages, read the jacket copy, often borrowed a book with Helen's grudging permission, and read it at Miss Skattergoods's library or at home that night. It took some doing, but he had always liked memorizing lists — of baseball statistics, capitals, titles of *Star Trek* episodes.

He would show Helen, he thought. He could sell *The Makioka Sisters*. He could sell whatever she and her store could dish out.

"I need something," said Theresa, wheeling in the twins. They slept. It was safer that way. "Something to write. I write many, many books."

"Really?" said Johnny.

"In Polish, many, many. In English, I enjoy writing *Middlemarch*."

—

Someone loves me, someone loves me not. Someone loves someone, someone loves someone not. Thump thump, thump thump. Helen ran along the side of the road. Thump thump, like a dog, she thought. A dog preoccupied by a stupid letter. The love letter had been sent to plague her, clearly. It was a riddle sent by an amoral god. No, Helen decided. This was no poetic Greek myth. This riddle was sent by the amoral Greek god's incompetent secretary.

When she was almost at the beach, Johnny passed her in his ridiculous car. He drove too fast and too close. Had he noticed her? She watched the large wide end of the navy blue Lincoln Continental pull farther and farther ahead.

The car was there when Helen got to the beach. She stopped, panting, sweating, her head still filled with Goat and Ram. Who was Goat? She could be anyone and anywhere. She could be he and could be anyone, anywhere.

She saw Johnny in the water, quite far out, beyond the breaking waves. His arms looked white. He left a wake. Beyond him, two fishing boats crossed the horizon.

Helen pulled off her shorts and T-shirt until she was wearing only her bathing suit and her heavy socks and big running shoes. She looked down at her feet. Oh, for God's sake, no one can see you, no one's here except Johnny, and even he is far away, a bobbing head on the horizon. She wondered if he took out the diamond stud in his ear to swim. She had often wondered if the diamond was real. She liked jewelry, liked to talk about it, it was a habit she had picked up from her mother and grandmother, who often spoke of nothing else. She rather liked the way the earring looked on Johnny, too, but the impulse behind it was obscure to her — what did it mean, exactly, when a twenty-year-old boy wore an earring? — and made her feel culturally out of touch.

She left her stuff piled on the hood of his car, ran across the sand, and dove beneath a wave. The shock, the sudden cold, was a triumph, an affirmation of her superiority as a rational being who could choose discomfort for the higher good of physical fitness. The water here was dark and heavy with seaweed. It seemed both fresh and full of decay. The sea frightened her, and she swam as if she were being chased. Some people, she knew, relaxed in the water. Helen swam in a near frenzy. Sometimes, when a wave or swell smacked her in the face, she experienced a sickening, hardly conscious recollection of the car accident, the speed of it, the whirl of indistinguishable objects.

At sixteen, the accident had made her merely angry. Lying in the hospital, in the emergency room, as doctors tried to stanch the flow of blood from her lacerated face, she had wondered if her belt, her favorite belt, was ruined. It was so inconvenient, a car crash. How dare this happen? She had almost died, but all she knew, as she almost died, was a prickly irritation, as if death were a curfew, a punishment she could talk her parents out of. Now, twenty-five years later, she understood that she had almost died; she had even gotten used to the idea. But familiarity bred horror, not contempt: death lived in the world, disaster descended from the mountaintop. They were real, death and disaster. Worse, they were plausible. If one let one's wild teenage boyfriend drive one around a sharp curve on a country road at night at seventy miles an hour, one went through a windshield. Therefore, one drove oneself. This was Helen's credo. It extended beyond automobiles. She could have crocheted it on a pillow, hung a sign in the store, tattooed it on her chest: I'LL DRIVE.

It wasn't until she got out of the water that Helen could relax, and then she would fling herself rather dramatically down on the sand and feel the warmth of the sun or the chill of the breeze with so much gratitude that she sometimes pretended not to feel it at all. Her relief, profound and thrilling, was excessive. She disliked excess. It was unnecessary, wasn't it, by definition. She would lie on the beach and feel the sand coat her body. With her eyes closed, she would let her breathing slow, and then, more often than not, fall asleep.

Today, seeing Johnny right there before her, sitting on the sand peeling an orange, she tempered her exit from the water, shook her hair like a wet dog, and sat down heavily beside him. She gave a quick appraising glance at him, at his legs, the wet, baggy red bathing suit, his chest and arms. He had no bulk, just the long, supple build of a swimmer. He was wearing his earring. The sun was visible now, like a little angry eye. The sand was warm, on top. The air was already hot and close around them.

"When I peel an orange . . ." she said.

He looked at her blankly. "Excuse me?"

"Nothing. Just thinking. How peaceful and pensive you look, all alone with an orange. Where's your boom box? Your Walkman? What kind of a young person are you, anyway?"

"I thought it was you," he said. "Swimming."

With her feet, she burrowed until she felt the cooler sand, a shade darker, wetter. Johnny held out a towel, and she felt the dampness when she took it, even though she was so wet. It was his towel, the one he had just used, and this secondhand intimacy made her smile at him.

She was amused by the response to her smile. His whole face changed. His pouting, down-turned mouth lifted. His eyes, normally so big and staring, had receded and softened. She liked his face. It had a pushed-in quality, irregular, like a boxer's face. He was relieved, she saw, he was lonely and young and wanted her friendship, and she was gratified. She put her arm around his shoulders, which felt warm and dry, and said softly, "Johnny, I think you should come have dinner with me tonight. Do you eat alone in that depressing way students do? Do you eat at all, that's what I want to know. I'll cook for you." And I won't tease you, she promised herself. You're very brave to spend the summer in this town. Why *are* you spending the summer here? I must ask you tonight.

He accepted her invitation, obviously grateful, and she looked him over again, this stray she was taking in off the beach. He had appeared so pale in the water, but she saw now that he was tan. His bathing suit seemed too bright on the empty morning beach. He held a section of orange out to her. There were two white grains of sand on the fruit, more on his hand.

5

THE STORE WAS PARTICULARLY WELCOMING THAT
morning, dark and cool. Outside, it had grown absurdly
heavy with heat, top-heavy, unbalanced. Johnny looked out
the window at Main Street, at people walking by, mostly
women in wrinkled linen shorts, their polo shirts damp,
their faces red and excited as, complete strangers, they
nodded to each other, victims acknowledging the ghastly
community of disaster — blackout, earthquake, riots, *heat*.
The weather was all the customers wanted to talk about.
They sat on the couch, panting, their eyes adjusting to the
store's shade.

Now that Johnny had memorized book titles and jacket
copy, he wanted a chance to show off his knowledge. He
wanted to sell. If a woman came in and announced that
Virago had just put out a novel by Radclyffe Hall, one she'd
never read, he wouldn't even flinch. Yes, he would say,
though he'd never read Radclyffe Hall and had never even
heard of her or Virago Press until a week ago. Yes, we just
got it in, isn't it wonderful to discover books by an author

one loves. *Taylor's Guide to Ground Covers,* the new Knopf translation of *Buddenbrooks,* a Grisham, a Ludlum, *WAC Stats,* a book about Queen Elizabeth's dogs, *The Rituals of Dinner,* May Swenson, Zdenek Urbanek, Homer, O'Hara, Frank or John — Johnny would know, offer, fetch, describe, and sell.

He saw Miss Skattergoods pedal up on her bicycle, her helmet pushed back on her head, a Walkman strapped to her arm. Johnny knew her from the library and waved to her now, but she didn't see him as she locked the bike to a fence. Her family had not exactly founded the town. Before the Skattergoods, there had been a few trappers and farmers. But her ancestors had populated Pequot with their own, and Miss Skattergoods had returned to tend their books and papers and artifacts with a flourish, a carefree confidence, as if she were the library's eccentric new nanny. Miss Skattergoods saw nothing unconventional in Johnny's hobby. She found his frequent presence at the library, surrounded by Skattergoodsiana, perfectly logical.

The store was unusually busy, and Helen, with a slight movement of her head, indicated that Johnny should leave the new hardcovers in their cartons and wait on Miss Skattergoods. He knew it was an effort for Helen to share her concubines. He knew she was watching him with one yellow eye. He felt a surge of giddy, shameless pleasure, garrulous and expansive, as if he were on stage, as if his voice boomed magnificent lines, Shakespeare, Chekhov, Kaufman and Hart.

"What can I get you?" he asked. "What can I get you that you don't already have?"

Miss Skattergoods pulled the headphones down around her neck and looked about the store. "My great-aunt Patricia Skattergoods Randolph raised hounds," she said. "They all lived here, in this very house, together, Aunt Batty Patty and the dogs. A thinning gene pool is a terrible thing to witness. My mother was Italian, thank God. No, you can't help me, thank you. I like to browse. Check out the competition."

Disappointed, he went back to his carton of books. If he were selling, he knew what he would do. Today, in this heat, he would offer books as if they were cool drinks. Here you are, try this nice tall memoir of a year in Provence. Or a frosty British comedy. Or *Aquamarine,* doesn't that sound good on a day like today, a first novel, the heroine is an Olympic swimmer, cool and refreshing . . .

It was an art, selling books, a kind of theater, intimate and demanding. It was also a game. Watching Helen, he had gradually come to realize this. Name the shape, the customer shape; find the corresponding piece on the shelf; fit the pieces together; the puzzle is complete. Helen instinctively knew what someone would like. But she often was able simply to seduce customers into buying. She could talk a customer into buying (and reading and enjoying) the most unlikely books. Teenage girls read diplomatic dispatches under Helen's tutelage. Middle-aged men read short stories by avant-garde German feminists. She pushed only what she liked, but she liked many kinds of things and could see no reason that others shouldn't also, and all the reasons that they might. Customers felt the challenge and the lure. Buying a book from Helen was personal, an agreement, an assignation. J. R. Ackerley? I'll be there!

Helen nodded at Johnny again, and he approached an older man. Was this a test? To amuse himself as he checked books in, as he shelved them or dusted them, Johnny often plotted how he would sell them, too. The theory he developed he called the strategic war game method of sales-manship — and now he could test it out. Would Helen notice? Yes. The central control tower noticed everything.

Customer makes first move: "I want something, uh, I don't know — fun, something fun." Salesman interprets this to mean literary enough to be respectable, but not particularly challenging. Suggests new nine-hundred-page Southern novel, critically acclaimed bestseller. Customer balks. Salesman realizes customer has constructed bulwarks as backup defense, namely, book must be short as well as fun. Salesman launches new offensive. Fire one: nine-hundred-page Anglo-Indian novel. Customer coughs noncommittally. Fire two: new paperback of nine-hundred-page Latin American novel. Customer scratches head, looks at floor. Fire torpedoes: nine-hundred-page biographies of forgotten president and minor short-story writer of 1940s. Customer reels. Salesman moves in for the kill: Booker Prize–winning novel, short but first in a trilogy. Customer thrilled, relieved, surrenders, hands high in the air but with honor; buys all three and new John le Carré while he's at it. Cash register rings merrily.

That was how Johnny had imagined it. In fact, the man got discouraged after the Latin American novel and went off empty-handed.

"Johnny," Helen said. She held his chin in her hand. "Try to find out what they want. What they really want. Customers don't always say what they want, they don't even always know. That's why they come in — to find out. That's our job. It's not a trick, we don't trick them. If we do, they won't come back." She banged the side of his head with the palm of her hand. It was a playful gesture — probably. "You have to *listen*, Johnny. It's like making friends," she said. "But you have to make friends and be a good friend at the same time. All at once." She smiled. "Okay?"

"I need something to read," a man said to Helen.

Her attention shifted to him instantly and completely. "It's terrible to be between books," she said. And Johnny marveled at the tenderness of her voice. It suddenly seemed terrible to him, too, to be between books, though he was often between books for months and had never really noticed it before. "It's so disorienting, isn't it?" Helen was saying. "Like a divorce. An amicable one, but still."

"Yes," the man said. "Now I have to date again." He looked at Helen and gave a little, shy laugh.

"I just finished *Wild Swans*," Helen went on, taking his arm and leading him to the shelves. "The most wonderful memoir, a history of China, really, and I don't know which direction to go in next. Have you read it? I wonder if you'd like it. But what did you read last? Maybe I can read that. We'll help each other . . ."

Outside, the heat had gathered even closer, gray, soft, and spongy; inside Johnny wondered how to interpret Helen's advice. Should he be flattered that she took the time to help him? Should he be humiliated? "Listen," she'd said. He rarely listened. He thought constantly, daydreamed, planned and plotted. But listen? Now he would have to listen. He *would* listen.

"What?" he said, startled.

Helen pushed some Jiffy bags at him. "I said it's so fucking hot I don't want to go to the post office, so would you please go?"

He walked across the street, his feet sticking to the melting tarmac. He inhaled heat, exhaled heat. Should he have gone away, like Matt, his college roommate? To Mexico? Or anywhere, hiking or bicycling or prowling museums? He could have worked in a bar, maybe, in another state, another city, someplace new. Anchorage, perhaps.

What was the drinking age in Anchorage? But this was someplace new. This was also someplace rent-free. And he liked being on his own, he liked taking up a whole house. He got up each morning almost reeling with isolation, a pioneer surrounded by miles of waving prairie grasses. The huge house, the little town stretched out before him; the hours, too, awaited him lightly, patiently.

Sometimes, usually in the evening, walking through the empty rooms, he changed his mind. He longed for someone else's cooking. He longed for human companionship, even with the unpredictable Helen. Just trying to sell a book to some weary, sunburnt, perspiring customers was a social gala, a convivial change from his usual routine of unpacking, stacking, counting, hauling. I am a beast of burden, he sometimes thought, looking at Helen as she reached out her hand to some thunderstruck customer. *She* is a beast.

"Go ahead," Helen said, when a young woman came in and stood looking uncertainly around.

Johnny went up to her. "Can I help you?"

"I need a book."

Thank you for that illuminating piece of information, he thought. "For yourself?" he asked.

"Um . . ."

Sometimes, when he was angry or nervous, Johnny could feel his eyes bulge. He knew they did because people told him so. But sometimes he could actually feel them protrude.

"Um . . . yeah, I guess so."

"A novel? Biography?"

"Oh, okay, a novel . . ."

⟁

The bell on the door jingled as a customer left and the store was suddenly silent, empty. Johnny wanted to throw himself on the couch and close his eyes, but Helen threw herself on the couch and closed hers first.

"You're learning," Helen said, her eyes still closed.

"I sold a copy of *The Snows of Kilimanjaro,*" he said, "and *Cold Comfort Farm.* They liked the titles. I tried to find out what they wanted. I tried to listen. That girl said she was too hot to think. Was that okay? Do you think I was, um, frivolous? Do you know what I mean?"

I hate melodrama, Helen was thinking through Johnny's voice, as distant as the rustle of leaves. I like clarity and humor. I like sense. And when I do like sensibility, which I often don't, I like it crisp and straightforward. Reading someone else's love letter is not sense. It makes no sense. Reading someone else's love letter is a treacly, sickening sensibility, perfumed heavily with someone else's scent. It is melodrama, by definition. She made a disgusted sound.

"But I did sell *Love in a Cold Climate* as well, so maybe it's okay . . ."

"You did?" Helen said. She laughed.

Helen's partner, Lucy Dodge Hall, the ghost of the attic office, appeared in the doorway.

"Make more money," Lucy said. "*Please,*" she added politely, and went back upstairs.

⟶

When he got home, Johnny took a beer out of the refrigerator and thought of calling his former girlfriend before heading over to Helen's for dinner. He wasn't sure he actually wanted to talk to her, but he felt a vague loneliness. Carla had not wanted him to come to Pequot. She sulked and spoke of almost nothing else for a full month. He should stay on campus with her, take courses. They should hitchhike to Colorado, wait tables, and ski. Did people ski in the summer there? Well, if not, he should bring her with him to Pequot.

"You'll find someone else," she had said. "You'll leave me. You'll forget me. Men are all the same. You just don't get it. Abandonment is a form of rape."

And then she had looked him in the eyes and delivered the final blow, the one she believed he could not withstand: "You're afraid of commitment."

Commitment? he thought. To what? Sharing a dorm room? Pooling our allowances?

"I just want to get away from everything," he said.

And now, alone in a strange house that belonged to his parents but not somehow to him, he was away.

He looked at the phone, repeated Carla's number in his head, thought of her face, her nose, of which she was quite proud, a snub nose, just a little too snub in his opinion, a bit on the porcine side; her eyes, dark and sincere; her blond hair that she constantly pushed back from her face or threw back with a flick of her head. The smell of her shampoo returned to him, sweetish, like jam. After months of sticky, fruity scents, of anguished discussions of their relationship (discussions that began the moment they had a relationship), of hearing passages of Anaïs Nin read aloud, he had started to feel heavy and dull and ominous in her presence, as if he were drunk.

Johnny was appealing to girls. He was good-looking, re-ally handsome on some days. But he'd always been such a scrawny bug-eyed kid that even after he grew, and grew into his big, round eyes, and occasionally suspected he was good-looking, it was never something he felt. This made him more appealing. People thought he was modest. He wasn't. He believed deeply in his own superiority, but only deeply. On the surface, in his immediate responses, in his daily life, Johnny worried and judged and brought himself to task. Only secretly (and sometimes it was a secret even from himself) did he know that things would work out for him, that he could take the world and convince it to do what he asked.

This is where I wanted to be, he thought. That thought comforted him, and he left for Helen's.

—

When Helen watched Johnny leave the store, she wondered if he would change his clothes for dinner. Change to what? A different white T-shirt? An alternate denim shirt, untucked, a conjurer's cape billowing behind him as he passed the air conditioner? Khaki pants, Birkenstock sandals. It amused her that they dressed alike. Would she change for dinner? Change to what?

I know I'm in love when I see you, I know it when I long to see you. Reading the letter over and over, she had begun to feel as if the letter were reading her. Together they sat on the couch. Together they contemplated the nature of love. *I'm racked by love as if love were pain.* Wooed by its earnest, edgy passion, Helen was now not only convinced the letter had been meant for her, and her alone, but was half in love with Ram herself.

She put the letter in her bag, a huge, ugly canvas sack, battered and shabby, which she always meant to replace and never did. She looked at the bag, once black, now a grubby gray, stuffed with books she had to read and mail she had to answer, and she sighed with disgust as she always did before hoisting it on her shoulder.

She wanted to read the letter at home, in complete privacy, just the two of them, before Johnny came if there was time. At the market on the way home, she thought of the letter, folded, flattened between the letters of Elizabeth Bishop and a Vietnam vet novel. She held a small soft lettuce and passed her fingers over its leaves, separating them, examining, looking for nothing at all.

Helen bought the little lettuce. She bought Parmesan cheese. She bought a loaf of bread and some pasta, blueberries, basil, and a large ugly mushroom. She went to the liquor store and bought a couple of bottles of merlot, sure that Johnny would not, and stuffed them into her canvas bag. She held the bag of groceries in her arms, the smell of the basil rising from the brown paper.

As she cooked, the wooden spoon knocked comfortably against the pan. She enjoyed the act of cooking, but since Emily had gone to camp, Helen hadn't done it much. She ate salads and bread, or a banana, scrambled eggs, a peanut butter sandwich. There had been times in her life when eating alone was dreary. This was not one of them. Cooking was lovely, but there was also the daily, palpable pleasure of not making a meal. She could have an apple for dinner, a bottle of beer for dinner. But now the steam rolling in a warm fog from the pot removed her from that sparse and solitary happiness to the realm of aproned, sloping-bosomed maternal kitchen marvels.

Her own mother had never cooked. They'd had a cook, who was also the housekeeper, who'd also straightened Helen out on the facts of life. "Standing up?" she remembered Dinah saying, trying not to smile. "No, honey. You've got the picture wrong in your head. Mostly." Helen used to watch her cook. Helen's daughter liked to watch Helen cook, often helping. Emily's eating habits had become increasingly narrow, though. A courageous eater as a small child, snacking on cold Brussels sprouts to the astonishment and envy of the parental world, she had developed other less impressive but equally eccentric tastes recently. She had become a vegetarian, except for bacon and hot dogs. And then, the only vegetables she liked were radishes and half dill pickles.

Helen thought how much she missed Emily. The sound of her pounding through the house, the detritus of her games, the whining that she had "nothing to *do,*" all appeared to Helen now as shining details of a life almost unbearably full, euphoric and miraculously hers. Her existence was blessed by her child's childhood. And that blessed intensity would return soon, with Emily, it would come back to her. She would see it drive up in the camp's bus and scoop it up and bring it home again, tuck it into its bed, shake it conscious each morning, buy it new shoes and pencils. Those things Helen could control (her body, her speech, her workdays, her manner, her friends and acquaintances), she did control. What she could not control, she regarded as insubstantial or as inevitable. Most of her feelings she deemed insubstantial and she sent them packing with barely a nod of recognition. But her feelings for her daughter she recognized as inevitable, irresistible, and she reveled in them.

In this sturdy domestic moment, Helen felt a benign satisfaction with all around her, particularly, though, with herself, the center of all around her. How thoughtful of me to invite poor Johnny to dinner. Then she wondered for a moment whether perhaps he liked only radishes and bacon, too. Maybe it was a generational development. Was he of Emily's generation? Not really (Emily was only eleven), but he was closer in age to Emily than to Helen. Had they both watched *Sesame Street* as toddlers?

Helen poured herself a Scotch and went to her bag, which she'd left lying in the hall, to have a quick look at the letter. Who had written it? Why had he not just signed his name? What was he afraid of, ashamed of? Why a goat? Why not a duck? Did Ram watch Marx Brothers movies? Did Goat? Oh, yes, she, Helen, was Goat. She heard a car pull up, glanced in the mirror, took her drink, and went to the door to meet her guest.

—

Johnny arrived in his blue Lincoln at exactly eight o'clock. He was punctual. It seemed unnecessary not to be punctual. He sat in the car, though, for several minutes, reluctant to leave the haven of the worn, cracked leather. He pulled at a rip in the upholstery and wondered what he should have brought. His experience with dinner parties was limited. He had a sense that one ought to bring something. But what? He had tried to remember what his parents brought with them. A bottle of wine? He'd considered it, but his ignorance about wine was too profound. What if he brought a terrible wine, a ghastly year from a preposterous province of the wrong country? A clown wine? Helen would laugh at him again, and think, There, there, poor child with his little offering. Would she drink it politely, the way his mother used to wear the terrible jewelry he bought her at Woolworth's? No. Decidedly not. She would laugh, hold the bottle up with affectionate contempt, and say, "Aren't you sweet." And if he were lucky, she would not say the rest, only think it: Johnny, dear, leave the wine to the grown-up, to me.

And so I have, Johnny thought. I've left it to you, you old witch. And he looked at her house as though it were a candy cottage. There, waiting for him to jump inside, the oven, preheated.

Why did I come? I could have gone with Jennifer or Kelly

to a movie. Why doesn't Helen invite them to dinner? Why am I the chosen one? Maybe she wants to fire me. Maybe she needs someone to repair the back steps.

He picked at one of the holes left on the seat by his grandfather's cigar ash. His grandfather had been silent and remote but kind. He was the relative one turned to — for a summer job, for money — the relative of last resort, the relative one was most ashamed to approach, the relative who never said no. Johnny missed him, when he smelled cigar smoke or saw a suit of a certain medium blue color. When he drove the car with the windows open, he sometimes recalled driving his grandfather on a fishing trip. "Slow down, Johnny," his grandfather had said. "Johnny, it's a dirt road. Slow down." Johnny had been going only twenty-five miles an hour and could not understand his grandfather's concern, until they both realized the volume on his hearing aid was turned up full blast and the soft, passing breeze of the open windows swirled dangerously in his ears, the gales of a hurricane.

She won't eat you up, Johnny, he said to himself as he stood in the driveway facing the big white house. She felt sorry for you and invited you here for a good meal. She misses her daughter and is feeling motherly. You're doing her a favor, too. He relaxed, imagining a plate of pot roast, a pale dune of mashed potatoes, the inviting gray of over-cooked string beans. He looked up at the house. It was large, regular, and white, a red brick chimney at either end. Eighteenth century. He knew, before he looked, that the stable would be a hundred or so feet to the left. Hey! he thought. I know this house. She lives in Everett Banks Millerton's house. At the library, he'd just read a reference to the house in a triumphant letter from a Reverend Matthew Skattergoods, a distant cousin of the owner and a colonel in the Revolutionary army, to E. B. Millerton, an elderly Royalist by this time decamped to England. "The rooms, uncommon large, suit us nicely," wrote Reverend Skattergoods, apparently house-sitting for his relative.

Do not imagine that the vista, however pleasing, makes us forgetful of our responsibility to you in your absence. You will find it interesting, though, to be kept informed of all the progress taking place here after your unfortunately hasty leave-taking. You will remember how in the past we would complain of the black flies leaving us in blotches and pray they would not continue past the 1st July. It seemed but part of the Commission given to the destroying Angel, and this we knew, and ought to have felt, our highly favored Country had sinned, with a high hand, against "High Heaven." Well did we join in the lamentation of the humble prophet "Woe is me for I am of unclean lips and I dwell among people of unclean lips." Since your departure, you will be surprised and gratified to learn, these same black flies have not seen fit to return. In this house, they might well be kept at bay by the cooling breezes of the ocean swells. But in the rest of the region, I suspect a higher agent.

Helen stood at the door and watched Johnny. He didn't see her. He sat moodily in his big car, staring. She remembered sitting in the car in that driveway, listening to sylvan rustlings and neighborly lawn mowers. It was a family habit. Her mother sat, too, her elbow on the wheel, her chin in her hand. Sometimes they sat together, the two of them, talking for ten minutes, twenty, sometimes for an hour, their

heads facing straight ahead (no eye contact, like two ana-
lysands without their analysts, without their couches), her
mother laughing and vigorous, Helen thrilled to be in her
company, to have her alone, all to herself, in the intimacy
of the parked automobile. In the summer when it was hot,
with the windows rolled down, they would hear the cicadas
and they would know it was late, time to go in although
the day lingered oddly on. In the winter, blowing on their
hands, they would spout white breath as they spoke, about
nothing, really, until the cold became unbearable and they
would run into the house. There Helen would see her
mother caught up and borne away by telephones and
housekeepers, by her father if he were there, by letters and
books and the dolorous Romantic music she favored —
borne away from Helen's exclusive claims like a showgirl
lifted on the shoulders of a chorus of top-hatted dancing
men. Helen had learned to share her mother, but she had
never gotten used to it.

She still liked to sit in the driveway when she got home,
partly to recall those lovely, stolen talks, interludes in her
real life, meaningless to the progression of her days, but full
of a larger charm and significance that she felt even now.
And partly she sat in the empty car because she was reluctant to leave its protection. There was nothing to do in the
car once one had finished driving it. It was so private and
restful. This was when she felt most amiable, most kindly
disposed toward her fellow man — when she was alone.

She watched Johnny get out of the car. He looked at the
big house with something she thought might have been awe
— it was an impressive house — then turned his eyes down
and shuffled in.

"This is where I grew up," she said. "Then we, my mother
actually, rented the place out for years. I've been renovating

it for years. By the time I finish, I'm sure I'll have to start all over again. It's old."

She said the word *old* with grudging respect. Johnny said nothing about E. B. Millerton. Either she already knew, or she wouldn't be interested. This was one of the things one learned quickly about one's hobby. He looked around as she talked and saw a careful, easy, modern living room, books on every wall (didn't she have enough at the store? he wondered), a bare floor, some kind of couch the size of a double bed covered with an Oriental rug that looked older than the house, a low leather armchair.

"Very nineteenth-century Vienna," Johnny said.

"Colonial furniture is too spindly for me," Helen said, a little surprised he knew there was a Vienna or a nineteenth century. "I stomp around, crash into it . . ."

She continued to talk and supposed the chatter was meant to ease his discomfort. But was he uncomfortable? The foot shuffling, the head hanging — were they signs of shyness, or just signs of youth? Either way, it made her feel old.

"Sit down," she said, and her voice sounded to her like an owner's voice, and he obeyed her, well trained, good and loyal, bred that way.

Johnny sat in the armchair, grateful she had bossily ordered him to sit, leaving him time to collect his thoughts, happy in the large living room, its windows looking out onto a lush garden, a few fruit trees, then rows of dark pines. Beyond them, he knew, was the beach: cliffs high and sudden, dropping, without warning, to the din of the waves below.

In *Litchfield's Coastal Travels in the Americas,* he remembered, this place was described as "land not fit for culture, but useful in its ocean aspects." Where was the view now? The garden stretched out in a soft drift, colors jumbled any which way, an unmade bed of red and yellow and pink. Then came the trees. Apple, plum. And the Japanese black pine. Brought here a hundred years or so ago, they were everywhere in the Northeast now, their clumps of needles full as brooms, brushing the skies of highway dividers and shopping mall parking lots. But soon they would all be gone, he knew. They had thrived ridiculously in the New World; and they would perish here, millions of them, infected by a New World virus carried by a New World wasp.

"Johnny?" Helen stood before him. How had she gotten there? She was bending toward him, her face almost level with his. She knocked gently on his head, as if he were a door.

"Those pine trees will all be gone in a few years," he said. "Then you'll have your view back."

Helen looked at him curiously.

"I will?"

A dog, a very old dog, slid from beneath the divan or couch or double bed, whatever it was, stood up, stared at Johnny, sniffed, then walked crookedly, slowly, away.

"That's Jasper," she said.

"Hi, Jasper," he said.

"He'll be gone in a few years, too, won't you, Jasper? Do you want wine, Johnny? Go into the hall, in front, and get the wine, would you? It's in my bag. I have to cook. Pour yourself a glass." She put two wine glasses on a small table by the bed with the rug on it. She handed him a corkscrew. "Me too."

Dear Goat,

How does one fall in love? Do you trip? Do you stumble . . .

Johnny squatted on the floor above the canvas bag, its

worn gray mouth splayed open, the letter spread before him, staring up at him, daring him to read on.

I have fallen in love without taking a step.

Who had fallen in love without taking a step? How *do* you fall in love?

Is there a precipice, from which you float, over the edge, forever? . . . I feel your hair brush my cheek when it does not . . .

The hall was spare and pretty, boarding-house chic. There was one chair against a wall, its paint peeling in picturesque fashion. But it was piled with old newspapers, which spoiled the effect. Johnny read the letter again and felt that he, himself, must surely never have fallen in love. *You'll see,* said the letter. He read it once more, and then, in the thrill of eavesdropping, again. *How does one fall in love?* He reached into the bag, beneath the letter, to pull out the dark bottles of wine. He slid them, one in each hand, along the sides of the bag, not disturbing the letter in the center. The letter, white and crinkled, stared back up at him. It had obviously been folded before, but so oddly, so unevenly. The creases themselves had a sense of desperation. I only wanted the wine, he thought. I went to the bag in the hall for the wine. I didn't know it was the bag for the love letters, for Helen's love letters. I don't even like wine.

Who wrote this love letter to Helen? He felt sick with curiosity. Perhaps Helen had written the letter? Perhaps she'd left it there for him to see? Left it there for *him?* He couldn't actually imagine Helen in love. Not lost in love like the letter writer. Much less leaving a letter in a bag for him. He read the letter again, realizing as he did that he'd memorized it, that his eavesdropping was not limited now to this moment, but would stay with him. He pushed the letter away, back in the bag, between two books. If she had left it out for him to see, to torment him in some way, which she was just capable of doing, she would see it covered up and know he had read it. If she hadn't, no one need be the wiser.

"Johnny?" She called him from the kitchen. "Find it?"

"Yeah."

I found it. I found it, Helen. And now I know something about you. But what?

He opened one of the bottles. He poured two glasses. She smiled at him when he came into the kitchen. She touched her glass to his and drank. She put her glass down on the counter. She put one foot up on a chair, noticed a loose shoelace, and tied it. *When I tie my shoes* . . .

Johnny reached toward a bowl of fruit that stood in the middle of the table. He picked up an orange. *When I peel an orange* . . .

They stared at each other for a moment.

"Not now," Helen said.

"Not now?"

She tapped the cool skin of the orange. "For dessert."

—

Back in the living room, Johnny knelt down to pet the dog and wondered who was in love with Helen and why. Then he wondered if he should have changed his clothes. Helen was wearing a clean black T-shirt and black jeans. Evening wear. Then he wondered what to say. *Is that too banal for you?* He imagined most things were too banal for Helen, but could a lover consumed by fiery passion be one of them? Or was a lover on fire the most banal of all?

"So why did you come to spend the summer in this hot little town?" Helen said.

Johnny hesitated. She had asked him this question before and had not waited for his answer. But now Helen threw herself, with a contented sigh, onto the double-bed couch, and because she was practically lying down, having kicked her shoes onto the floor, waiting silently, he thought either he was meant to join her there in some amorous activity, or that she had prepared herself to actually listen, comfortably, to his answer this time. The latter, however improbable, seemed the more likely of the two. "I don't know," he said. "Free rent." He asked her if she knew whose house this had been originally.

"Some English sailor, I think."

He told her about Millerton, naval commander and politician, who had arrived early in the century as a young man and set up trading posts with the several tribes of Indians whose lands intersected on his own; who had lived with his mistresses as if they were wives, an Indian wife and an Irish indentured servant–girl wife. On this land, outside this stable, yearly conferences of Indian chiefs were held.

He paused, looking for signs of boredom.

"At the same time?" Helen asked.

"What?"

"The Indian mistress and Irish mistress. Simultaneously?"

"Apparently."

"Those Puritans. Nice furniture, too." And she waited for him to continue.

"Millerton exported black cherry lumber to the English furniture makers, actually. And, um, from this house, he imported settlers, farmers and craftsmen. He speculated in real estate, too. He went back to England as an old man. Royalist. Lost everything."

Then Johnny told her that he'd run across Pequot in a book he was reading in an American history class.

"I was reading about a battle that took place in Recklesstown. It was supposed to take place, anyway, but the British passed by a stream — it's the one where the Spinning Wheel Restaurant is now — and they stopped, had a swim, a rest. They didn't march by the town till the next day, and by then the minutemen had all gone home. Anyway, I was reading about this. And then I saw in a footnote that Recklesstown later became Pequot."

"That's my town," Helen said. "A town with a famous battle never fought."

"A town with aliases."

"I thought it was always named Pequot. Do you like your name, Johnny?"

"It's John, actually. Only my parents call me Johnny," he said, although he'd already informed her of this on the first day of work.

"And me. I call you Johnny. Do you mind?"

Johnny thought about it. "Not anymore," he said.

"Helen has no diminutive," Helen said.

"I know," he said. He laughed.

"Did we once talk about this?" Helen asked, and Johnny nodded.

"Oh." And she began to tell him about a new paperback edition of a Lore Segal novel.

But he was watching her now, as she spoke, instead of listening. He looked at her feet. Her feet were bare. Her toenails painted red. Funny, to paint your toenails, which few people saw, and not to paint your fingernails, which everyone saw. I'm one of the few people, he thought. He wondered if her toenails had had polish on them at the beach. Had he simply not noticed? Why was he noticing now?

"Let's eat," Helen said.

"Pequot was once called Point Caviar," he said. "Because

so many sturgeon were caught and shipped. You know the old railroad tracks? Near the yacht club? That's from the sturgeon-fishing days."

"What a protean town. What next?"

Johnny shrugged. He had no interest in what next. How could one know what next until it was no longer next, but was now, which made it, almost immediately, then?

She pointed to a chair at the round, battered oak table. Is this where Ram, the man who wrote the letter, sat, staring across the table at Helen, unable to eat? Two place mats had been laid out, black rubber flecked with yellow and turquoise and red, as if someone had made a huge black, spotted rubber meat loaf and sliced off these thin slabs. Johnny, admiring the way they looked with the red flowered damask napkins, the mixed-up silverware, all large and expensive but none of it matching, realized he had meat loaf on the brain. Though the warm kitchen smells did not much resemble meat loaf, it was true. More like spaghetti.

"Pasta," Helen said, carrying in a large, flat white bowl.

"I love pasta," he said. I eat it every night, he added, to himself. It's the only thing I know how to cook. And she asked him more about Pequot, and he told her.

Helen is listening to me, he thought, but it's her listening that makes me speak in the first place. It was a gift, the way Helen listened — like a beautiful singing voice. Helen attended, when she chose, easy and kind, her eyes fixed with a gentle intensity on your own. And yet you knew how impatient she could be, how demanding. And so her approval gave you the feeling of having been chosen, sheltered. For that moment, that one lovely moment, Helen was protecting you from something — from Helen.

Was this why people fell for her? Was this what Ram

saw, what Ram heard? Or was it the way she somehow held your glance, her eyes slyly taking you in as she overwhelmed you? There was something inevitable about Helen, a gust of temperament, of kindness, of intolerance, a demanding warmth.

Jesus, Johnny, she's just Helen, your noisy boss. She's okay-looking for a middle-aged woman. She's funny when she wants to be. So some guy fell for her. A guy named Ram. Some guy who's into astrology. Hard to imagine Helen letting someone call her Goat. Hard to imagine Helen entertaining serious thoughts about astrology. But why imagine Helen at all? The real thing was more than enough.

"Come to the picnic tomorrow. You are coming, aren't you?" Helen said.

Was he going to the fireworks? He loved fireworks. Pequot held them at the beach each Fourth of July. The Police Athletic League sold tickets, fifteen bucks a car.

"I didn't get a ticket."

"Come with me. Come on, Johnny. We sit near the cannons. Did they ever fire those cannons? At the British?"

"No."

"But you'll come to the fireworks anyway, won't you?"

"Yes."

———

She wondered about Johnny and wanted to know more. He sat in her chair, at her table, spread in so many directions, his limbs stuck out this way and that like hands on a clock, a minute hand, an hour hand, a second hand, a hand for the alarm. He pointed everywhere at once, a crazy compass. Where was north, anyway? Where am I? said the compass. What difference does it make? answered the compass. I am here.

Helen liked him and felt he was worth following up. But then, suddenly, she wanted him out, him and all his hands and directions, all his possibilities, out of her house, out of her sight. They drank their coffee, and Helen drummed her fingers on the tablecloth, distracted now, aloof. Johnny watched the fingers, as if they danced, in leotards, on a stage. She had big hands. Her nails were short. The fingers thumped, large dancers, clumsy dancers. He was moved by them. They thumped so seriously, like big-boned children on a school stage.

"Do you receive much mail?" she asked suddenly, when they'd finished. "You know — letters."

"A few. From my parents, mostly. You certainly do."

"Yes."

And the conversation was over, as if it had been snapped shut.

———

Johnny drove home full of food and wine and a feeling, an obscure feeling. Was it gratitude? Or annoyance? Was it pleasure? Or was it rage?

He smelled the stale cigars of his grandfather, a fragrance of the past, faint but unmistakable. The night was mossy and hot, and his open windows roared around him. Helen had stretched out on her carpet-covered divan, a pasha in black jeans, and listened gloriously. She had seated him at a round table and fed him. She had spoken to him softly, about her daughter, her mother, and grandmother. They were all coming home, she said. She was wary of so many women in her house, wary of so much family in her family. Helen had confided in him in a small way, a friendly way. And he had been lulled, like a child by a song.

"Towns are my hobby," he had said, stupidly.

"Lucky towns," she said. Then, suddenly, "Towns are like marriages. Bad marriages. Multigenerational bad Mormon marriages. Towns are full of fools."

"Fools are my hobby," he said. And she laughed.

Then Helen had done what Helen did. She turned, suddenly sour, like milk. He felt a quick, sharp distance. Not again, he thought from deep within his comfortable, companionable mood. But there it was — the empty boredom of her eyes, the distracted banality of her conversation, then the simple, straightforward impatience, the smooth superiority. He wondered what he was doing there. Surely he had invited himself? He had pushed himself on her in some way. He was curious and uncouth, a hanger-on, the blackened boy chimney sweep who had wandered into her ladyship's pastel bedroom.

There is no class system in the United States! he wanted to shout. Get off your high horse! But Helen, on her high horse, had already galloped out of earshot.

"Good-bye, Johnny," she said.

What have I done? he wondered as he shook her large abstracted hand. He had allowed himself pleasure and comfort in her company, in her confectionery house, only to be tipped helplessly into the witch's waiting oven. What an ass, he thought. But whether he meant Helen or himself he could not decide.

⌒

Too much fraternizing with the help, Helen, she thought. It won't do. She wondered if Johnny ought to go out with Jennifer or Kelly. Jennifer, she decided. Kelly was less intelligent. She would see what she could do about Johnny and Jennifer. She took her bag and her letter from the hall up into her bedroom, read the letter again, got into bed, read a happy Elizabeth Bishop letter about a macaw, wished she was in Brazil, then wrote a letter to Emily.

Dear Emily,

I miss you. Bailey has killed 14 moles, 6 mice, and 1 bird. Jasper sends his drooly, snoring love. It's been really hot here. The black flies are gone, though. Do you have enough After-Bite? Grandma Lilian and Grandma Eleanor are coming for a visit. We'll try on hats and play poker. Lucy got a tattoo on her ankle.

One of the college kids working for me, a guy named Johnny, came for dinner. He said our house was built by a man married to an Indian woman and an Irish servant girl *at the same time!* He ran away during the Revolutionary War. Not Johnny. The guy who built our house. I wonder how his wives managed in London, where everyone was so proper. Send candy. I miss you terribly, I love you.

Love,

Mommy

Johnny got into bed with a beer and turned on *Mystery Science Theater* 3000. It was one he'd already seen, with Joel and the two robots watching a biker movie. The bikers began to scream at each other, waving broken bottles. "What is this — *The McLaughlin Report?*" said Joel. Johnny wondered what Helen was doing now. Was she watching *Mystery Science Theater* 3000? Or Letterman? Was she reading? Sleeping? Sleeping with whom?

The phone rang, and for a moment he thought it must be Helen. Why? She had never called him before. Certainly not at one A.M.

"John? Did I wake you up?"

Carla?

"I didn't wake you, did I? I'm on the road. Driving to Maine for a workshop."

"Hi, Carla."

"Advanced West African drums. Do you think I should transfer to Wesleyan? Oh, you don't care. But they have an excellent ethnic drum department. And a Javanese gamelan! I'm outside of Pequot now. Can I stop by? Spend the night? No strings attached. I just can't find a motel. Fucking July Fourth."

Johnny gave her directions to his house and waited for her downstairs. When she drove up, he felt the stirrings of sexual desire, which he thought was too bad because he was so tired and Carla was basically such a pain in the ass.

"You look great," she said, touching his bare arms, poking his chest. "Working out?"

"Swimming. Where are you going in Maine? Are you hungry or anything? Want a beer?"

After they had sex, Johnny held her in his arms in his parents' bed, fruity shampoo scenting the air, Carla's beautiful breasts resting against him, Carla's gentle trivialities murmuring in the night.

"My energy is so diffused in the summer."

Johnny thought of Helen. What would she make of Carla?

"Drumming centers me."

Johnny told her it was good to see her. Which it was. He liked sleeping with her. But he thought, too, that it would be good to see her go the next day when she continued her trip north.

"I think I'll stay one extra day," she said, kissing him. "Go to the fireworks with you. The workshop doesn't start till the sixth."

"Great!"

"I'll come to the store."

"We're closed tomorrow."

"We?"

6

JOHNNY DIDN'T WANT TO DRIVE TO THE FIREWORKS with Helen now that Carla was coming. He thought the extra passenger would annoy Helen, and if not the extra passenger per se, then perhaps this extra passenger. He called Jennifer instead and arranged to go with her and Kelly.

"Can we go in your car, though?" Jennifer said. "Does it have a bar and a whirlpool? We won't fit in my Hyundai anyway."

Johnny drove the three girls to the beach, where a policeman in white gloves took the big cardboard ticket Jennifer held out the window for him. Other policemen waved cars in confusing directions.

They found Helen manning a long table covered with a red-and-white-checked cloth and a dozen bowls and plates. She smiled, shaking Carla's hand when Johnny introduced them.

"John loves his job," Carla said. "He uses the first person plural for the store. He's a supportive person."

Helen flashed a glance at Johnny, a moment of eye

contact full of questions, full of conclusions: Your girl-friend? Not very keen on her, are you? I mean, you've never mentioned that you had a girlfriend, though why shouldn't you have a girlfriend? She looks a little like Doris Day, even with the brown eyes. Is that what you like — Doris Day?

Johnny heard the questions and looked down at the sand. He saw a spent shotgun shell, a crab shell spotted like a leopard, a cigarette butt, and a straw.

Carla thanked Helen for letting her join the picnic, explaining she was on her way to an African drumming workshop.

"Ah," Helen said. "You drum."

"I'm into authenticity, kind of."

In a rush of malevolence for which she couldn't account, and utterly unable to help herself, Helen said, "What's your sign?"

Helen, you bitch, she thought, watching Johnny blush the way he did. You condescending bitch. So she takes bongo seminars. You used to macramé. Although you never actually studied it, did you? Maybe Carla takes macramé classes, too. Droopy hammocks for plants, ugly belts. Helen smiled an indulgent smile at the memory.

"Aries," Carla was saying. She nodded a few times in a thoughtful manner, then said, "You must be an Aries, too. We're so direct."

Johnny looked down, then silently pulled Carla away to see the cannon that never fired a shot. He stood with his hand on the rough black surface. He glanced back at Helen. He realized he could not take his eyes off her. She unpacked plastic forks and spoons. She smoothed the checked tablecloth on the folding table. She pulled more bowls from paper bags — fried chicken, sliced steak, potato salad. She peeled Saran Wrap from the bowls. Johnny watched her. He watched her hands crumple the plastic, drop it in the bag set aside for garbage. He heard her say, "Oh shit, what will I wrap leftovers in?" and retrieve the crumpled wrap.

George was there, too, and his wife, Nancy, a very beautiful blonde, her hair cut just like Johnny's, which gave her a sensible, no-nonsense look. *And gives me a nonsense look,* Johnny thought.

Johnny watched Helen flirt with George, flirt with George's wife. She kissed each of them on the mouth. She left her hand on Nancy's arm. She smiled at them, served them, laughed at whatever they chose to say. Lucy arrived with a cake decorated with strawberries and blueberries to look like the American flag. He saw Miss Skattergoods nearby, on a folding chair, sipping a drink. She waved a hand at him, trailing cigarette smoke. Kelly and Jennifer, giggling and whispering, took off on a journey to the ladies' room and took Carla with them. They seemed to know everyone along the way, stopping at blanket after blanket. Barry and Eliot set up their chairs and argued about who had been responsible for dropping, and breaking, an enormous bowl of tabbouleh in the parking lot. Johnny glanced at all of them, then looked back at Helen. *I look away from you, sometimes. Then I look back.*

❦

Helen laid the food on the table the way she always had, the way she had for as long as she could remember, ever since she could reach the table. The menu was still the same — fried chicken, marinated steak sliced paper-thin, potato salad. Over the years, as the picnic had grown to include other people, other dishes had arrived with them. But Helen's contribution was unchanged from her mother's offerings forty years ago. The same bowls, enamel, brought back by her mother from a trip to Norway before Helen was born. The same beach, a rocky crescent. The cannon. The dark water. The line of dry seaweed. Lines of gulls standing on glassy blue patches of wet sand. Lines of children running back and forth to the water, back and forth. Ladies walking two by two, friends, a stroll. A line of sails beneath a line of pink cloud. Helen remembered when she first drew a beach, in art class at summer camp, age four. She drew a blue strip and a brown one. But she put the brown strip on top by accident. Normally, she thought, things came in lines at the beach. Tonight the beach was so crowded it looked more like a maze.

She took paper plates out of the picnic basket, saw Kelly, Jennifer, and Johnny's girlfriend, or whatever she was, threading their way back to the table through sand castles and beach towels and blankets spread with food. How silly Johnny's girlfriend was. Pretty. But Jennifer would be much better for him.

Janet passed by carrying a huge picnic basket. She was meeting one of her dates. "His wife left him for her helicopter instructor," she said. "And he pats his hamburgers with napkins. At restaurants."

Helen put plastic forks and knives and spoons on the table and watched George. He was helping Lucy find room for her cake, the berries plump and bright on the white icing. What if George *had* written the letter? What if he had written it *to her*? What if, after all these years, he had finally fallen in love with her? She wondered if she were in love with him.

George was walking toward her. A fife and drum band in Civil War uniforms marched past. Wrong war, she thought. The sky got darker. Too quickly, she thought. George stood beside her now. Too close? Helen saw Nancy from the corner of her eye. She wanted to lean forward and touch George's lips again with her lips, as she had when he'd arrived, his cheek with her cheek, and then she would know, as if his cheek were a letter, and she could read it. There was a sudden shaft of lightning, long and jagged. Helen felt her hair stand up, the hair on the back of her neck.

Everyone's hair stood up, for a moment, strands floating in the air. Except Jennifer's. Everyone rushed toward the cars. George grabbed Helen's arm and pushed her into his car. She saw Nancy in Johnny's ridiculous car, the two of them laughing, the three girls in the back seat. George was beside Helen, a bucket seat away, tense, frowning. Helen wondered what she would normally say to him, for she found herself speechless. You wrote it, didn't you, George? You wrote that letter. We've resisted each other for years. I wonder if we will this time? She looked at him, at his face in profile, his features easy and graceful in a way that made his face a pleasure to look at without drawing attention to this fact, his hair almost white, long, brushed back from his forehead. She waited for him to say something, to give her some clue. Like, "Oh, by the way, Helen, I accidentally sent you a love letter the other day. I have, also accidentally of course, fallen passionately in love with you, but as you know I'm happily married and don't wish to jeopardize that relationship, what with the child and all, and of course longevity leads to longevity if you know what I mean, we humans being such creatures of habit. But I have fallen head over heels, let's face it, and there's only one face I see, as you know, having read the letter, which I didn't really intend to send, you know, but, the human unconscious being what it is . . ."

She waited.

George stared anxiously out the windshield at the dark beach. "I really do not want to be hit by lightning," he said. "Such a cliché."

Then there was no more lightning. There had been no rain. The whole thing lasted less than five minutes. The sky got lighter. The sun began to set properly. They ate and picked sand from their chicken in the pink light.

Such a cliché? Helen thought. Was falling in love a cliché, too? *How does one fall in love?* She passed Johnny several times as she offered people food, carried garbage to the cans, replenished platters. This was her picnic, primarily, and she acted the good hostess. She passed Johnny, but when he wasn't surrounded by the three chattering girls, he seemed always to be looking the other way when she got near him, looking down at his plate, up at the sky, out to sea.

———

Lucy came and stood beside Johnny. "All these children," she said.

Johnny had hardly noticed them. But they were everywhere, digging, running, squealing. What was Helen's child like, he wondered. He'd seen her picture. She looked nothing like Helen. But was she like Helen in some other way? Did she take pleasure in people the way her mother did, the way a herpetologist takes pleasure in reptiles?

"I always used to worry that I'd lose one of my kids here. In the dark," Lucy said.

"Where are your kids?"

"Law school."

Johnny thought, How old is Lucy? She looks younger than Helen. But her kids are older than I am. "How about

your husband?" Johnny asked, astonished at his own bold-
ness. Lucy never mentioned one, after all.

"Law school," she said.

———

Helen, walking by with an armload of trash, saw Johnny
talking to Lucy. Why won't he talk to me tonight? she
wondered. Why is he avoiding me? I think Lucy's avoiding
me as well. I don't know why I think that. But I do. Why
is Lucy talking to Johnny? They never speak to each other.
Not much anyway. Johnny should be with some nice young
people, girls his own age, even Carla.

"As a woman," Carla was saying, "I have trouble with the
militaristic basis of Fourth of July fireworks. But they're so
totally exciting!"

———

"Do you miss being a lawyer?" Johnny asked Lucy.

"No. I love working with Helen. I love Helen. Don't
you?"

"I love Helen," Helen heard Lucy say.

She continued walking, quickly, the sand cold beneath
her bare feet. *Typically stupid choice. . . . It's all wrong and
you know it. . . . You are all wrong for me . . .* I'll say, Helen
thought. *You are all wrong for me, I know it, but I no longer
care for my thoughts unless they're thoughts of you.*

Lucy?

Helen thought, It could be anyone. Anyone here could
have sent me that letter. Almost. Anyone here could be in
love. In love with me at this very moment. Maybe it wasn't
meant for me, but maybe it was. I received it, after all. It
came to me at my address. It's my letter.

"It's mine," she said aloud. And someone here is mine.

The sky got darker. The flag cake was cut. Helen dabbed icing from Lucy's lips.

The air is still.

"Isn't the air still?" Helen said.

"No, Helen. It's windy."

I no longer eat, I forget to eat. . . . when I peel an orange . . .

"How's your appetite these days, Lucy? Do you like oranges? I've often wondered — do you cut your fruit?"

Lucy chewed her cake and stared thoughtfully at Helen.

"Or do you peel it?"

Lucy laughed, pushed a finger at Helen's chest, and shook her head. "That's private information, baby."

Johnny, close to them in the near dark, listened and watched. Lucy? he thought. Could Lucy have written the letter?

"Fuck you," said Helen, taking Lucy's hand and steering the last bit of cake into her own mouth.

"Just like a wedding," Lucy said.

Jennifer and Kelly and Carla, all pals on a beach towel now, pulled Johnny beside them. He noticed their long, bare legs, stretched in the sand. Each had a green plastic strip that glowed in the dark around her neck.

"Here, Johnny, we bought one for you," said Carla, slipping it over his head.

He saw Helen, her face lit by a citronella lantern, watching.

"Thank you," he said to Carla. He could smell her Jell-O soap smell.

"This is kind of like Take Back the Night," Carla said.

"It is?" said Kelly.

"I think it's like opera in the park," said Jennifer. "Have you ever been to the opera in Central Park?"

I lived overlooking Central Park, Johnny thought. I saw the leaves turn, acres of them, from above, like God. In Pequot, the leaves are all around you.

He dug his foot into the sand, homesick. Kelly and Jennifer asked him to join them in their blanket hopping. He shook his head. "Go ahead," he said to Carla.

"Great," she said, obviously annoyed. "Sure."

Johnny heard jazz coming from Miss Skattergoods's radio. He hated music at the beach.

"Johnny." It was Helen. She sat beside him. Her leg, the white denim of her leg, almost touched his leg, the white denim of his leg. "Did you notice that you and I dress alike?"

He nodded.

"What are you thinking about? You look very blue." She put her hand on his. Then suddenly: "Am I an Aries? When *is* Aries?"

Johnny allowed his hand to feel her hand. The touch of her spread. Her hand stayed where it was, but he felt it everywhere, roaming across his body. He looked at her, but her head was back, her eyes closed. Her face was tired. He felt he had to speak. A defense against her touch.

"I was thinking that in New York I looked down on all the trees from my window. In Pequot, they're all around me."

She turned and smiled at him. Then the fireworks began. She pulled her hand away, turned her eyes to the sky.

"Aries is the ram," he said.

She jerked her head around and faced him.

"You're a Capricorn. Goat. Sign of the goat."

He could feel her eyes on him. He looked up at the fireworks. A bar of linked burning colored lights drifted down from the sky.

"That looks like a menorah," Barry said.

"Oh, you think *everything* looks like a menorah," said Eliot.

When I tie my shoes, when I peel an orange, when I drive my car . . . "When I drive my car . . ." Johnny said.

Lucy stood beside them, several green plastic necklaces around her neck.

"Are you selling those?" a man asked her.

"Don't be ridiculous!" she said.

"When I drive my car," Johnny said, turning to face Helen's stare, "I see you sometimes. Running."

———

Helen sat in her car, the post-fireworks traffic jam even worse than usual. A policeman directed her to turn left. She did, and faced another car directed to turn right by another policeman. Their headlights shone at each other. Hemmed in on every side, no place to turn or even back up, Helen sat passively, watching the other car try to maneuver its way out. It was such a large car. It was Johnny's, she realized, as at last it managed to turn and pulled away, across her bow, like an ocean liner passing a fishing boat. Kelly and Jennifer had given him their pass and he had driven them in his big car. Why hadn't he come with her? Afraid of the boss? Helen saw the two girls silhouetted in the back seat, the other girl in the huge front seat with him. Before Helen could follow, another car slid into the space behind him. She felt suddenly impatient and honked her horn absurdly.

At night, when she drove past the curve on South Beach Road, with its yellow signs glittering their warnings, she felt a sickening recognition, the lights of the car bleaching the darkness and the memories. *When I drive my car,* she thought. When I drive *my* car, Johnny, I think of crashing.

Lightning doesn't strike, George, not usually. But what if it strikes twice?

"That's why I wear a seat belt," she said, aloud.

The letter had been singing in her head, like a child's song, all evening, as the fireworks exploded and she served potato salad and watched George. Georgie Porgie, it sang. Kissed the girls. Lucy kissed the girls! it sang as she stood close to Lucy, imagining a passion between two close, distant friends. She heard the letter and wanted to cry out, Stop chanting! the way she did when Emily endlessly repeated "Girls go to college to get more knowledge, boys go to Jupiter to get more stupider." Was the letter a chant? A song? The letter was a mystery. But not like the mysteries that lined the store's shelves. Mysteries have endings. Mystery readers like mysteries because they know everything will come out in the end. You don't know how exactly, but you know it will. Customers had explained that to Helen, and she understood because it was how she felt about any novel, really. But letters? They're just moments, aren't they? Helen thought. What happens in the end? Well, that depends on when the end is. Uncle Joe and I are well and enjoying the pot holder you sent. That's Monday. On Tuesday, Uncle Joe could have a heart attack. Quick! Send a new letter! That's the end of Uncle Joe! Is it the end of the letter? No. There's still Aunt May. She's thinking of moving to Florida now. Love and kisses. Each letter ends with a plea to continue. "As Ever, Ram." And why does the letter end at all? Because the information is conveyed, all the information? Or because the doorbell rings? Or has the space run out on the note card decorated with the Audubon flamingo print? Perhaps the letter writer is hungry, sleepy, gets a cramp, is seduced by a lover waiting impatiently, naked, listening to the scratch, scratch of the pen. The pencil breaks, time to pick up the kids, the toast pops, Oprah's on, have to pee, take a nap, run five miles. Feed the cat.

Every letter reaches out, she thought, tries to hold on. My letter wants to hold on. But it's just a letter, a moment that passed, a matter of circumstance. *As ever.* Is anything as ever?

Back at home, Helen realized she was just a wee bit drunk. Her room was hot. She thought of Johnny the other morning on the beach, handing her a section of orange, Johnny holding an orange in her kitchen. She was hot, and she wanted an orange. She sat in a pool of light from the lamp beside her bed. Her hands were sweating. Even her hands. I'm a voyeur, she thought, watching my own life.

She lifted the letter from her shabby gray bag, held it in both hands, and tore it in half, then in half again, then again and again until she held only little ragged pieces in her hands.

"Oh shit," she said.

It took her over an hour to tape it back together.

7 ′ ′ ′ ′ ′ ′ ′ ′ ′ ′ ′ ′ ′ ′ ′

THERE WERE TWO BEACHES IN PEQUOT, A DRAMATIC
ocean beach pounded by mountains of waves, great watery
alps of them, and a small, rocky crescent on the bay where
mothers took their toddlers and gulls dropped clamshells
with a clatter. The fireworks had been held on the bay
beach, and Johnny returned there the next morning, his day
off. Bits of garbage from last night's picnics lay on the sand.
This early in the morning, it wasn't six yet, the beach was
empty, free of babies, even of runners, even of Helen in her
nylon shorts, her body glistening with sweat. He thought of
her body, adult, healthy, solid — almost massive compared
to the slender girlish body of Carla, or of Jennifer or Kelly.
He wondered if Helen was older than his mother. For a
moment he couldn't remember how old his mother was.
Forty-eight? How old was Helen? She looked nothing like
his mother, seemed nothing like his mother, a trim and
orderly woman who did what she had to do quietly and who
appeared to find her life, her husband, and her children
mildly amusing, as if they were eccentric, beloved pets.

He parked the huge car and looked back at it fondly, a

deep blue, a monument of a car: This car is dedicated to all the cars everywhere, in every age, who have served the cause of cars. He thought that when he next went to the library he would have to begin research into the history of the Lincoln Continental.

On the beach, his shoes in his hands, he stood in the water, the rocks slippery and sharp beneath him. He was the only one there. The water was cold. It was so cold that for a moment he could imagine the air was cold, too. Carla had not spent the night of July Fourth with him. She had driven off as soon as they got back from the fireworks, saying, "I forgot what a male asshole you were." Johnny, feeling only slightly guilty for ignoring her all evening (who had invited her to come, anyway?), waved good-bye with relief. It was too distracting to have Carla around. What she was distracting him from he wasn't sure, but he was glad she was gone.

Johnny picked his way carefully to the jetty of large rocks at the southern end of the beach and sat down to have his breakfast. When he was in high school, his mother had worried about his breakfast. That was part of her job, she had informed him, to worry about his breakfast. And as he didn't much like breakfast, being always too much in a hurry and too anxious about the hurry he was always in, she had come up with a plan that satisfied them both, an attractive breakfast gesture, "a Potemkin village breakfast," she said. As he rushed out, his shirt untucked, his books spilling from his backpack, she would stand at the door and drop a hard-boiled egg in one hand, an orange in the other. "There," she would say, satisfied, knowing he would eat neither.

All morning at school he would roll the egg and the orange around in front of him on the desk. The pale brown eggshell kept remarkably cool. The orange, if held just a little bit closer to the face, gave off the scent of a land a thousand miles away.

For years, he did not eat these breakfast orbs. They formed a daily sensual still life, hauled from Biology to World History, casting faint shadows on the shiny tops of a dozen desks. He liked having them with him. They lent an aesthetic dimension to his classroom hours. He got into the habit of the orange and egg. And then one day they looked so lovely, the egg light and subtle, the orange vibrant and scented, that he'd eaten them. The egg first. Then the orange. He still treated himself to this breakfast every once in a while.

When I peel an orange, he thought, I think of you. You, Helen. Yeah, you. When I hold an orange, when I eat it, when I wipe the juice from my lips, I think of your lips. I think of your hand taking a soft, bright section of fruit from my hand. I think of your hand taking my hand, of my hand taking yours. I think of that fucking letter, and I think of fucking you. And I think I've gone crazy.

He looked at the shed skins beside him, eggshells, white today, cradled in a large piece of orange rind. A gull, large and comically sinister, sidled up to him, opened its beak, and let out a harsh cry, almost a bark. The bird tilted its head and eyed him with its one visible, avid eye, and it reminded him of Helen.

He covered his face with his hands. What's wrong with me? I can't stop thinking of Helen. Helen. A middle-aged woman. Helen. Helen. Your name sounds different to me, difficult, as if it were in another language. Helen, my boss, who bosses me around, who thinks I'm a child, whose child I could be. And he could see her arm as she handed a customer a neatly gift-wrapped book, the inside of her wrist, smooth and revealed.

Three cormorants sailed past, their throats curling up from the glassy water. A mockingbird hooted and whistled, one call after another, a show-off, a comedian of the tree-tops. Johnny sat on the beach until others came. He felt the warmth of the day press closer and closer. He saw the slate gray of the sky turn almost white. Where did the pale, flat water end and the pale, flat sky begin? He watched the children with their buckets and their mothers. Which were the weary mothers, the ones who were there because the child would not sleep past dawn? Which were the con-scientious ones, the ones who came to provide an early-morning experience of nature for their progeny? It was an idle question. He was not interested enough in the an-swer even to inspect the faces of the women or the state of their clothing or the make of their cars. It was not even his question, really, just one he felt he ought to ask, a question inherited from some overheard conversation, or from a book. It could have been something his mother had said once. He didn't know. His thoughts were often not his own. Sometimes he bored himself.

Am I waiting for Helen to show up? he wondered. Or do I want to make sure I leave before she arrives, which she could do at any moment, sweating and out of breath, push-ing the damp hair from her forehead? He got back in the car, bringing his eggshell and his orange peel with him.

＿

Johnny drove from the beach onto an ugly commercial four-lane road called the Highway. Although it ran right through most of Pequot, the Highway was not considered part of the town. It was a foreign road, necessary but never accepted, like Turkish workers in Switzerland. There had been battles fought in Pequot, or very nearly. There had been industries and crops and feuds in Pequot, formerly Point Caviar, formerly Recklesstown, formerly Skatter-goods, formerly Brown's Mill. Through all the names, the Highway had been called the Highway. A straight ribbon of car dealers, carpet stores, supermarkets, and fast-food res-taurants, it passed through much of the residential neigh-borhood and stopped abruptly at a little patch of woods. Here stood the abandoned Pequot sanitorium, which sepa-rated the actual village from the rest of the town and the rest of the world. A statue of a minuteman knelt at the edge of the woods, its musket aimed at the Highway. The village hid behind the statue, exclusive and battered by the sea on a short, wide peninsula.

Johnny drove along the Highway and across Brown's Bridge, once the site of Brown's mill, now the site of a nineteenth-century hat factory being turned into a luxury hotel. Everywhere he looked, he saw what was no longer there. He missed New York, but he had come to love Pequot, for, like New York City, it seemed to him a soil deep and rich, blooming with its own past. At Waiting Junction (where the minutemen had waited for the redcoats who never came) the car wash that stood there was of no con-sequence to Johnny, like make-up applied badly to a beau-tiful girl.

When he got to the woods and the minuteman statue, instead of going right to get to the village and Horatio Street Books, Johnny turned left, entering North Pequot. This part of town had once been called North Todd, not because there was a South Todd, or an East or West or even a plain Todd. But because Mary Todd Lincoln had passed through the town (in a carriage; she did not stop), and, anticipating that the neighboring areas would also change their names to commemorate her visit, the townspeople had considered their geographical relationship to their neighbors and chosen what they considered to be the correct directional nomenclature.

Johnny parked in front of the library, a big, stone Victorian barn built at the behest of Miss Skattergoods's grandmother and given to the town with the understanding that one floor be devoted to the town's history, which pretty much coincided with the history of the Skattergoods family. Each day, Miss Skattergoods dusted the archival shelves with a feather duster, played Count Basie softly on a boom box beside her desk, and at five o'clock, promptly pulled a couple of bottles and an etched crystal glass from her bottom desk drawer and made herself a cocktail.

"Gin and lime juice," she would say. "Keep away the scurvy."

The Skattergoodses had originally come over from Britain in the seventeenth century on the *Willing Wind*. Johnny had read the journal kept by Jebediah Skattergoods describing the trip, a dull, uneventful journey — no death, no starvation, no storms, just heat and trepidation, bickering, worms in the biscuits. Jebediah came with his wife, Constance, who was barely mentioned in the journals, though he did note the cost of her passage. They had settled in what was then known as Brown's Mill (after Joseph Brown, who had a mill a little way up the river — Muddy River then, Pequot River now). There they had raised their two children, Thomas and Thomasine. In a cave.

Kind of like Siegmund and Sieglinde, Johnny thought.

Miss Skattergoods, who was so forthcoming about so much of her family history, was a little sketchy about what happened next. But a new generation of Skattergoodses was produced somehow (like Siegmund and Sieglinde indeed!), for two generations later, the Skattergoods family had bought Brown's Mill and most of the surrounding land and renamed the area Skattergoods.

"With a name like Skattergoods, love it or leave it, I say!" explained Miss Skattergoods.

Johnny sat at a long table. Journals and letters regarding Pequot's history were spread before him. None of the letters was a love letter. They were mere scraps of communications, bland requests, bland acknowledgments. Something was to be bought, something had been bought. Something was to be sold, something had been sold. There was a sequence, of which each letter was a part. Could this be done? Please do it, then. Thank you for having done it. A beginning, a middle, an end.

Was there a sequence of which the love letter, Helen's love letter, was a part? Were love letters like merchant letters requesting six bolts of muslin? Could Goat please love Ram at his or her soonest possible convenience? That was the idea, wasn't it? One thing led to another. But what thing led to this letter? And what would the letter lead to? Perhaps it had already led to something, and he would never know. Johnny stared at the documents before him, but in his jealousy of someone involved in something, he barely noticed them. I will never know, he thought. I will know only this one moment, a lone integer, a single letter.

He wondered what book the love letter writer had thrown out the window. Who would throw a book out a window, anyway? Once Carla had thrown his CDs out the window. What book was it? What floor? Helen would never throw a book out the window, although he did notice she tore the covers off mass-market paperbacks with an odd combination of boredom and zeal, like a child pulling wings off a fly — in a factory exclusively devoted to fly-wing removal. He had been shocked to discover that one did not return to the publisher a mass-market paperback that didn't sell — one returned the cover. Saved postage. Libraries are more civilized places than bookstores, he thought, the stacks of faded volumes standing like levees before a flood. But then he longed to be in the bookstore, watching Helen tap the keys of the cash register, climb a ladder, lick a stamp.

At five o'clock, Miss Skattergoods skipped to her desk, pulled open the drawer with a creak, and removed a bottle, another bottle, a glass, and then another glass. "Join me?" she said.

Johnny took his glass, and they sat side by side, each in a huge leather armchair facing an arched window. He longed to tell her. He could explain: he had seen a letter, and he was caught somewhere in a sequence of events leading to other events, about which he knew nothing except that Helen loved someone or that someone loved Helen.

And what about me? Johnny thought. And he realized he was almost trembling at a thought and had to steady his drink. He was almost trembling at the words that formed in his head. The light dimmed. The small, formal garden, which Miss Skattergoods also tended, blushed, then receded. Birds called out and insects answered. I love Helen.

"The cocktail hour," Miss Skattergoods said with a contented sigh. Count Basie murmured among the bird songs. "All of civilization has led up to this moment, Johnny." Then Miss Skattergoods laughed gaily. And Johnny, unable to think what else to do, joined her.

Helen's voice, deep and booming one minute, a caress the next, echoed in his head. "You have to listen, Johnny," she had reminded him again one day as he sat on the high counter. And she put her hand on his thigh. She had patted him kindly. On the thigh. And he had listened.

———

For one week it rained in Pequot. The heat was still, as if it were the inside of something. There was thunder and there was lightning, but the sky did not stir even then. *Leaves hang unruffled by any breeze.* There wasn't even the shudder of a breeze. All breezes lay comatose, exhausted from the heat. Johnny's leather dress shoes grew a pale green moss. Outside, at night, frogs bellowed triumphantly. At the beach, the leaden water met the leaden sky in a sluggish, unwholesome union. All was wet, from generation unto generation, from sea to shining sea.

Johnny stood behind the counter on the prow of the ship of Helen's store. I'm just the cabin boy. I should be fetching the skipper's cocoa. But I can pretend to be captain, grasp the tiller, squint toward the west in search of land. See which way the wind blows.

Behind him was Helen's voice, a low rumble of displeasure breaking like waves over the more solicitous tones of the salesman hawking clever, arty postcards. Johnny turned toward the sound. She was sitting on a step in the back with the card salesman. Floppy catalogues of postcards of pigs in humorous positions and attire lay across her knees.

"I actually hate these," she was saying.

"How about Christmas cards? Time to think about Christmas cards."

"I'm not ordering Christmas cards in July."

"Oh, Helen," said the salesman with a sigh.

"Well, these are nice," she said then, and it was as if her

voice were a movie star and had slipped into something more comfortable.

The salesman smiled at her. Was he dazzled? Johnny wondered. Like a guy in a black-and-white movie on TV, when the girl comes out in a satin negligee? I'm dazzled. Why am I dazzled? Is Helen dazzling? She sits on a wooden step. She is wearing blue jeans. She's wearing a sleeveless white shirt. Her arms are muscular, but they have that softness of age. She's too old for me. She's too mean for me. She has no interest in me. I can see the curve of her breast against the shirt. What is it like to touch her breast? Do her breasts sag? Why don't I mind? Why do I want to know so much? Why am I dazzled? God, am I dazzled.

The rain banged on the air conditioners. It was midday, but the store was dark except for the lamps. Johnny rang up a sale and smiled and talked to the customer about the rain as he had talked about the heat only one week before. He forgot what he was saying as he said it. He turned back to watch Helen and the salesman as they flipped through scenes of Paris, babies, automobiles, Felix the Cat, 1950s barbecues, Audubons, poets, and popes. Kelly offered him a corn muffin. He shook his head. *I no longer eat, I forget to eat. . . . When did this happen? I haven't even blinked. . . . "There's only one face, it's all I see, awake or asleep." . . . I feel your hair brush my cheek when it does not.*

Oh, Helen, Johnny thought. At least you don't smell like Jell-O. Your soap smells like soap. Beautiful, clean soap. You don't read Anaïs Nin. Anymore. And you don't know my secret. Though I know yours. Whatever it is.

"Johnny," she said when the salesman left. "Jennifer liked those short stories, too. I told her you recommended them."

Touch me, he thought. Put your hand on my arm. On

117

my shoulder. Stand close to me, so close I can smell your skin and feel its warmth.

"Johnny? The collection you told me to read, which I liked so much? She read it. She liked it. You two have a lot in common."

He looked at the bit of bra that showed, lace, and at the cleavage above it. I'm a peeping Tom, he thought. I should be out holding hands with a sophomore, or surfing or playing volleyball or something. Driving too fast.

"I can't go myself," Helen was saying, "but I have these two tickets."

He looked at her throat, a little thick, the smooth flesh creased twice. The warmth and sweet smell of her words moved toward him on her breath.

"Johnny, are you listening?"

Listen, Johnny. You have to listen. Yes, Helen, I'm listening. But all I can hear is the pounding of blood in my ears, pumped there by my heart, my poor heart, out of control, my heart out of its mind.

"So you can both go together. I love Buster Keaton. You love Keaton, don't you? Jennifer does. I guess. She didn't actually say so, but she was happy to take the ticket. Maybe she thinks I meant Diane Keaton. Or Michael Keaton. She thinks she's going to see *Batman*. No. She must like Buster Keaton. Of course she does."

She smiled. She was through. She turned. She stood in front of the shelves of new hardcover fiction. She leaned forward over a first novel and from its bright red jacket blew away an imaginary speck of dust.

——

Sometimes Johnny tried to picture what it would be like with Helen. Would he walk down the street holding her hand? Would she lie beside him at the beach, stretched on a towel, face to face, her fingers on his cheek? People would notice. He would notice them noticing. Could they go to a concert? Sit beside each other watching — who? Tina Turner. Such great shape for her age! they would say. Like you, he would think, looking away, hoping she did not guess his thoughts. At home, he would watch MTV. She would watch VH-1. Both would see Mick Jagger's face, now old as well as wasted.

Johnny thought, I don't care about any of that. You can listen to Linda Ronstadt for all I care. Barbra Streisand. He looked in the mirror, and thought, What do you see? When you look at me? A bug-eyed kid with hair in his eyes? A virile young man? A boy with a questionable grip on the alphabet? He looked into his eyes as she would look into them and wondered what color they were and wondered if she wondered. Were they blue or were they green? Helen's eyes were brown, except when they were a predator's yellow.

He tried to imagine what it would be like with Helen sometimes, but all he could really imagine was Helen, so clearly; all his senses welcomed her, held out their arms to see her and touch her, breathe her in, savor her, listen to the low melody of her voice. They would be together, alone. His desire was so modest. To put his lips to hers. To feel her hair against his cheek. Just once. And once more.

⟁

Helen watched Johnny leave with Jennifer. His long hair flipped as he walked. Jennifer's smooth bald skull slid lightly into the night. They were gone. Helen's encouragement seemed to be paying off. Were they going to dinner? To fuck on the beach? No, surely not. Not yet. Maybe he would take her to the Chinese restaurant, the same one Helen had gone to as a child, the Golden Dynasty Palace. Moo goo gai pan. She remembered dropping something into a glass of water, a roll of paper or a shell, something the waiter always gave her, and watching it unfurl. She remembered the feel of the red banquette, Leatherette stuck to the underside of her knees. She remembered fucking on the beach, too. Only the woods, with all those damp twigs, was worse.

Helen closed up the store and on her way home stopped at the library. Miss Skattergoods was sitting cross-legged on her desk, drinking Bombay gin.

"Johnny usually keeps me company," Miss Skattergoods said, pouring a glass of gin and lime juice for Helen. "But you'll do."

"He went out with Jennifer," Helen said. "The bald one." Johnny was a minor. Helen wondered if it was legal for Miss Skattergoods to serve Johnny Bombay gin, even with lime juice mixed in.

Helen signed out a collection of love letters by famous authors and a volume of correspondence between Edmund Wilson and Nabokov. Was that a kind of love, too? The two friends were brilliant, but who was nastier? Who more bitter? One minute Nabokov, Wilson the next. That was the drama of the letters, and she looked forward to the contest. She opened the other collection and read a letter from Edith Wharton to her lover, W. Morton Fullerton. "There would have been the making of an accomplished flirt in me, because my lucidity shows me each move of the game — but that, in the same instant, a reaction of contempt makes me sweep all the counters off the board & cry out: — 'Take them all — I don't want to win — I want to lose everything to you!'"

Nice punctuation, Helen thought.

She drove home and wondered what Johnny and Jennifer talked about. Maybe they blossomed into partners in a brittle and brilliant exchange, like Wilson and Nabokov. Maybe they reverted to slack-jawed teen jargon. Maybe they played the game with insight and skill. Maybe they lost themselves, or wanted to, like Edith Wharton. Helen would never really know. She would alter their conversation if she was there to hear it. Like Heisenberg.

They have to talk about me at least a little, though, she thought. What did they see when they saw her? It shocked her sometimes when she said something that revealed to herself how old she was, something like, "Oh, yes, I went out with someone like that twenty-five years ago." How could anyone have been old enough to go out with someone twenty-five years earlier? She was glad not to be twenty anymore, it was true. Twenty was a difficult year, and sad. First her father's death, then her mother's move, which seemed to confirm the loss of her father somehow. But now she was twice twenty and then some. Anyway, what had it been like, to be twenty? She could not remember because she could not distinguish. She had been Helen MacFarquhar then, just as she was Helen MacFarquhar now.

It had stopped raining at last, and a calm, clear chill had moved in. Helen loved weather, all weather. It was so utterly beyond her control. She could not predict it, stop it, encourage it. She had no responsibility at all toward weather. Weather was liberating. She drove home with the window down, the noise of the crickets mingling with the chirp of the car's loose fan belt. Interspecies communication.

—

Johnny sat at the espresso bar with Jennifer. They thumb-wrestled. He won.

"You won," she said.

"My thumbs rule."

"Yeah, they're okay."

She looked at him in a friendly, noncommittal way. He wondered how often she had to shave her head to keep it looking like that. Most girls who looked like Jennifer turned out to be ill-tempered substance abusers who fancied themselves artistic. But he was beginning to see that Jennifer was actually of a rather sunny disposition, a cheerleader type who fancied herself artistic, though it wasn't yet clear to her which art exactly.

"Should I shave my head?" he asked.

"What is your deal with my hair? Anyway, Helen would fire you. Don't you think Helen is incredible? For someone her age?"

Yes, he thought. I do think she's incredible. I want to throw her on the mass-market paperback table and fuck her. Don't you, Jennifer?

"She's a bitch," Jennifer was saying. "Isn't she?"

He nodded, thrilled that she was talking about Helen. She always talked about Helen, which was why Johnny had begun to hang out with her.

"It's liberating to be a bitch, though," she said. "You have to be a bitch. Just to hold your own. Well, *you* don't. You're a man —"

He laughed at the thought of himself as man.

"I aspire to being a bitch," Jennifer said. "Just like Helen."

"Me, too," Johnny said.

He ran his hand along Jennifer's bald skull. "Brings you luck."

She coughed and said she wanted a cigarette but didn't have any because she didn't smoke.

"So we'll go to that movie next week," he said. "Buster

Keaton. Do you like Buster Keaton or did you just not want to make Helen mad?"

Talk about her more, Jennifer. You have one of those girl crushes, the kind girls get on their French teachers. I have a crush on her, too. The kind that Greeks get on queens named Jocasta, the kind that blinds you.

"Both," Jennifer said. "I started working out, you know. At Barry and Eliot's gym. Where Helen goes. God, is she cut. Have you seen her without a shirt? Do you know she grew up here?"

Johnny had an unsettling vision of Helen working out, of sweat shining on her face, patterning her T-shirt. But she apparently didn't wear a T-shirt. Just one of those sports bra things? Or had Jennifer seen her in the locker room, changing, and there admired her muscle definition? Aroused and annoyed, he wondered if he could ask Jennifer.

"She brought me flowers from her garden yesterday," Jennifer was saying. "I took them back to the dorm. It gets so dreary there. She said, 'Here, put these in your dorm room. Dorm rooms get so dreary.'"

"Very thoughtful," he said. He longed to listen to others talk about Helen, but he was afraid to say anything at all about her himself, afraid his secret would show somehow. "Why didn't you go home for the summer?" he asked Jennifer. Why doesn't Helen bring me flowers? he asked himself. I don't like flowers, but so what? She thinks even less of me than she does of Miss Cue Ball. He looked affectionately at Jennifer.

"Can't stand my mother," said Jennifer. "Helen's probably a wonderful mother. Strict sometimes. You have to be. But then I bet the two of them — the daughter, right? — I bet they sit up late at night sometimes, looking at the stars or drinking cocoa, talking."

"What can you talk to an eleven-year-old about?" Johnny said. I'm nine years older than Helen's daughter. Helen is twenty-two years older than I am. What can you talk to a twenty-year-old about? That's what she thinks, if she ever thinks of me at all.

"I don't know," said Jennifer. "Life?"

—

At home in bed, Helen heard the death cry of a mole. The Wilson-Nabokov letters lay open across her knees. The death cry of a mole was harsher and more rhythmic than the squeals of a dying mouse. She had come to make this fine distinction after years of overhearing the different sounds of the final moments of her cat's victims and then finding the corresponding rodent corpse on her doorstep the next morning.

She was glad Jennifer and Johnny were making friends. She noticed they hung out together now, sometimes with Kelly, sometimes without. She noticed, too, that Jennifer had begun bringing her things, just like the cat. Not mice or moles but bagels, glutinous health-food-store cookies, a surprise cappuccino from next door. Helen liked devoted staff. If you had to have staff, that is. Perhaps Johnny would bring her things, too. And Lucy. Everyone. Perhaps she would require it. Part of the job description.

She thought Jennifer had mentioned a boyfriend, which was inconvenient. But the boyfriend was far away somewhere, which was better. It was summer. They were young. And Johnny was so good-looking. His eyes sometimes startled her in the store, bright in the gloom of a far-off corner, green and sudden. Then he'd turn away and she would feel almost bereft. He was far more intelligent than she had thought at first. He seemed to have memorized the stock, for one thing. Not just the titles, but some quick sense of the books themselves. He had studied books in college which she considered popular novels — books by Philip Roth or Mary Gordon. Imagine. They were classics now, along with T. S. Eliot and James Joyce. Which he had also read, in class. She wasn't sure what he read on his own. Macho-austere short stories, yes, like the book he'd recommended to her. A little highbrow sci-fi, too, she imagined. They all did. Though she had never seen him with any. She did sometimes see him in the poetry crypt. And leafing through the military histories. If Johnny had written that letter, which of course he had not (everyone ties his shoes and peels an orange, after all; everyone drives a car), if he had, though, what book would he have thrown from the window? She thought she might ask him. If, Johnny, you were to throw a book from the window, what book would it be?

Helen had arranged a shelf full of Barbara Pym novels in the room that was to be her mother's when her mother came to visit, hoping they would somehow soothe her. Red meat to the parental beast. But what if her mother threw all of them out the window, onto the lawn? What if the letter had been written by her mother and she had developed this new habit, pitching books out the window when she was annoyed? Her mother was so often annoyed. The complete works of Barbara Pym would be quite insufficient.

Perhaps George would come calling and pick all the Barbara Pym paperbacks up off the ground, give them to a patient, a chaste patient, several patients, a stable of them. He would pick up the books from the wet grass and cradle them in his arms, like apples fallen from a tree. The bounty of nature, he would think. He would come back with a basket, waiting for more English novels with perfect pitch to fall to the ground. Would Helen be able to charge him for them? she wondered. Under those circumstances?

She considered the question carefully, from all different angles. She felt she was approaching some sort of insight on the subject. She was satisfied. She forgot what she was satisfied with. George? She considered George, his quiet, insinuating calm. Underneath this unruffled exterior, said his eyes, underneath, underneath. . . . What was underneath? she wondered. The bottom.

The mole had stopped crying. Helen shook herself fully awake, surprised she had been asleep. She turned off the light. *When I lie down each night without you.* . . . Without who? she wondered. Or was it whom?

8

JOHNNY WATERED THE FLOWERS HIS MOTHER HAD planted. He watered the weeds, too, for they were everywhere in the garden, taller and grander than the yellow and orange lilies. Did they need water, after all the rain? They certainly needed something. Perhaps he should have bailed out the garden instead, with a bucket. He anticipated criticism and annoyance when his parents came back next month. He wasn't sure what he had done wrong — at least, he wasn't sure of all the things he had done wrong — but he did recognize that the garden held a prominent position on the list, with only the bathtub situation farther up in the hierarchy.

He went in the kitchen and looked at the stack of dirty dishes, at the spaghetti sauce, dried, and dark as blood, adorning so many surfaces. He'd been up most of the night, the TV on incoherently as he tossed in his bed. He got a Coke and went back outside in an unfocused, dull despair. The store wouldn't open until two o'clock. Mondays were always so slow. There was plenty of time to clean the kitchen. He should clean the kitchen. The bathtub, on the other hand. . . . The bathtub could perhaps be replaced. He wished he could pick some of the flowers in the garden and bring them to Helen, as Helen had done for Jennifer, but Helen would think he was insane, Jennifer would laugh at him, and the flowers were half-dead anyway. He could bring weeds. I have nothing to offer, he thought, and threw himself down on the lawn and fell asleep.

Helen rang the bell. Johnny's car was parked in the driveway, big enough to be its own address. She rang again. Surely he was home. Where else could he be? It seemed extremely inconsiderate of him not to be home when she had taken the trouble to stop by unexpectedly.

She'd already been to Barry and Eliot's gym, where she saw little Jennifer, her smooth pate bobbing up and down in the Gravitron. Then Helen had driven to the bakery. I'll drop by Johnny's and bring him a bread, she thought. One always needs a bread, a fresh French bread, still warm. He'll put jam on it for his breakfast. I'll make him coffee. Really good coffee. And she stopped at the espresso bar and bought some absurdly expensive beans.

"Johnny!"

He didn't answer. The house stood high on a hill. She'd never visited Johnny's parents here, though they frequently saw each other at a mutual friend's. Helen wondered what the driveway was like in the winter. She thought it was good that an adult was checking up on Johnny while Mark and Vivian were away. She heard the hissing of the hose. It was hooked up just to the left of the front door behind a huge wall of rhododendron. She followed the green twisting tube past the garage, where there were skis and bicycles, a saw-horse, and the inevitable red Volvo station wagon, then around the side of the house. The hose stopped, abandoned in a scraggly, neglected flower garden, the spray attachment cutting off its juices, which dribbled desperately out the edges. Someone had left the hose on. Johnny, no doubt. She felt a twinge of irritation at him, as if it were her hose, her neglectful child. She went to turn it off, then came back, squeezed the handle, and released the pent-up water in a great, noisy, mildly obscene squirt. She watched the arc of water. Watched it shower onto the ground, watched it shower onto someone asleep on the ground, onto Johnny, asleep on his back on the grass. Oh dear, she thought, then was distracted by the sight of him there, the realization of his legs, his baggy soccer shorts draped across his thighs in iridescent nylon folds, his half-naked body, his arms stretched above his head.

He sat up, wiping spray from his face.

"Johnny!" she said. She smiled and spoke in her dog-trainer voice. But she felt oddly unsure of herself. "Sorry. Didn't see you."

Johnny stared at her. His face and bare chest were dripping. But what a nice face and bare chest, she thought.

He wiped his wet face with his wet arm.

"You left the hose on," she said.

He opened his mouth, then closed it, his expression confused. "Helen?" he said finally.

"It almost burst," she said. She walked over to him, sat next to him, turning to put her hands on his shoulders. "You're so wet."

He put his wet hands on her waist. He pulled her against him. He kissed her on the mouth.

⌐

Johnny felt the warmth of the sun on her skin, felt it against his cold wet cheek. He felt her in his hands, a firm curve

129

of torso. He held her, hung on to her with all his strength, as if he were falling. I am falling, he thought.

—

Johnny is grabbing me, she observed neutrally. She could have been noticing a cloud pass over the sun. Or the sun break out from the clouds.

He pulled her to him, and she thought how hard his chest was against her, how shapely, like Achilles' armor. His kiss was brief, as if he'd changed his mind.

But he hadn't changed his mind. They drew back, looked at each other, and Helen saw his eyes had narrowed in an almost petulant determination. Helen saw his greed and his beauty and his youth all laid out before her. She forgot to wonder what he saw before him. She took his hand and led him through the back door. Or perhaps he led her, up a flight of creaking steps, into a bedroom, past piles of discarded clothing to an unmade bed. I shouldn't be doing this, she thought. I shouldn't be doing this. I don't even know if I want to do this. I've never wanted to do anything as much as I want to do this. I shouldn't want to do this. Thou shalt not lie down with the lambs. Or something.

"Helen," he said, almost angrily, and she was startled, as if he'd told her the time and she were late. He put his hands on her face. Young men are so young, she thought. Youth is so smooth and so hard. And then she pushed him down on his smooth, hard back and took his smooth, hard arms and pinned them to the bed and kissed him back.

—

Helen left him sleeping, a prince fallen among dirty laundry. She turned to look at him from the doorway, almost afraid. He had taken her by surprise. And she had liked it.

But I hate surprises, she thought when she was home, in the shower. The shower sometimes soothed her, protected her, allowed her to feel sympathy for her fellow man from a comfortable, isolated distance. Today, it simply made noise, made her wet, rinsed away a morning in bed with a man.

Man? she thought. Boy. And she wondered how he had dared to grab her like that, to kiss her. She was his boss. She was old enough to be his mother. She was his mother's friend. And his father's. She deserved a certain respect. Did he think she was so lonely, so desperate, so *old,* that she would be unable to resist his charms? She had been unable to resist his charms, it was true. But I am not a schoolgirl, she thought. I have slept with far too many men to make a fool of myself over this pretty juvenile. I choose whom I fall in love with. I choose who falls in love with me. Romance is ridiculous. I'm too old for it. And too smart. She stood in the shower. She looked down at herself, and the sight of her own naked body made her think of his pressed against hers, and she caught her breath and the force of her desire enraged her and she leaned her forehead against the cold tile and wept.

—

Johnny got to the store late. Helen had written a love letter and left it for him to see. He had kissed her. She had kissed him back. They made love. He said these things over and over to himself. But when he walked in and saw Helen, his thoughts seemed like nonsense rhymes. He looked at her, then ducked his head in a misery of confusion, with no idea what to say or do. No smile leaped to his lips. No frown. No words burst from his heart, or even from his head. He looked at the floor, waiting. How could he know what to do now? They had barely spoken. She left while he was asleep. Why? Was she angry? Disappointed? He was meant to be the young stud, perhaps. Had she expected him to perform in some particularly virile manner? But it was she who had performed. He was stunned at being in bed with someone who. . . . Well, let's face it, he said to himself, someone who knew what she was doing. He blushed at his own thoughts. It was as if she were some well-trained Oriental courtesan, the way he had just described her. He felt disloyal, disrespectful. And yet it's quite true, he thought. And he looked up at her in a sudden burst of longing. But Helen was checking in a new shipment, and she had turned her back.

—

Johnny took it badly. Helen's shoulder, the shoulder he had pushed beneath his own, was now a cold shoulder. She addressed him in tones so bland he barely recognized her voice. Had he dreamt the whole thing? He stood in the store in a kind of shock. He watched Helen flirt with her customers. The hands around their hand, the laugh, the unexpected kiss, the joke, the perfect book. She listened. She pushed aside a strand of someone's hair. "Hi, honey," she said when people came in. "Thanks for stopping by," she said when they left.

Helen charged for gift wrapping if the customer annoyed her. He'd seen her give someone the finger, down low, behind the desk where they couldn't see it. The customers would never know what she was really like. Look how vulnerable she looks now, talking to that man. Look how he wants to put his hand on her shoulder. He stops himself. She hands him *The Oxford Illustrated History of Christianity*.

"Tell me more the next time you come in," she says to him. "Please."

"I will," he says. "Thanks. I will."

How can she go on like that? Johnny wondered. Listening. Why won't she listen to me? Or allow me to listen to her? But the customers crowded around her, screening her from his view, nudging her away. He saw her smile as a distant flash, too distant for him to hear the thunder. Nothing was ever said about the morning they had spent in each other's arms. Nothing was ever said about anything. And he watched Helen and her customers, and he thought she was just an old fraud, a conjurer who had arranged the mirrors and dimmed the lights and cut him in two with a phony sword.

Johnny stayed near Jennifer as much as he could. He hung on her words about Helen, content to be left dangling from them, meaningless and unnecessary. His friendship with her took on a new, desperate quality. They went to see Buster Keaton in *Sherlock Jr.*, as arranged by Helen. They went to other movies with Kelly. Sometimes they would get ice cream at the beach or drink beer at Johnny's parents' house. One night the three of them went to a bar at which Kelly spent much of the evening pondering whether she should pierce her nipple. Which one? Johnny wondered.

Jennifer, inspired by Helen, had decided to become an academic. "Helen almost got her Ph.D., you know," she said one day, lying around her dorm room with Johnny while Kelly was at work. "She never finished her dissertation. About some fascist English guy. He had a magazine and wrote novels and did paintings with lots of gears or smokestacks or something. Who can I study?"

"Same guy," Johnny said. "Borrow Helen's note cards."

Jennifer stretched out on her bed. Johnny, sitting on the floor, leaned against Kelly's bed. The room was plain and grim, but there was a pretty white pitcher filled with black-eyed Susans and some purple flowers he didn't know the name of.

"Helen give you those?" he asked.

"Yeah. She's been so great. Are you guys, like, having a fight or something?"

"Who?" he said.

"What do you mean, who?"

"Because she doesn't give me flowers? Because I don't bring an apple for the teacher every day like you? I'm not fighting with her. I just don't like her. She's a bitch."

Jennifer turned on her side and looked down at him.

"You said so yourself," he said.

"Did I?"

Their faces were close. Her arm dangled from the bed, her hand resting on the floor. She lifted it and pushed his hair behind one ear. He wondered if he should lean toward her, if he should kiss her, reach for her, pull himself onto the bed with her. All he had to do was move, just a fraction of an inch in her direction. She wasn't dying to sleep with him, he could tell, but she was bored and she liked him, and so she would.

"Hey, baby." He wiggled his eyebrows and tapped the ash off of an imaginary cigar. Like Groucho. It was something his father did when he didn't know what else to do.

"Asshole," Jennifer said, tossing a dirty sock listlessly in his direction. "God, you're boring today."

"I'm going to the beach."

"Helen runs to the beach every morning," she said, sitting up. "She told me that. How many miles is that? And back. No wonder she's in such great shape. God, if I could look like that at her age. I wonder how old she really is —"

"Forty-two," Johnny said. When I drive my car, he had

said to her on the dark July beach. When I drive my car, I see you running.

"And she works out, too. I think Barry and Eliot both have big crushes on her. She gave me the best book to read last week. . ."

Johnny lay back, closed his eyes, and luxuriated in the exquisite pain of Jennifer's conversation.

—

Helen saw them together and knew she'd been right: Johnny belonged with Jennifer. They were seeing each other every day, it seemed. And hadn't she, Helen, gotten them together in the first place? What had happened that morning between herself and Johnny was an accident, a matter of circumstance. Mere circumstance, she said to herself, emphasizing the mere. She had been there. He had been there. She'd awakened him, from a dream perhaps. Neither of them had thought. They'd just responded to the fact that they were there, two of them alone, together.

Helen was angry, that much she knew. But was she angry at Johnny for his presumption? Was she angry at him because his presumption had been correct? Or was she angry because she had given in to his whim? Or because that's all it was, a whim? But why shouldn't I give in? she wondered. And what's wrong with a whim? I've given in to whims before. Of course, they were always my own whims.

It meant nothing, she thought. He's said nothing about it because there's nothing to say. It was an accident. Accidents happen. We put them behind us. We wear seat belts. I wear a seat belt when I drive. I'll drive — that's my motto. When I drive my car. *When I drive my car* . . .

An accident, she thought, as George came into the store.

And she flung herself into his arms, grabbed him, and shook him. What am I doing? she thought, laughing to cover her confusion, at the same time noticing with pleasure the strength of her own arms.

George laughed, too, pushed her away, and said she needed a vacation.

I don't want a vacation, she thought. I want you. At least, I want you to want me. And she took his hand, gently this time, and pulled him with her into the military history room and stood so close she could feel his breath on her cheek.

"George," she said. She noticed he'd gotten a haircut, just an inch or so. Did Nancy cut his hair? Sit him down in the kitchen with a towel around his neck? Or did he go to a salon and listen to loud music with clips in his long, wet locks? Helen had cut his hair once when they were teenagers. It had come out uneven and much too short. His mother cried when she saw it.

"George, I had a dream about you last night," Helen said. She was still holding his hand. He looked down at the two hands.

"Really?" he said. He sighed. "I once dreamt my furnace caught fire and I kept trying to turn it off. There was an off switch. But I flicked it and flicked it and nothing happened. The fire wouldn't go out. You were standing beside me."

Helen let his hand drop from hers. He had dreamt about fire? *I'm on fire.* Was George on fire? Was it really him? Such a lousy dream pun, though, that she'd lit his fire. And him a psychiatrist, too.

"What was your dream?" he asked.

Helen had not, in fact, dreamt about him last night, or any night, for that matter. Last night, she had dreamt about being at the opera. Suddenly she was in the opera. She didn't know the words to the songs. She didn't know the tunes. And then it was a ballet. She didn't know the steps. She watched the others move their arms, swaying beautifully, and she didn't know how to move.

"I dreamt we went to the opera and then we were in it and didn't know any of the words."

"Very revealing. What opera?"

"I don't know."

"Very revealing."

They stood like that for a moment. Helen wondered if he had made up his dream, too. I certainly hope so, she realized.

"Shall I take you to the opera, Helen?" He put his hands on her waist.

No! Helen wanted to cry out. I don't want to go to the opera with you. Did you write that letter? Was it you? I don't want a love letter from you. I don't want you after all. Sorry. Wrong number. Dial again. "I think operas are silly," she said. She could smell the starch in George's crisp white shirt. He always wore white shirts. Why? Very revealing. Of something.

Lucy and a customer walked by. The customer did not notice them, but Lucy did.

George pulled back, then looked at Helen with an amused expression. "You're kind of a horrible friend to have, Helen," he said, kissing her on the cheek. And he left without buying anything.

"You know," Lucy said later, "you're bad for business."

⬤

Each day Helen watched Johnny and Jennifer and Kelly share their lunches, make plans to meet later, sometimes leave the store together. Jennifer had decided to become her protégée, she noticed with some satisfaction. And Kelly,

Jennifer's shadow, went along for the ride. Helen looked at them, one with her hair shaved off, the other with her nose newly pierced, and she wanted to kill them. She had hired two wholesome college gals and wound up with bright-eyed, cheery little ghouls. But still she liked them and encouraged their devotion. It was pleasant to have these slender, shyly arrogant young girls fussing about her. She felt her power over Jennifer. And she felt her power was stronger than Johnny's. I can take her away from you, Johnny, she thought. I can keep her for myself. I can keep all of them for myself. Sometimes she looked at the letter, and thought, Good. Someone is suffering for me. I don't care who.

"I like only women no men cat," Theresa the Polish nanny said, petting Charlie, the tabby from the neighboring espresso bar, who had wandered into the store.

"Your cat only likes women? And not men?" Lucy said. "Really?" She had brought Helen a cup of tea from upstairs, and now went back.

"I grrr my cat men."

Helen gave Theresa her change and put her copy of *Mrs. Dalloway* in a bag.

"Enjoy it!" she said.

"Enjoy me!" Theresa answered, and wheeled the twins out.

Once in a while Helen would see someone she knew from her childhood. Women came back loaded with babies in backpacks; guys came back, balding, to visit their parents and wandered into her store. She also had customers who'd been friends of her parents. At first she'd gotten this latter group mixed up, especially the women. Was that the ophthalmologist's wife or the orthodontist's wife? Had the psychiatrist's wife become a personal trainer or a real estate agent or a musicologist? One day a tall handsome man came into the store, greeted her with an affectionate kiss, and said, "God, that night we went skinny dipping, Helen. I've never forgotten it." Then he bought a copy of Victoria Glendinning's biography of Trollope, whispered "Ah, high school" and that he often thought of her breasts, kissed her again, and left. She looked at his American Express receipt and saw his name, Robert Collins.

"Who was that?" Jennifer said.

"Yeah, who was that?" said Kelly.

Who was Robert Collins? Helen had no idea.

"I have no idea," she said.

She heard Johnny snort. A derisive snort. I don't allow derisive snorts from employees, she thought. She turned and glared at him.

He was halfway up a ladder. His red cap was on backward, a flannel shirt tied around his waist. Above his shorts his back was bare.

"Johnny, put a shirt on. We're not at the beach."

He turned and smiled at her, a slow, contemptuous smile. Then, never taking his eyes off hers, he untied his shirt, put his arms slowly in, buttoned it partway, and stood, still balancing on the ladder, looking somehow as undressed as he had without the shirt.

"It's so unfair that guys can take their shirts off," Jennifer said.

"But he couldn't, could he?" said Kelly. "So what's so unfair?"

Helen and Johnny looked at each other and she wondered who would blink first.

"Sorry," Johnny suddenly mumbled. For a minute Helen felt sorry for him, but then he scowled and shrugged and went back to his shelves, and the minute was over.

9 ⸌⸌⸌⸌⸌⸌⸌⸌⸌⸌⸌⸌⸌⸌⸌⸌

ON SUNDAY MORNING, ALMOST ONE WEEK AFTER
the morning she and Johnny had made love in his unmade
bed, Helen ventured up to her attic. In the endless renova-
tion of the endless house, the workmen had finally arrived
at a room beyond which they could not go. Helen had
always carefully avoided going up there herself. Old junk
and mold and mouse droppings — the attic depressed her.
There were nesting squirrels too sometimes. For years, she
had just closed it off, hoping it would somehow disappear.
But here it still was. Helen sneezed, sat down on an old
chair on top of what she believed she remembered calling
a granny dress, and thought, This is everything I left behind
when I moved to New York.

She had named her store Horatio Street Books out of
nostalgia for her last address — and because it had a slight
Shakespearian ring to it. Did Johnny miss New York? Hadn't
he said so once? What difference did it make where a
twenty-year-old lived? A twenty-year-old had no reason to
be there, or anywhere else.

I do have a reason, Helen thought. I have a reason to be here. I chose it. And I was right.

Her conquest of her own house, though, was somewhat less complete than her conquest of the town. When she moved back to Pequot, Helen took one look at the house and set out to find Ray Bean, whom she remembered from the old days, and there he still was in his hardware store surrounded by sparkling chains of varying sizes. Can after can of varnish and paint, hooks and ropes and toilet seats, sat where she remembered them, all clean and dusted and inviting. Don't buy that pretty red axe, she had to tell herself. Just throw yourself on Ray's mercy and get out.

Ever since, with six months off here and there, Ray Bean, contractor and mayoral hopeful, had driven up her driveway each morning in his van. Recently, his new assistant, Howard, drove up, too, but he came in a BMW. Howard had just been laid off as an account executive at a downsizing corporation.

"Mort!" Howard would call to Ray, slamming the screen door. "You here?"

"Hey, Mort!" Ray would answer. "Where you been?"

They always called each other Mort.

"Mort?" Helen asked.

"Mortimer's," Howard said.

"Restaurant," Ray said.

Helen wondered what life would be like without them. Idle speculation.

The two Morts had finished most of the upstairs rooms and were now cleaning out the attic, a large repository of rot as well as cribs, high school English papers, miniature plastic horses, labeled envelopes of shed baby teeth, and racks of musty clothing. Wedgwood ashtrays were brought down.

A shawl; riding boots with patent leather tops; chaps as stiff as cardboard; a picnic basket from Hammacher Schlemmer, covered in thick green mold. Bell-bottoms. Hideous paintings in even more hideous frames. Two guitars. An aquarium. Bicycle pumps. Bicycles. A moped.

In the last ten days, Ray and Howard had taken two tons of rotting junk to the dump. Still, the house looked like a rummage sale after the ladies had rummaged but not bought. A heavy, musty smell rolled down the stairs like fog.

Helen sat on the plywood floor, two old hatboxes full of letters beside her. She browsed through the box of her mother's and father's letters first. "Dear Mac," said one dated April 10, 1951. "The enclosed little tidbit I dragged forth from my recipe file where I've had it 'salted' away for years. It's for your fiancée. However, you may take a small peek before you hand it over." It was signed by someone Helen had never heard of. She tried to imagine her mother as her father's fiancée. As for her father, sometimes she could hardly remember him at all. Other times, his presence was so vivid she thought she heard his footstep on the stairs, coming to kiss her good night.

"Husband Conserve" was the name of the recipe enclosed in the letter. "Select the best man and brush him carefully to rid him of any indifference."

Poor Daddy, Helen thought.

"Lift him gently into the home-preserving kettle and tie him with strong cords of affection which are not easily broken . . ."

Poor *Mommy.*

"Do not sear him with sarcasm . . ."

Helen wondered if her father had actually shown this to Lilian. Maybe he'd hidden it. Maybe he'd opened it, read it, and put it in a drawer, like the love letter.

"Stuff him one hour before taking him out or before asking

a favor of him. . . . Serve him daily on a platter of strength and courage, garnished with clean shirts and collars."

In just one generation, this horrible husband recipe had gone from being quaintly ridiculous to grotesque. Is that how far she was from Johnny? The distance of the husband conserve? She thought of how close she had been to Johnny, touching him, feeling his naked weight.

She folded up the recipe and began to dig through the other box of letters, most written to her when she was in France for her junior year. In one envelope, two pieces of cardboard, inserted to protect a photograph, remained, but the photo itself was gone. She remembered it, though. Her boyfriend of that long-ago era sat in an armchair, one foot in its heavy Frye boot up on his knee, a book on his lap, a bottle of Heineken in his hand. Then she read the letter that had accompanied the now lost photograph.

"Dear Beauty," it began, and went on to describe his unbearable loneliness, horniness, and the new Bob Marley album. Letters are so indiscreet, she thought. They're so exposed, so vulnerable, so naked — they're even worse than snapshots. In a picture you smile or stick out your tongue. Cheese! It's for all to see. Even a candid snapshot is taken in public, a public place where people look at other people and display themselves to the world. But this — no one was supposed to watch this. Tampering with the mail was a federal offense. And this letter was written in private and sent to only one person, only once. Now here I am reading it twenty years later, a stranger with the same name and same genetic composition.

Many of the letters were love letters. Unlike the letter from Ram to Goat, though, they were rather jaunty, confident, bawdy. "Your thighs! Have you still got them? Why not leave them here next time? For me?" "I have used the ruler you so considerately sent and have confirmed the measurement in question . . ." There were references by one boyfriend to Jake the Puppet, who seemed to be his dick. The name in one return address read "V. Oglio Scopare," which Helen thought she remembered meant "I want to fuck" in Italian. There was also a string of world-weary laments and naive hyperbole, contradictory, repetitive, often ungrammatical and occasionally illiterate, that seemed to pass easily from letter to letter, regardless of who wrote it: I've been through this before . . . I've never felt like this before . . . I know you'll never hurt me . . . I know love is pain. Helen read letter after letter, the crinkle of the stationery beneath her fingers blending with the chatter of squirrels on the roof.

She wondered if Johnny wrote letters like this to girls. Would he write a letter to Helen? Worse, would he write a letter about Helen? Had he told Jennifer? No. Jennifer was far too taken with Helen still. If she had known, she would have cooled. But she was still fetching bagels, mimicking Helen's way of speaking, an ardent, slender little parody. "Oh, *please*," she said, catching Helen's elongated sarcastic vowels exactly. She greeted the customers with a surprised delight verging on wonder which was identical to Helen's. Helen rewarded her with reading recommendations, flowers from her garden, the occasional private chat. She knew Johnny noticed. She thought again of Johnny, his eyes closed, his face above hers, his breathing broken with hoarse gasps. He had called out her name.

Helen stood up and looked out the attic window at the lawn, at the trees, at her garden below. It was so quiet she could hear the surf breaking against the rocks. She tried to remember the boys who had written these letters, boys from long ago. She remembered the way they smelled, the nicotine stains on their fingers, the fit of their jockey shorts. She remembered them without remembering which was which, like the lines in the letters.

—

Lilian called while she was still in the attic, and Helen ran downstairs to answer the phone, clutching the hatbox of letters.

"Did I make you rush in from the garden? I'm sorry. What are you hacking away at today?"

Helen's gardening, while frequent and energetic, was confined primarily to pruning. She loved pruning. Or deadheading. So satisfying. Planting was merely a means to that end.

"I was in the attic." Helen sneezed, exaggerating the sound for her mother.

"Bless you."

"You know, mother, Ray and Howard are still working and will probably always be working, as long as the earth revolves around the sun."

"Very conscientious."

"Working *here,* on this house. It's livable downstairs, but it's still kind of a demolition site upstairs . . ."

"We'll stay downstairs."

"Ah."

"You don't mind, do you? We'll pretend it's the depression and we all have to live together."

"Let's pretend it's the war and pretend there's rationing, too."

"Can you stand it?" her mother asked then.

Helen did not answer. Of course she could stand it. For one thing, she had to stand it. It was her mother's house. For another, she missed her mother. How often did she get Lilian to herself?

"And Grandma Eleanor?" Lilian said.

Almost to herself.

"I don't know why she wants to come," Lilian was saying. "Just to annoy me. She's already complaining about the damp. Well, you're a generation removed. Grandmothers and grandchildren get along because they have a common enemy. I can drive you both crazy."

"You have such insight, Mother," Helen said, and hung up rather giddy. They would arrive in two weeks and spend all of August with her, just like the cicadas. Emily would be back in the middle of August. Maybe she'd get a letter from Emily soon. The campers had to write every Sunday, and Helen usually got her letter by Tuesday. When Helen was a child at camp, she'd been forced to write on Sundays, too. She'd been so outraged that she'd put a blank piece of paper in the envelope as a protest and sent it to her mother. How could I have done that? Helen wondered. It was so cruel to my mother. Though, actually, Lilian hadn't seemed to mind at all. Maybe I'll send her a blank sheet of paper today. For old time's sake, Helen thought. She heard Ray's van and looked out the window. Howard's BMW was right behind it.

"Mort!"

"Hi, Mort."

Helen held the letters in their hatbox on her lap. She remembered when she was twenty and lived with her parents and screwed in their bed when they went on vacations. Her father had died that summer. And now she would live with her mother again.

"It's only temporary," her mother had said. "Everything is."

Helen flipped through more letters, too bored now to read more than the return addresses, until she came upon a folder that made her blood run cold. "Poems," it said.

"Oh God."

Inside were lined blue and green pages torn from a spiral notebook, each covered with several poems printed in a tiny hand, *her* tiny hand, and piled in with flimsy onionskin pages on which these same poems had been typed up.

"Love Poems," said one typed sheet, the title sheet of a large bundle of typed pages.

"Oh God."

"More Love Poems," read another.

Helen moaned and covered her eyes. She had been certain for years that this early oeuvre had been lost. But here it was.

> Surge of
> ululations of retreat,
> as we in waves soft . . .

Helen held the onionskin, stunned by embarrassment.

> little
> nectar
> leaves
> tiny voluptuaries . . .

There seemed to be quite a lot of leaves in the poems.

> woods are piled with years of
> leaves discussion piled soft be-
> reaved of stampened clayed in
> dirt ingratiated mirth . . .

Helen started to laugh. Stampened?

"Oh! Look! This is the best!" she said, and stood to read the poem aloud to herself.

> There are no
> curtains
> on my bedroom windows
> but were they shaded
> with even the heaviest foldings
> of the deepest red velvet
> these, even these, dark weighty drapes
> would spread at your sign
> would quiver, and lift apart
> unhesitatingly, to reveal me
> to you, that your heat might
> linger
> on my naked arms and legs,
> etc.

The "etc." was good. She recognized herself in the "etc." But the rest — could she ever really have felt this way? She could no more write a love poem like this now than she could a love letter. Did Johnny write preposterous poetry? She thought of the love letter, now back in its drawer at the store. She thought of Johnny as she had last seen him, leaving Horatio Street Books with a sullen nod, unshaven, his eyes puffy, his skin gray. Probably up all night drinking, banging little Jennifer. Good. Go get her, Johnny. I'm a lot more than you could ever hope to handle.

She looked back at the sheaf of papers in her hand. What a sap I was, she thought. And what a poet.

> Penis
> Flashing red
> Sliding to the sky . . .

It, the penis, proceeded to sing and fly, if she were

interpreting the verse correctly. Lots of singing, flying, wandering, rustling, dreaming, in all the poems. She seemed to have favored short broken lines and large romantic thoughts.

> endless rhythms
> love distortion
> wavy heat.

Helen bundled the poems back in their folder. Should she lock them up with the love letter in the store? What? And risk spontaneous combustion? Or, worse, spontaneous generation? Anyway, someone might find them there. Should she throw them in the truck Mort and Mort left parked on the lawn, loaded with old cribs and KLH speakers, waiting to go to the town dump, now known as the Community Recycling Headquarters? No. What if they blew away into someone else's garden? What if the poems got recycled, and someone read them on a cereal box? The poems smelled of mildew, just slightly, like cologne. The dog waddled in, sniffed her leg, and waddled out again. She couldn't throw them away because someone might find them. She couldn't keep them because someone might find them.

Helen put the poems in the back of her closet on the floor behind the ice skates and shoe polish. It's only temporary, she thought. Everything is.

Then she went out into the garden. It was a beautiful day for pruning.

10 ′ ′ ′ ′ ′ ′ ′ ′ ′ ′ ′ ′ ′ ′

JOHNNY SWAM IN THE EVENINGS NOW, WHEN HE knew Helen would not be at the beach. He swam for an hour, for two hours. Sometimes it would get dark and he would see phosphorous with every stroke. Jennifer told him he had a great body, and sometimes, in his sleepless wanderings around his house, he would stop and examine his chest and arms, run a hand over the curve of a muscle. Then he would resume his pacing, or aim himself out the door. In the moonlight, the trees rushed toward the sky. The moist smells of the earth ascended. Mist rose from a neighbor's heated pool. Once he saw a deer and thought, You don't belong here either. He walked to the beach, to the town with its dark stores, its dark bookstore. One night, he walked to Jennifer and Kelly's dormitory. He arrived at dawn, too embarrassed to wake them, and turned around and hitchhiked home. He couldn't stand to be alone at night after that. He began to sleep in Jennifer and Kelly's dorm room on the floor.

On the morning of one of his days off, he woke up late from his spot on the floor among the stacks of CDs, the

Coke cans and sweatpants and lace underwear that surrounded him. Kelly and Jennifer were gone, and he got up,
already dressed, and went to the library. Miss Skattergoods
was reading, a cigarette dangling from her mouth, her feet
on the desk.

"Hello, darling, where have you been this last week?"
She ran a finger over the stubble on his chin.

Johnny shrugged.

"You, too?" She smiled and went back to her book.

Johnny spread his documents out, but they held no interest for him. He missed New York. This town was a
posturing, polished, superficial dump. He sighed. Look,
Helen is just a middle-aged woman, he told himself, a
housewife divorcée, languishing in ennui, who had a little
fling. How was it that I got flung, though? And then he
thought of that morning, of putting his hands on her arms,
of pulling her to him, kissing her. How had he ever had the
nerve? He still didn't understand it. He had stood beside
her in the store so many times thinking, All I have to do is
lean, give in to gravity just a little, and my lips will be on
her lips. And, absolutely still, he would feel himself moving
toward her. He never moved toward her, not really. Only
stood and felt the pull of gravity. Until that day in his
backyard. He buried his head in his arms, the papers wrin-
kling beneath him. I'm out of control, he thought. Better to
go back to Carla and her dramatic readings of Alice Walker.

"Johnny," said Miss Skattergoods, "let's close up shop and
go get drunk."

It was five o'clock. He'd been sitting for hours doing
nothing, daydreaming about a woman he detested, about
the way her shirt, unbuttoned, fell from her shoulder.

Miss Skattergoods locked the doors and led him around
to an old stable, now a garage.

"Get in," she said, opening the door of a shiny black Porsche.

"Nice car."

She nodded in agreement. "It's new. I needed it."

Johnny hastily fastened his seat belt as they roared out onto the quiet street. In a kind of trance, he watched the streets fly by.

"Are you in a hurry?" he asked.

"Bad mood."

"Oh."

"You too."

Johnny nodded, then sat passively. Perhaps Miss Skattergoods wanted to be fucked by a boy, too. He should advertise. Bored? Tired of men? Try a boy! Twenty-year-old. Nice-looking, bright, available for one-night stand with mature woman. But Miss Skattergoods was not interested in sleeping with him, he was sure. She lit a cigarette and, holding it in her left hand, which was on the wheel, she pinched Johnny's chin with her free hand. The car screeched around a curve.

"Cheer up, Johnny. You're far too young to die."

"I'm twenty," he said.

"Are you? I forgive you."

He waited, looking at her curiously, rather rudely, he imagined.

"I'm sixty-one," she said. "Tomorrow. Are they going to let you into this bar?"

"I have a fake ID."

"In case you decide to buy a shotgun to murder your parents. Like those boys in California."

"Yes."

They were out of Pequot now, away from the shore and farther into the country. Miss Skattergoods braked, the car lurched and stopped in front of a low, wood-shingled, dreary-looking bar. Inside it was dark, practically empty, and they sat at a booth and drank boilermakers, one after another, as the bar filled up, men mostly, the occasional couple, and Johnny told her he was in love with someone he should not be in love with, though he was careful not to say who, and she said, "Oh yes, me too, darling, that's why we're here." And they drank some more, and then more, and Johnny watched Miss Skattergoods, drinking Scotch only now, and the more they drank, the more Johnny realized that Miss Skattergoods was right, that was the motive, and she was right about their purpose, as well, that they were in the bar to get drunk, and, sure that he could meet this goal, he drank with a will and a feeling of accomplishment until, his mouth dry and his eyes heavy, he found himself blinking in the morning sun, the leather of the Porsche's seat stuck to his cheek, the sound of Miss Skattergoods's breathing beside his ear.

He sat up straight and saw, through the windshield, the little cedar-shingled building and the neon light, now turned off, spelling out the word TAVERN. Miss Skattergoods opened her eyes. "Good morning," she said briskly. "Don't you feel better now, Johnny? Clears the head."

She drove him home, just as fast as before, the CD player blaring Louis Armstrong, and dropped him at his doorstep.

"Bye, honey. We'll have to do this again some time. See you later!" And she drove off, a cigarette in her mouth, her engine roaring jauntily.

"Happy birthday," he called after her. He staggered inside, showered, and realized his car was at the library. He looked for the keys to his parents' Volvo, but couldn't find them. More trouble when they got back. He was supposed to have used it now and then, or at least started it up, but he had forgotten its existence until just this moment. He cursed Miss Skattergoods, his parents, and himself, as slowly, unsteadily, he bicycled to work. He wondered if he should have eaten. He'd eaten very little recently. Didn't have the stomach for it. This morning, he wasn't sure he had a stomach at all. He felt weak. The ride was downhill mostly. He was sure he'd feel better by the time he had to pedal home. Anyway, he could probably get Jennifer or Kelly to give him a lift. He felt queasy, but he couldn't remember throwing up last night, so perhaps he hadn't and perhaps he wouldn't now. He remembered quite a bit else about the evening. Miss Skattergoods had insisted he call her Skat. He let her beat him at arm wrestling. He told her about his life in the city, his friends, his parents. She told him nothing about her life in the city, nothing about her friends, and he already knew all about her family. "I've retired," she said simply, when pressed about her unhappy love affair. "I've retired from all that." He never told her it was Helen, he remembered. Was it really Helen?

When he got to the store, he saw he was early, and as he walked in, he saw that Helen was, too, that no one else was there, that they were alone. He considered turning around and walking out. Instead, he stood just inside the door, staring and a little dizzy.

"Hi," he said. His head pounded and he suspected he was listing to one side. He walked toward the couch.

She looked skeptically at him. "Rough night?"

"Helen, I know you're not . . ." and he felt himself falling as he spoke. He put a hand against the wall to support himself, sank onto the couch, felt the cushions against his face. I know she's not what? he wondered. What was I going to say? What is Helen saying? He heard Helen's voice but not the words.

"Helen?" he said.

And he felt Helen's hands, and her arms. His face was against her breast. She stroked his cheek. She said his name. She kissed him.

How do you fall in love? Do you trip? Do you stumble? He put his face against hers, and he thought he told her he loved her. "I am in love," he whispered. "I know I'm in love when I see you." But she didn't answer, and he wondered if he had actually said anything, actually quoted that letter, the letter he'd seen in her bag.

"It's not polite to read other people's mail," Helen said at last. Then she helped him up, drove him home in her car, home to her house. Lucy will be in soon, she'll take care of the store, she thought. I'll take care of you. And she put him in her bed.

"Take off your clothes," she said.

He did, sitting on the bed, as she stood before him. She was watching.

"You're very beautiful, Johnny," she said.

Take off your clothes, he thought.

She shook her head, as if she'd heard him, went out and came back with toast and tea and aspirin and a glass of cold water. She sat on the bed beside him as he ate.

"Sorry," he said.

She put her hand on his cheek, ran it down his neck, onto his chest. "This is a bad idea," she said.

"I know," he said. He watched her unbutton her shirt. She let it fall to the floor. She slipped out of her jeans. How solid she was, he thought, how full and rounded, how soft, how strong . . . His adjectives stumbled incoherently. He realized with a start that she was beside him, against him, and he felt her body with something very like fear, then threw himself onto her with no fear and no thought at all and hardly knew what he was doing and hardly cared.

———

Helen's eyes were open, her face pressed beneath his. She could see nothing, so close. He breathed against her, his chest pushing into hers, up and down, his breath ruffling her hair. She could smell stale tobacco, although neither of them smoked. It was a memory, the boy from long ago with nicotine stains on his fingers. When you speak of this, she thought, hearing the words in Deborah Kerr's accent, and you will . . . be kind. She laughed.

"What?" he said.

"Nothing." Just a movie. A terrible old movie.

"What? What are you laughing at?" he raised himself on his elbows, looking down at her. His hair fell on either side of his face and brushed hers. His cheeks were pink from exertion, like an ice-skating child's.

"Oh, Johnny," she said, pulling him down, putting her arms around him. "What are we doing?"

"Fucking," he said, lifting his head again to smile, to kiss her.

Fucking, Helen thought later. Exactly.

Helen made dinner, which they ate in bed.

"There wasn't anything here. I don't cook much when Emily is away," she said. She put a tray of scrambled eggs and toast and sliced tomatoes on the bed between them. Johnny thought, I am Emily. She is feeding me and tending to me. I'm just a child to her, someone to look after. She was wearing his shirt, a blue oxford shirt with the sleeves torn off. It struck him as so improbable that Helen was wearing his shirt, as if that were what all this had been leading up to. It struck him as intimate beyond even sex. Her body in his shirt. His shirt on her body.

—

Confused and nearly dazed with desire, Helen sat on the bed watching Johnny eat. She couldn't eat at all herself. Her thoughts were physical, her passion like a blast of wind. It had no context, no history, no ambition beyond itself. There was no question of whether or not Johnny was a suitable mate. He was so patently unsuitable. There was no possibility of a serious relationship. She did not have to calculate whether she would be able to tolerate this or that characteristic, whether this encounter could lead to something deeper. It couldn't. And yet it in no way resembled the various casual sexual adventures she'd had over the years, curious plunges or tired acquiescences or bored exercises in power. Now there was only a joyous need. How odd, she thought. How uncharacteristically romantic. How overwhelming. How young he was, and excited.

"Johnny," she whispered, later, kissing his neck, her tongue moving down his arm, rubbing her face on his flat stomach, and she wanted to say, I've never wanted anyone this way. I've never felt this way. She ran her face along his legs, his thighs, her tongue tasting his skin, and she wanted to say, your body makes me tremble with desire, makes me want to crush you in my hands, fills me with tenderness and rage. "Johnny," she said instead.

—

Outside, the crickets began, soft and light in the tall grass of the field. Helen heard them as she lay beside Johnny. Did crickets fall in love? Or just sing about love? She

157

wondered if Johnny heard the crickets. He was on his back, his eyes open. It was a warm night and he lay naked and uncovered. Helen looked him over, his large, squared-off male feet; his legs, which stretched out, long and unconcerned, tan, the hair bleached almost blond by the sun; and then. . . . And then. What does one call it? Helen wondered. Even in thought? A penis? Penis is a ridiculous word. A dick? Cock? It all sounded lewd in such an uninteresting way, and she felt lewd in such an interesting way. Member? Member of what? Prick, schlong, schmuck, pecker, Jake the Puppet? None of them was right, she decided. But the simple, silent recital of these words had aroused her. Remarkable, she thought.

She heard the weird song of a raccoon.

"What on earth was that?" said Johnny.

"Raccoon."

"Do you think it's rabid?"

"I'm rabid, Johnny," she said, rolling on top of him.

"Yeah," he said, laughing. "You are."

———

Johnny sat up looking out at the blue morning sky. Helen had left him and gone running. He couldn't believe she was gone. He couldn't believe she had ever been there, with him. He thought of her, of her body, of the flesh of her arms, the curve of her belly, her thighs soft and rounded against his face, the smell of her, the smell of sex, warm, everywhere like a melody — he thought of all this with something like reverence. The tenderness he felt for Helen was too forceful to be tenderness.

He stood up and saw himself in the mirror. The dog came in, looked at him, and lay down. Johnny heard its tail thumping on the wood floor. He wanted Helen to come back. He wondered how, now that he'd been with her, he could ever be without her.

He pulled on his pants and went downstairs. Helen had made him coffee, or made it for herself and left him some. He looked around him, at her kitchen. He walked through the house. He strutted, really. He knew he was smiling idiotically. He looked through the French doors at the garden, opened them, stepped out, careful to avoid a dead rodent on the flagstones, and breathed in the morning.

"Bingo!" he said.

———

No one knew they were sleeping together. In the store, the tension surrounded them, but still no one knew. Helen saw Johnny standing behind the counter. She caught his eye, he looked back at the cash register, stared at the keys. "Nine ninety-five," she called to him gently. The color rose in his cheeks as he punched in the numbers and took the customer's money. Had the customer, a professor of Animal Behavior from the college, noticed Johnny's behavior? Or hers? Helen realized that a man in a green polo shirt was facing her, waiting for something, probably for her to finish her sentence. She looked at him, helpless.

"See?" his wife said, poking him in the arm with her elbow.

See? See what? Did they know, had they guessed? She was a cradle robber. She was sexually harassing an employee, and would have been sexually harassing an employee at the workplace at that moment if all these people would just leave. Did everyone know? Could they tell?

"Look," Helen said desperately, seeing Miss Skattergoods bomb down the street in her new black Porsche. "Miss Skattergoods, guardian of Skattergoods Library. She bought herself a Porsche for her birthday."

"See?" the woman said, poking her husband again, nodding at him in a way that was both intimate, as if they were accomplices, and accusatory.

Helen relaxed. She remembered them now. They hadn't noticed anything. They hadn't seen that her attention, the attention she so carefully lavished on her customers, was being drawn forcibly away from them by a boy eating a bagel behind the counter. This wife always poked her husband knowingly and said "See?" no matter what Helen said. From the corner of her eye, Helen watched Johnny chewing, watched his mouth. My knees are getting weak, she thought. They are actually getting weak. She felt them trembling, felt a lightness. She tried not to groan out loud with desire.

"I just wonder if he has the experience," the man was saying.

Experience? Helen thought. Johnny?

"I mean, I like Ray, but the other candidate for mayor worked for IBM."

"Oh. *Ray,*" Helen said. "I hope Ray doesn't get elected mayor before he finishes my house. Though he never has in the past."

"See?" said the wife.

⌐

They left the store separately, often at different times. But once in a while, Johnny couldn't tear himself away, and he would wait for Helen, hanging around, trying to make himself inconspicuous by helping out. In this he had to compete with Jennifer, who often worked extra hours just to be with Helen. Johnny was careful not to horn in on their exchanges. He didn't want to make Jennifer jealous, didn't want her to suspect anything. He didn't want anyone to suspect. It was no one's business but his and Helen's. He realized how much his other relationships with girls had been involved in publicly displaying them. A beautiful girlfriend; he was associated with her. She had chosen *him*, not someone else. He had chosen this girl, and she had accepted him. They would walk across the campus holding hands, claiming each other. But Helen was private. All he wanted from her was her. Helen was a secret, his secret: his and no one else's.

He did occasionally wonder if Miss Skattergoods had guessed. She watched him so closely sometimes.

"Feeling better, honey, I see," she said when he went back to the library two days after their drunken night together. He had spent those two days at Helen's. It was Helen who dropped him off at the library. Miss Skattergoods was sitting on the edge of her desk reading a letter. She folded it carefully and put it in the envelope and stuffed it in the back pocket of her khaki shorts. "I'm feeling better, too, aren't I? Yes, I am. Your car is very impressive," continued the librarian, "parked out there in front of the library. It looks as though you've been working day and night."

"Oh, I have been," he said. It was an impulse, a moment of mischief which he immediately regretted, for Miss Skattergoods narrowed her eyes, tilted her head, and smiled rather slyly before going off to the stacks, a large pink feather duster in one hand, a cigarette in the other. She was singing "Me and Mrs. Jones" quietly, under her breath, but he heard it.

". . . got a thaang goin' on . . ."

⸻

Johnny got home to Helen's before she did. Howard and Ray, the resident, or nearly resident, workmen, had not been around recently, Helen explained, because Ray was fund-raising and canvassing for the primary. Helen had given Johnny a key and he walked through each room, pretending he owned the house, Everett Banks Millerton's house. The dog followed him for a while, then got tired and collapsed and began to snore. Johnny looked in the refrigerator. There were two apples and a bottle of Evian. He wondered what was in his own refrigerator. He hadn't seen it in days.

Millerton walks past the tents of the Pequot Indians erected on his property by the trade representatives of that native nation. He smells the smoke from their cooking fires. He steps through his garden, his hunting dog at his side, out into the field. He doesn't see all these black Japanese pines because they haven't yet been introduced to the North American continent. He walks to the cliff's edge and gazes toward home, toward England. But I have left all that behind, he thinks. This is my home now, this wild and untamed land. Here have I set down my roots, among this brave people who have no need of roots. Johnny looked out across the water, one hand on his chest, imagining the thrill of being a man in a new land.

"Neat trick," Helen had said, when he'd told her more of Millerton. "Bourgeois comforts, bohemian conventions."

"I don't think those terms are really appropriate," he said. "I mean, historically, you know? It was only the eighteenth century."

"There has always been a bourgeoisie, I don't care what anyone says," Helen said. "The cavemen had one guy who put bearskin rugs on the floor of his cave, who cared which way the grain went on his oak club. The guy who bought the first wheel. The bourgeoisie make the world go around. Don't ever forget it."

"Spoken like a true shopkeeper."

Johnny looked out at the sea now. The waves were loud and exuberant, crashing onto the rocks below. Sometimes Johnny wished he lived in another time, wished he could see what he read about, wished he rode a horse across dirt roads instead of driving the biggest car ever made that was not a limousine. But today he would not have traded his place in time with anybody. Everett Banks Millerton, with his two mistresses, still did not have Helen. And he, Johnny, did.

As he walked back to the house, he passed a bank of wild raspberry bushes, and he went into the kitchen to find a bowl. He banged around, wondering why all people didn't keep their bowls where his mother kept hers, until he found a green plastic one with a lid, which seemed perfect.

He walked back toward the raspberries. The late after-noon heat was unruffled by breeze or noise. *Leaves hang unruffled by any breeze. The air is still. I have fallen in love without taking a step.* Two small parchment white moths circled each other in their flight from bush to bush, flower to flower. He thought he saw a hummingbird, then recognized it to be an insect of some kind. The garden surrounded him in a fragrant, vaporous tangle. As he passed an apple tree, his foot caught on an exposed root. When he looked down, he saw a pink worm working its way up through the soil. The apples, still green, hung above in their sweet, light scent. Johnny, a city boy, stood among the bees and plucked the dark raspberries from the fierce little vines, and he felt tears come to his eyes. Tears of what? he wondered. Just generic tears, tears of emotion, not some emotion, but emotion itself. The bees buried themselves in the honeysuckle blossoms, pushing deep into the funnels of transparent yellow petals. He plucked one of the flowers, pulled the end off carefully, tugged on the tiny string until the honey appeared, a drop. He put it to his lips.

11

THE TIME HAD COME TO CHANGE THE DISPLAY
window, and Helen removed the old books, dust jackets
faded by the sun, the paperback covers curling inside the
rubber bands she used to keep them flat. She cleaned
the shelf with Fantastik, cleaned the glass with Windex,
began loading the window once again with new volumes of
fiction and biography and history and poetry, looked out
at the street and wondered why biographies of poets sold
better than poetry itself. She saw Lucy coming, claiming the sidewalk with her bustling determination. Helen
waved.

"Helen," Lucy said when she came in, looking around to
see if anyone else was there. But the store was empty
except for Helen on her knees in the window like the doggy
in the song, the one with the waggly tail.

"Ruff, ruff!" Helen said, but Lucy seemed not to understand the allusion.

"Helen, I really have to speak to you. I've been wanting
to say something, but it's really a little embarrassing. It's
difficult even to bring up the subject . . ."

Helen snapped a rubber band around a paperback, then snapped it again loudly, then again and again, rhythmically.

"Could you stop that, please? It's really annoying."

Helen stopped and looked grimly at Lucy. She hoped this was about George. Lucy had seen her throwing herself at George. But then, over the years Lucy had seen her throwing herself at a lot of people. Lucy, more than anyone else, knew how little it meant. No, this talk was not to be about George. Helen knew exactly what Lucy wanted to talk about. She could not hide the truth from Lucy forever. They worked together. They were friends. Lucy knew her as well as anyone did. Of course Lucy had guessed. But how depressing. One had no privacy. One was so transparent. Helen realized she was humming, not even a tune, just a buzzing tone.

"Helen! What is wrong with you?"

"Sorry. What? What do you want? I'm very busy." Helen pointed to the books piled in the window. "See?"

"I want to know about, about, well, if you have any, um, feelings. Or secrets, say. Or secret feelings. Of some kind. That you want to talk to me about."

"No."

"What?"

"No, I don't have any feelings, secrets, or secret feelings."

Lucy tapped her foot. "Yes, you do," she said.

"No, I don't." Helen crossed her arms. She felt sullen and defiant. No one could make her tell. It was nobody's business but her own. It was a secret. Why was it a secret, though? Because it was easier that way? Because she was embarrassed to be ensnared by a twenty-year-old? Because of what people would think of her, a desperate old cradle robber? She had no explanation. It was just a secret. A wonderful, glorious, outrageous secret.

"Look, I'm sorry. This is terrible. I'm as embarrassed as you are. But you can talk to me, Helen. I'm very . . ." she paused, and Helen wondered what she would say. Sympathetic? Understanding? Surely not. Lucy was kind, but as a white-haired senator is kind to the son of his longtime maid, the talented one who wants to go to law school. Noblesse oblige toward family retainers was the philosophic basis for Lucy's relations with the outside world. This involved generosity but certainly not understanding or sympathy.

"I'm very *discreet*," Lucy said, finally.

Helen smiled and turned back to the window. "So am I."

She heard Lucy walk away, heard her at the desk rummaging around, heard her return. Turning, she saw Lucy dangling the letter, the anonymous love letter, criss-crossed with Scotch tape.

"I understand," Lucy was saying. "I understand why you never told me, never could show me the letter. And I understand why you left it in that drawer, where I was bound to see it someday — and bound to understand."

The letter.

"And I do. *I understand*," Lucy said. "I understand everything, Helen. You don't have to explain. All those references to oranges and shoelaces and driving cars and my eating habits . . ."

When I tie my shoes, when I peel an orange, when I drive my car.

"Look, let's just talk about it, okay? This isn't easy for me, either, Helen. But these things are never easy."

Which things? Helen wondered. Letter things? Love things? Lucy things?

Lucy sat on the windowsill beside Helen.

"Helen?"

The sun was hot on Helen's back.

"I know it's hard for you, too," Lucy said.

"Well," Helen said. She looked at Lucy holding the love letter. "I guess."

"I feel better now," Lucy said. "I know we'll work it out."

"We will?"

"Helen, we've been friends for such a long time."

Lucy wrote the letter?

"You wrote the letter?" Helen said. "To me?"

"Me?"

Lucy stood up, a look of polite horror on her face.

"*You* wrote the letter to *me*, Helen. I'm not in love with you. You're in love with me. It says so. Quite clearly." Lucy pointed to the letter. "Here." She tapped it authoritatively.

"Lucy, I'm sorry, I've never been interested in women in that way."

"Sometimes this happens late in life. It's not that unusual. I'm not condemning you, Helen. I'm flattered —"

"Well, don't be. I did not write that letter to you. Did you write it to me?"

"Of course not. I actually find it quite easy to resist your charms, Helen."

They glared at each other, insulted.

⸺

Helen explained the circumstances of the letter to Lucy, who forgave Helen for both having secretly been in love with her and for never having secretly been in love with her all in one august gesture: a wave of her hand dismissing the whole episode accompanied by a short exhalation of breath resulting in the word "Poo!" and a polite smile, which indicated that all was not only forgiven, all was positively forgotten. Then Lucy pored over the letter and offered various interpretations and theories as to who might have written it and to whom, none of which, to Helen's relief, included Johnny.

—

Johnny and Helen walked on the beach. They held hands like teenagers. He is a teenager, Helen thought. Nearly. I am not. But she felt like one, as desperate, as confused, as reckless. They walked on the beach holding hands, in the dark where no one could see them, though once the head-lights of a car entering the parking lot leaped toward them, then passed. The moon appeared, a sliver cutting through the clouds, mirrored, a dash, a hundred dashes, on the rippled water. The sand was wet. Helen put her hand around Johnny's waist and felt the movement as he walked beside her. I want to fuck him, she thought. All the time. But worse, I want to be with him all the time. I like him. I'm crazy about him. She sighed. I'm very, very fond of him.

"I love you," Johnny said.

You're just a kid, she thought. You don't know anything about it.

"I love you, Helen. I don't care if you think I'm ridiculous for saying so. I do. And I'm right to. And furthermore, you love me."

"I can't see you tomorrow night," she said after a while. "I have to have dinner with George and Nancy. An old invitation. It's George's birthday."

"I'll wait for you."

She thought of him: pacing, staring out the window, tapping his fingers on the sill. She liked the idea of Johnny waiting for her, his shirt thrown casually over a chair, his eyes enlarged with impatience.

"Is that okay?"

"Yes," she said. "You wait for me."

There was no question of bringing Johnny along. What would she say? This is my date. This is my adopted son. This is my lover, and is he ever. This is my *boy*friend.

———

She stood in George's living room watching him make martinis. He loved to make martinis and to discuss making martinis. He handed one to Helen and she sipped it and thought the taste was miraculous, incorporating three states all at once, liquid, vaporous alcohol, and a solid icy chill. There were quite a few people. She knew some, recognized some from the store.

"I like the Mazda 929, but I wish the trunk were bigger," she heard someone say.

"There's that new Volvo wagon."

Lucy was there, and Helen was sure she was thinking of the love letter. She gave Helen a smirky, knowing half smile each time their eyes met.

"George?" Lucy whispered at one point. "Is it? Did he write it?"

Helen shrugged. She didn't know, though she was sure that if he had written it, he had not written it to her. She whispered back, "Miss Skattergoods?"

Miss Skattergoods was also present, looking uncharacteristically elegant in a green sleeveless linen sheath.

"Helen," she said. "Did you like that funny collection?"

She'd found a book of eighteenth-century courtship letters for Helen, a correspondence between a Dr. Franklin B. Hough and his fiancée, Mariah Kilham, in one of which Dr. Hough wonders what her plans are for "life," then quickly worries that "perhaps I have offended a sense of delicacy or excited surprise, that so early in a correspondence or at all an allusion has been made to a theme of momentous importance which but few persons who attain mature age do not discuss inwardly and in the silent recesses of the heart, if not otherwise." That was his proposal of marriage.

"He lists the books in his library," Helen said. "As a form of courtship. It's very sweet."

"One of his patients married an eleven-year-old. Did you read that part?"

Helen had. He wrote: "Often did he have to call her home from play *with other children* to get his dinner," she remembered reading.

"Helen, you know, you've gone through nearly every collection of letters I have in the library. Are you writing a book?" Miss Skattergoods asked. "A scholarly monograph! Or are you composing your own letter? A long, lovely one. Studying the form? Who are you writing a letter *to*, dear? *Do* you write?"

"Helen," Lucy said quickly, "has become interested in the letter as a genre. Haven't you, Helen?"

"She certainly has," said Miss Skattergoods.

"I write postcards," Helen said. "Postcards only. I don't write letters. Do you write letters, Miss Skattergoods?"

"Frequently."

"I *read* letters. We have a bond." Helen noticed her voice. It was edgy. Why had Miss Skattergoods mentioned the eleven-year-old? Anyway, Johnny wasn't eleven. Emily was eleven, but she remained quite single. It was just a coincidence that Miss Skattergoods had mentioned the eleven-year-old bride. Even so, Helen was annoyed. She didn't like Miss Skattergoods questioning her reading habits. It was intrusive, a breach of confidence. Book lists were personal, like Dr. Hough's library inventory in his love letter.

She saw a man, an English professor, to whom she had sold a guidebook to Mexico just the other day, walking toward her little group with his wife. Was that, too, privileged information, selling a travel guide? she wondered. Could she say, "Hey, where did you decide to go in Mexico?" Was there confidentiality between a librarian and her patrons, a bookseller and her customers? What if he were sneaking off to Mexico with a nubile student?

"As a birthday present," Nancy was saying, her arm around George, "we're going to Antarctica."

"Really?" said the English professor, encircling his wife suddenly with his own arm. "So are we!"

The four of them forced smiles and looked at each other, a little disappointed.

Helen glanced at Lucy, who nodded. They would order guidebooks to Antarctica in the morning.

"Send us postcards. Don't forget. With penguins," Helen said. "Does Antarctica have a post office? People only write when they're away on a vacation, don't they? If then. They used to write all the time. About everything."

"You know," George said, "Freud introduced the Oedipus theory *in a letter*. The letter to Fliess. Imagine introducing a theory in a letter these days."

An older woman, a doctor who had emigrated from Vienna whom Helen recognized from the store, said, "The dear old Oedipus theory. When I was younger, a thousand years ago, I went with my husband and son to a rather august gathering of physicians. We were sitting across the table from a beautiful woman. She must have been seventy. Delicate. Delicious. She was flirting with my son. My sixteen-year-old son. He was delicious, too, I admit. I heard her later, nearly whispering, saying to him, 'Everyone I've been with I've made very happy,' that sort of thing. I went to bed that night, and said to my husband, 'I'm having a heart attack.' It wasn't a heart attack, of course, but it was my heart. The dear old Oedipus theory. Or would that be the Jocasta theory? She was a countess, I believe."

Helen said, "I don't feel well." She got up, went to the bathroom, looked at herself in the mirror, thought, I am a bad person and I will go to hell, thought of Johnny waiting impatiently for her at home, and thought, I am a bad person, I will go home to Johnny.

—

When she got there, Johnny was not pacing or staring out the window. He was sprawled in bed eating a peach, writing a letter, watching MTV, and reading Diana Trilling's memoir of her life and marriage to Lionel Trilling. Helen had left the book beside her bed, meaning to read it herself.

"Do you know who Diana Trilling is?" she said. Helen was of a different generation from the Trillings, but Lionel and Diana Trilling were figures of her intellectual coming of age. To Johnny, though, she suspected they must seem like figures from early American history. She had noticed that while Johnny liked to read contemporary authors on his own and had studied the classics of modernism in school, there was a whole period of which he was almost completely ignorant. It was too early in time for him to have been there, too recent in history to be covered in classes. A mention of Mary McCarthy or Edmund Wilson, of Jean Stafford or Robert Lowell or Delmore Schwartz or Randall Jarrell was met with a blank stare.

Johnny was looking at her. "I do now," he said.

And Helen was sorry she had asked, sorry she had put him on the spot. Why should he know anything about them? Why should he know anything at all? He was so young. He had time to learn whatever he needed. He should be watching a baseball game, not reading the memoir of a fierce intellectual warrior.

"Why aren't you watching a baseball game?" she said. The MTV logo came on. The show was called *Alternative Nation*.

"What *is* alternative music?" she asked.

He thought for a minute. Then he pointed at the screen and went back to his reading.

"Ah." She watched the show, her head on his shoulder as he read. After ten or twelve videos, which she rather liked, she thought she detected a pattern. White boys, once in a while a girl. Images and design once considered signs of modernism; cutting and camera angles once the province exclusively of the avant-garde; ironically apocalyptic rather than merely apocalyptic lyrics; voices and tunes far more melodic than heavier rock or rap but less obvious than pop; a droning instrumental accompaniment, often acoustic; bad posture.

"Look," she said, taking out her folder of letters and poems, extracting an old concert program, and hiding the folder again in the back of the closet. "I found this when I was going through stuff from the attic."

"The Fillmore East?" He looked at the cover, decorated with swirling Art Nouveau psychedelic nudes. Inside was an ad for a record by the Mothers of Invention.

"Frank Zappa," Helen explained, pointing at the picture.

"I know who Frank Zappa is, Helen. Who did you go see?"

"Well, this particular time seems to have been a Buffy Sainte-Marie concert. That's a little secret, Johnny. Between you and me. She's a rather icky folksinger, and I wouldn't like this lapse in taste generally known. I was very young. Younger than you."

In the program there were ads for antique clothing calling on cats and chicks to be groovy, ads for records and concerts by Procol Harem, Blood, Sweat and Tears, Butterfield Blues Band, Jeff Beck, Jefferson Airplane, the Incredible String Band, Vanilla Fudge. Helen read the names out loud.

"I saw Dylan," she said. "I saw Janis Joplin. I saw Cream."

"Did you get stoned, trip on LSD, all that?"

"Well . . ."

"Afraid of corrupting me? Setting a bad example? I already took LSD, Helen. It sucked. I thought my tongue was really long. What a mom you are. But luckily you're not my mom!" He grabbed her and kissed her. "Did you go to Woodstock? I saw the movie."

"No. I was in the hospital. Car crash."

She remembered waking up in a small room. Her grandmother sat beside her, holding her hand. A vase of yellow tulips sat on the windowsill, which she could see out of the corner of her eye. She couldn't move her head. She felt her face, felt the line of stitches running along her jaw, a smaller one on her forehead. She wondered if her favorite belt had been ruined, if her jeans, the tightest and most worn pair she had, were lost. If she would miss Woodstock.

"Who were you writing to?" she said to Johnny, looking at the sheet of paper still on his stomach.

"My mom and dad."

She picked up the letter. He didn't protest.

Dear Mom and Dad,

I hope you're still having a good time. Everything here is under control. So don't feel rushed. If you're having fun, feel free to stay on longer. I can man the fort, so to speak. Do you remember where you left the keys to the Volvo, by the way? Just wondering. Did you get the mail I forwarded? The weather has finally calmed down. It's not raining. It's not jungle hot. The wild raspberries are out. I'm getting some work on my paper done. The librarian is quite a character. My job is okay still. Miss you. But don't feel you have to come home right away. Or anything.

Love,
Johnny

She thought of her friends, Mark and Vivian Howell, Johnny's parents, Johnny Howell's parents far away in Texas reading this letter, and it was as if she had written a letter to them herself: My good friends, I am happy and thriving, and all thanks to you! What a surprise! What an adventure. I am "educating" your little boy! He's not so little, either! He's in good hands, too, my hands, and I'm doing my very best. You don't mind, do you? Everyone who's been with me I've made happy. That's what the seventy-year-old countess said, and I'm only forty-two. He's a lovely boy. Delicious. I know how much you love him. I have a child, after all. I'll treat him as if he were my own son. The dear old Oedipus theory.

"Oh God," she said.

"What? Bad letter?"

"Your parents. Your poor parents. I've betrayed them. I've betrayed myself as a parent."

"Helen, I'm not a child. And you're not my mother."

"They'll never forgive me. Except that they'll never know. Unless they guess. My mother always guessed everything. They'll read that letter and think, English translation: Don't come home! I'm doing something you wouldn't approve of! I've been seduced by that awful Helen who stomps around in blue jeans and can't bear to grow old." Helen laughed. "They'll be home like a flash."

"You're not old," he said without much conviction,

"I'm old and wise in the ways of the world. That's why you like me, darling."

"Yeah, that's true." He kissed her. "Do you really think they'll rush home? Will they know?"

Soon she'd be getting letters like that from Emily. Would she know? If she knew, what would she do? She put her arms around Johnny. Freud's letter to Fliess. George had gone to his bookcase to find it. He read it to his guests: "I can now understand the riveting power of *Oedipus Rex*," Freud wrote. Oh, so can I, Helen thought. Or is it the riveting power of Johnny himself? Or of youth; or my own age, a *force majeure,* driving me to this boy beside me, his head on my breast? So improbable, so inevitable. She kissed his hand, the one that held the peach.

"In that Trilling book," he said comfortably from her breast. "Why is everyone always so mad at everyone else? Are they all crazy?"

Am I going to have to explain anti-Communism and anti-anti-Communism to my little lover? Helen thought.

"This peach is awesome," he added, and held it out for her to bite.

Awesome. Instead of cringing, as she once would have, she let the echo resound in her head, music, a song that only Johnny could sing. Johnny. So young. Sometimes he said, "I'm like really psyched." Sometimes he said, "So she goes, 'Johnny!' and I'm like, 'Jennifer!'" He said things were excellent. He misused the word *hopefully* and overused the word *totally*. She, who interrupted complete strangers to correct their usage, wanted to correct nothing. How many men had she tried to change, to mold, to dress, to educate? But when she looked at Johnny, when she held him in her arms, she wanted to whisper, Don't change! I have no stake in you, no need to change you, no desire to mold you, to educate you. Dress you? I'd rather undress you. We don't belong together. But you belong to me. I want you not as you might be. I want you as you are.

"Yes," she said. "Awesome."

—

Johnny lay beside her stroking her hair. Would his parents rush back? He remembered sitting on the stairs at home, Helen marching past him in nothing but his shirt, her legs brushing his face. Would he now see her, a demure friend of the family, sipping a glass of white wine in the living room, chatting about roses with his mother?

"When they come back," he said to Helen, "don't change."

—

In the store, Johnny often found himself lingering in the poetry room reading love poems. At least, they were love poems to him. All poems are love poems, he thought. He read Wordsworth and Marvell and Keats and William Carlos Williams and Lowell and Emily Dickinson, Whitman, Edwin Denby, and Marianne Moore. He read whatever he happened to pull off the shelf. Linda Pastan and A. R. Ammons one day, Delmore Schwartz, Lloyd Schwartz, Harvey Shapiro, and Karl Shapiro the next. It was disorienting, and so struck him, disoriented as he was, as welcoming. He had no bearings, and caressed by the many breezes of language, he drifted and was comforted.

Helen, who usually spent any free moments in the narrow little room herself, now opened huge collections of letters instead whenever she had the chance. She scrutinized the mail, as well, examining typefaces, watermarks.

He asked her about it, but she said only, "That letter, the one you ought not to have read, is something of a mystery. Mysteries annoy me." Johnny often thought about the love letter himself. He could still see it lying in the shadows with the bottles of wine in her old black canvas bag. She had moved it to a drawer in the store and locked it up, and they had never really spoken of it. Once, he tried to ask her about it, and she said, "It was from no one to no one, and that makes it mine." That's all she would say. Even when he told her, "I wish it was from me, or from you to me," she simply answered, "So do I."

"Johnny," Miss Skattergoods said one day, hollering from her Porsche, as he stood in the store's open door. "Johnny," she said when he went out to see what she wanted. She handed him a book. "Give this to your mistress. Don't look so alarmed, dear. Your *boss*. She said she needed it for some horrible houseguest she's having."

"Oh. Yeah. Her mother's coming."

"Is she."

"And grandmother."

"Ah. And when do they arrive?"

"I guess tomorrow. Do you know them?"

"Do you ever really know anyone, Johnny? Stick to the lovely old past, don't you think?" And she roared off.

Johnny carried the book inside and thought of the past. He himself hardly had a past. Was that why he loved the past? Other people's pasts? But history wasn't really the past at all — it was what could never age.

He handed the book over the counter to Helen.

"What next?" she asked him softly.

"Next?" he said. "Next is more."

12 ' ' ' ' ' ' ' ' ' ' ' ' ' '

LILIAN AND ELEANOR ARRIVED IN A BOTTLE GREEN
Jaguar. It was an old Jaguar, but like a new Jaguar it broke
down regularly. Eleanor refused to sell it. She also refused
to drive it, and Lilian was at the wheel.

Grandma Eleanor stepped from the car. "I'm here!" she
said, holding her arms out, a cormorant on a post, a chorus
girl taking a bow, a butterfly, a crucifix, Helen thought. A
cross to bear.

"Grandma!" she said. "Mom!" she added, as her mother,
a cigarette dangling from her lips, her dark glasses pushed
up on her head, climbed from behind the wheel.

"Your grandmother is here," Lilian said. "As she has noted.
She's here and she's all yours. What you choose to do with
her is your business. But may I suggest strangulation as a
most satisfying option." She slammed the car door and
stormed, on her little feet in their little high-heeled mules
(it was a diminutive but fierce storm), into the house.

"She dislikes having an aged parent," Eleanor said in a
bland, even voice. "Imagine how I feel. With an aged daughter."

No wonder I'm such a bitch, Helen thought. Third-generation bitch. Nature and nurture, a conspiracy, a confederacy. Was little Emily also destined to this fate? Secretly Helen hoped so — she was proud of her grandmother, her mother, herself. But my poor Emily. Perhaps just this once, just this one generation could stay benign and sincere, perhaps she could stay at Camp Rolling Ridge, rolling over ridges until it was safe to come home, until she became an adult and home wasn't home.

Helen hugged her grandmother. She could feel her white hair against her cheek, smell her cold cream, her make-up, the sweet waxy smell of lipstick, as Grandma Eleanor kissed her, leaving, as she had since Helen was a child, two garish pink streaks on her face. She experienced the familiar sensation of hugging her grandmother after a long absence, and yet the moment pulled away from her, shyly, like a dog from a stranger. Johnny, Helen thought. Where are you now? Staring out the window, your jaw slack, your eyes glazed? Rubbing Jennifer's head for luck, your smile affectionate, contemptuous? Or are you selling one of my customers a book, looking up suddenly from the cash register with a flash of blue eyes?

Johnny, she thought, hugging her grandmother, then noticed over Grandma Eleanor's shoulder a moving van pull into the driveway.

"A moving van is pulling into my driveway," Helen said.

"I thought I might stay awhile," Grandma Eleanor said.

"Here?"

"For a while."

"A while?"

Lilian stuck her head out the door. "You're insane," she said to Grandma Eleanor.

"It's genetic," Grandma Eleanor said.

Helen took a deep breath. It's not my house, she reminded herself. I like my mother. I like my grandmother. I haven't seen them in a year. It's not my house. She watched the screen door swing forcefully shut behind her mother. She smiled, happy at the familiarity of the sight.

Lilian was severe and short-tempered with a throaty voice. She smoked in the bath. When Helen was growing up, her mother treated her like an adult who, for reasons no one cared to go into, was too small to reach the light switches. Helen trailed around after her mother in a soft haze of half understanding. Adult conversations, thrilling and somehow important, surrounded her, as indecipherable and compelling as new art. Lilian, propped against the pillows, would gossip mercilessly and good-humoredly into the telephone. Lolling on the bed, at the foot like a lapdog, Helen listened contentedly to her mother's side of the conversation.

Helen admired her mother, who either never stayed still or stayed absolutely still. As a youngish widow, she took up a desultory study of archaeology, which consisted mostly of visiting museums in European cities and going on digs in points farther east. She still traveled, having left a friend in every port. She had never thought in terms of a career. She didn't need the money and didn't seem to need the assurance of an academic post, or even an academic degree. She was a committed, energetic amateur. When she wasn't globe-trotting, she lay in bed manning the phone, dispensing advice, which she could, and did, give out on nearly any subject — and if she turned out to be right, so much the better.

It impressed Helen that Lilian had maintained so many close friendships from her childhood, from college, from every stage of her life. Women who wouldn't dream of speaking to each other all talked intimately to Lilian. The secret, Helen knew, was a combination of intelligence and interest. She, Helen, had inherited the intelligence.

My mother is interested in people; I am merely curious about them, Helen sometimes thought. Lilian regarded others as recipients of her energy, her counsel. She was imperious and generous. They were projects, her projects, and she worked hard at them. Helen saw this, saw the devotion it inspired in people, but she herself wanted only to let live and to live. She had escaped her mother's attention, for which she was grateful. Lilian, busy with bossing her friends about, had simply accepted Helen as a kind of silent accomplice, a junior member of the board, nonvoting.

Lilian never stayed anywhere very long anyway, Helen reminded herself. Neither did Grandma Eleanor. But unlike Lilian, who traveled obsessively, visiting ape preserves in Kenya and digging up shards in Turkey, Eleanor did not travel — she moved. She had moved so many times that she was now quite expert at it. She knew her moving man. She called Atlas Van Lines every few years and asked for him by name, Joe Clancy. And Joe Clancy would drive up in his giant moving van and load the boxes. Eleanor kept empty boxes, labeled and waiting, in the attic or the basement, depending on the house she was in at that moment. Sometimes she moved because her present abode was getting too big for an old woman like her. Sometimes she moved because it was getting too small. Sometimes the north was too cold. Sometimes the south was too hot. The east too wet, the west too dry.

"I want to spend some time with my family," she said now. "I'm getting older." She lied about her age, shaving off five years. "Almost eighty-five, after all."

"Mrs. Lasch!" It was the moving man, removing his baseball cap. He had a spiderweb tattoo on each elbow. "Welcome."

"Did you have a good trip, Mr. Clancy? Next time I'll travel with you. In the cab."

"You'd be safe with me, Mrs. Lasch."

"But would you be safe with me?" Grandma Eleanor shook her silver-handled cane at him.

"Maybe I should get a tattoo," she said to Helen as they walked in the door of the house.

"Like my friend Lucy."

"Like Cher."

Lilian was short and boyish, as insouciant about clothes as her own mother, Grandma Eleanor, was — was what? Souciant, Helen decided. Lilian threw her clothes on, threw them off, tossed her sweater here, kicked her shoes there. There was always the suggestion of vigorous movement in her attire. Her clothes were good, expensive clothes, and they didn't seem to mind her treatment of them. Like slumming debutantes, they were adventurous, reckless. Like Lilian herself. She and her Armani jackets appeared to have an understanding, not unlike an open marriage, a French *arrangement*.

"Coffee?" her mother said. She'd already found it, made it. She poured Helen a cup, and they stood at the sink, as if they were in a hurry, and Helen wondered again why her mother's coffee, made with Helen's beans and Helen's machine, always tasted so much better than Helen's coffee.

"You make the best coffee, Mom."

Lilian smiled. Helen noticed a ring, a sapphire, round and unfaceted, a ring she'd never seen before on her mother's left hand, on the finger with her wedding band.

"I never saw that. It's beautiful. It's really beautiful. When did you get that? I never saw that."

Her mother shrugged. "It was made for me. Last year. You like it?"

"I want it."

Lilian laughed. She put down her mug and embraced Helen. "My Helen," she said softly. "My dearest."

Helen felt her mother's hug from a vast distance, from childhood. She closed her eyes, pressed her face against her mother's hair, resisted the temptation to say Mommy.

Oh, Mommy, she thought.

"I love this house," Lilian was saying. "You've really fixed it up beautifully. Where is your poor old dog? Jasper!"

Lilian released her, and Helen whistled for the dog, who painfully emerged from beneath the chair he favored. The sun poured in through the big windows and he stood in a yellow rectangular patch of light, his tongue hanging, his tail lurching awkwardly back and forth. He barked.

"Here," Lilian said suddenly. She pulled off the ring and thrust it at Helen. "Take it."

Helen took it and put it back on her mother's finger.

"You're crazy, mother," she said.

"It's genetic," Lilian said, raising her arm dramatically and pointing a mighty finger at the figure silhouetted in the doorway, an elegant figure in a hat, flourishing her cane.

"I'm not conceited," Helen's grandmother often said. "I'm quoting."

And it was true. She took her new towns, neighborhoods, cities, states, by storm. Helen thought that the local Pequot inhabitants, possessing a blend of sophistication and provincialism that occurs only in those both very comfortable and very geographically isolated, would be charmed by Eleanor. Whether Eleanor would be charmed by Pequot was something altogether different. Having fled a small town to live in New York at an early age, having thrived there, turning herself from a poor seamstress into a well-known hat designer and then, with evident relief and pride, an idle Upper East Side matron, Eleanor might find Pequot as dull and limited as it in some ways was. Or she might see it as fallow ground, just waiting for Eleanor Lasch.

Eleanor always wore a hat. Not a petite perched lady's hat. Not a sensible canvas tennis hat, not a bright baseball cap. Not any of the kinds of hats people wore in Pequot. Eleanor wore her own hats, svelte, dashing fedoras. With her silver-tipped cane, she was the picture of elderly elegance. What Helen marveled at was not so much her perfect taste. It was her energy in exercising it. She tuned her look with gentle, meticulous expertise, a mechanic tinkering with his Daimler.

Lilian carried her one small duffel bag into the house. "*I'm* very considerate when intruding on my daughter, aren't I, cookie?"

"Very," Helen said.

"Am I intruding?" Grandma Eleanor asked, directing Mr. Clancy to put her Adirondack chairs in the front hall, as there was no room for them on the porch.

"Well, there's so much of you," Helen said.

"But so little time," said Grandma Eleanor.

So little time, Helen thought, and she pictured Johnny. Her grandmother patted her on the arm and smiled, and Helen smiled back.

"Yes," Helen said. "So little time."

"Oh, please," Lilian said.

Later that night Helen watched Grandma Eleanor unpack some of her clothes. It was Eleanor's gift somehow not to look eccentric, ever, no matter how polished and self-conscious her outfit. She was eccentric, of course. And the engine that drove her so smoothly through life was sheer vanity. Vanity inspired her, vanity sustained her, vanity rewarded her. Helen thanked the Fates that Eleanor was her grandmother and not her mother. A generation's distance muted Grandma Eleanor's effect, like the artful lighting of a photograph.

She would move into the big house in a big way, all those carefully marked boxes, all her furniture, nearly a century of it, hoisted by Joe Clancy and his twin spiderwebs. Eleanor moved often, but she never moved light.

"I have to think of more than myself," she would explain. "There's Lila, you know." Looming in the background of all family decisions was Lila, Eleanor's baby sister. Lila, a youthful seventy-nine, had lived in Florida for decades. She didn't move like Eleanor. She barely left her house in Palm Beach. For at least twenty years the two sisters had been promising each to join the other, each to welcome the other with open arms, neither of which did either of them ever actually do. But it meant that they both felt it necessary to maintain a household large enough for two (considerably larger, in fact — what if they needed live-in nurses?), just in case.

—

Helen lay in her bed without Johnny. Her house was full of women and boxes. She imagined Johnny in his messy room, asleep on his back, one arm flung across the bed, the other across his eyes. She had barely been able to speak to him today — a quick, awkward phone call, her mother around every corner, her grandmother shuffling from room to room.

"I love you," Johnny said. He had found a sweater of hers at the store and buried his face in the familiar scent, intoxicated, but he didn't tell her. "Send them away," he said instead. "You're mine."

Helen had listened with a shiver of pleasure. Was she his? He seemed awfully confident. From the moment she brought him home to her bed, he had become sure of himself. The awkward teenage lover seemed to have propelled himself into a new, reckless manhood. Young and afraid before, he now appeared too young to be afraid. Helen remembered being too young for fear. Vaguely.

Johnny said, "Stay at my house. Who'll give a shit?" Johnny said, "I love you, I love you, and I love you." He said, "Why don't we do it in the road?" Helen said nothing. Those are just lines from a song, she thought. An old song. Like me. I'm old enough to know not to do it in the road. That's where car accidents happen, in the road. Live and learn, Johnny. Learn and live.

She listened to the night noises rising with the warm air toward her bedroom window. The cicadas were out in full force. The sweetness of the newly mown grass made her rise and look out. The moon was not quite full, and she looked down at her garden, the pine trees, the sparkle of the water beyond. A mosquito buzzed by her ear. She realized she was waiting for Johnny. She stayed at the window, her cheek against the screen with its slight metallic smell, the mosquito invisibly circling her head, until the moon passed behind a cloud and the scene before her disappeared into muffled darkness.

Her mother filled the house with cigarette smoke and coffee cups. Grandma Eleanor, too, found the place comfortable, arriving expectantly at the table for breakfast, which Helen made for her and Lilian.

"Those birds! What a racket!" Lilian said. "The damp! Don't you feel hemmed in sometimes, with all these trees?"

Eleanor asked Helen if she would mind lending her the station wagon, as she absolutely refused to drive the Jaguar. "It's so unreliable."

Helen loved her car, a wagon she'd bought secondhand. When the door was opened and the ignition key turned, the car spoke. In a confident, Hal-like computer voice, it said: "A door is ajar!" Helen found the regularity of this communication reassuring. She liked to have a routine. "A door is not a jar," she would answer, each and every day, several times a day.

But today Helen silently drove off in the bottle green Jaguar and parked beside Johnny's deep blue Lincoln Continental, and rushed, gasping for privacy, into the bookstore.

Johnny looked up from a packing list. He held a pencil in his mouth, like a dog with a bone. He had changed his earring, she noticed, replacing the diamond stud with a small gold hoop.

Don't change, Helen thought. I turn my back for twenty-four hours and look what happens. She saw his lips part, watched the yellow pencil cling to them for a second, a fraction of a second. From the corner of her eye, Helen saw Lucy drinking a mug of coffee, watching. Johnny, she thought desperately. Johnny, you're too far away. Too many hours have passed. "Save me!" she said instead. "They're here for good. The women. They love me!"

—

For the next few days, Johnny waited for her every morning at the store in a torment of pleasure and resentment, a blur of need. He noticed the older couple, whom he and the girls called the You Sees. "You see!" the wife said, nudging her husband, when Johnny said good morning. He noticed Theresa thumbing through a glossy art book. "Too rich," she said. "I very, very rich," by which he knew she meant the book was too expensive for her. He noticed one of the twins handing him a wet zwieback. He noticed himself thanking the child, taking the gummy cookie from its sticky hand. He noticed that without Helen there the store seemed hollow. He tried to fill it with his own movement, with his own voice, but still he saw the absence of Helen throwing an arm over a customer's shoulder, or heard the absence of her voice murmuring a seductive, triumphant hello.

Where was she? Of course her mother and grandmother wanted to spend time with her. It had been a year, Helen said, and they needed her to referee, as well, for they couldn't stand each other. Still, Helen was a grown woman, the head of her own household. Adults could do as they liked, and wasn't spending every possible moment with him doing as she liked?

Where are you? he thought over and over every morning, until she pushed open the door, a burst of Helen. He knew she was on her way to him, each time. But then, of course, she would stop.

At night, Helen sat at dinner and planned how she would tell her mother. She knew she should just say, "I'm going out to see a friend." But then her mother would say, "Really? Which friend is that?" She knew she should just tell her mother which friend, but she also knew she couldn't. And if Helen lied, she would be caught, as she had always been caught as a teenager. She remembered sneaking out of the house, then sneaking back in hours later only to find her mother reading or listening to Mahler, but really waiting to pounce on her, pulling Helen's sunglasses off to check for dilated pupils. "You stink of marijuana," Lilian would say. She was not a strict parent, but she thought taking drugs was stupid, and it annoyed her to have a stupid daughter. She never told Helen's father, who might have really worried, and for that Helen was grateful, and to show her gratitude became more discreet, swigging Binaca before sneaking back in. But how could she be discreet now? Binaca would not help her.

Perhaps I won't see him, she thought. It is not written in the "Having a Secret Affair Manual" that you have to see each other every night. Tomorrow is another day. I'm an adult. I am a woman of a certain age, a certain stature, a great deal of self-control. I can stay home.

She told herself this as she plotted to see Johnny, for she had to see Johnny. The desire to see Johnny was what put her to bed at night and what woke her up in the morning. Seeing Johnny was the aim of all endeavor.

She said she was doing inventory at the store. The next night, she said the car needed gas. Then, she needed Tampax at the all-night drugstore. "And I took a drive. Such a beautiful night." Then she put on her running clothes and told her mother she was training for the marathon.

"Bad for your knees," said Grandma Eleanor.

"Don't get hit by a car," said Lilian.

Helen ran through the twilight to Johnny's, where, damp and gasping for breath, she faced him and, looking into his eyes, absorbing the violent intensity of his stare, she reached for him and thought, in a confused, ecstatic anger, that he was young and gentle, delicate as the petals of a flower, and she wanted to crush him, velvety and fragrant, in her hand.

Afterward, he looked at her with an expression somewhere between smug satisfaction and terror, and she herself wondered how this had happened — how sex, always a pleasant recreational activity, had grown serious.

—

For one week, Lilian complained about Pequot constantly. But she showed no inclination to leave. Why had she not brought a moving van as well? Helen wondered.

Her mother often pumped Helen for information about the natives and their habits, as if she herself had never lived in the town. "I like to know the lay of the land, that's all, dear. Any new people?"

"I don't know. I guess so. Hundreds. Oh, and one new old person. Miss Skattergoods, you know that old Pequot family, Skattergoods — she's come back from wherever she was. She took over the library."

"Did she?"

"She used to ride her bicycle. Very picturesque. Now she drives a Porsche —"

"*Does* she?"

"— like a maniac. Oh, and the ophthalmologist's wife, Janie McMillan, remember her? The shy housewife with her fussy Halloween cookies and Girl Scout troops? She's started a little advertising agency . . ."

But Helen saw that her mother's attention had already wandered. How alike we are, she thought.

—

"When do I get to meet them?" Johnny said.

"Are you going to ask for my hand?"

"Maybe."

"Are you chewing gum?"

"Maybe." He blew a large bubble, popped it with his

finger, and she remembered the tired taste of bubble gum and wanted to kiss him nevertheless. How, she wondered for the hundredth time, did this happen? Did I flirt with him? Not any more than with anybody else. Did I pay him? Bribe him? Threaten to turn him in to the immigration authorities? The likelihood of this big, gum-chewing boy falling in love with her was statistically nonexistent. Yet here he was.

"I'm too old for you," she said.

He grinned, stood close to her, pushed her hair back, leaned his lips to her ear, and whispered, "I know."

Jennifer came in soon after, carrying an assortment of coffees.

"One has steamed milk and regular coffee, one has steamed milk and espresso, one has regular milk and regular coffee. I don't know which is which, I don't know which is called what, and I don't remember anymore which I wanted."

"I want the biggest. And the hottest. I want the best one," Helen said.

"There's your car," Johnny said.

Helen saw her mother driving up, pulling into a parking space, walking toward the door.

"Yes," she said. She dreaded having Lilian meet Johnny. Or was it Johnny meeting Lilian she dreaded? "That's my mother." Her mother strode. That was the only word for the way she walked, a walk so full of purpose it was almost comical. Of course, I have inherited this walk, Helen thought. This comical walk.

Lilian quickly surveyed the place, saw that not much had changed since her last visit, asked Johnny where he went to college, told Jennifer her head had a lovely slope in the back, "which unfortunately you yourself can't see, but how nice for the rest of us," dashed upstairs to see Lucy, dashed down again, took several Nabokov novels without paying, and left, roaring off in Helen's car.

"My mother has a thudding ephemeral quality, if you know what I mean."

"I think she's cool," Jennifer said.

Was Jennifer's loyalty flagging? Helen wondered. Would Lilian become her new hero? Would Jennifer now smoke and call complete strangers "cookie"?

"She calls complete strangers cookie," Helen said, as a warning. "I've seen it."

"I think she looks like you," Johnny said.

Helen stared at him. She longed to look like her mother.

"No one ever says that," she said. "They say I look like my father. If they knew my father."

"You move the same way."

"I know."

"The way you walk," Johnny said softly. "The way you turn your head, so suddenly. Your hands . . ."

Helen noticed Jennifer, remembered she was there, saw how closely she was watching them.

"Thank you," Helen said abruptly. "Now who's going to phone in the order? Jennifer? Would you do that for me? Come on." She put her arm around Jennifer's waist and led her toward the phone. "If you do, I'll call you cookie in public . . ."

Jennifer giggled gratefully, as Helen had known she would.

⌐

One morning, when the womenfolk, as she had begun to call them, had been with her for two weeks, Helen got up early, before they were awake, and simply left. I have a business to run, she told herself. My business is not making breakfast for two perfectly capable women as they read the paper and argue about multiculturalism. She got to the store an hour before Lucy or Johnny or the girls and opened up with what was almost excitement. She swept the sidewalk, put out the mat. She vacuumed inside. She loved her store. It made very little money, but it belonged to her, she had made it, she made it run.

Helen remembered she'd meant to look up the burning boy. Love's the burning boy. She found it on page five of the salmon pink paperback edition of Elizabeth Bishop's complete poems.

Casabianca

Love's the boy stood on the burning deck
trying to recite "The boy stood on
the burning deck." Love's the son
stood stammering elocution
while the poor ship in flames went down.

Love's the obstinate boy, the ship,
even the swimming sailors, who
would like a schoolroom platform, too,
or an excuse to stay
on deck. And love's the burning boy.

"The boy stood on the burning deck," Helen said. "The boy stood on the burning deck."

—

The next morning she escaped again before breakfast, and when she arrived at the store found a note from Johnny, who had closed up the night before.

Dear Helen,

Do you want to redo the mass-market table? It's been awhile. Too long. What a long time it's been. I think the mass market table is calling out to be redone. Redo me! I did the trade paperback table myself. It wasn't the same without you. But desperate times call for desperate measures. As I applied myself to the task, it occurred to me that while our feelings rise against any arbitrary, individual compulsion of fate, such as is presupposed in Grillparzer's *Die Ahnfrau*, etc., the Greek legend, on the other hand, seizes on a compulsion which everyone recognizes because he feels its existence within himself. Each member of the audience was once, in germ and in phantasy, just such an Oedipus, and each one recoils in horror from the dream-fulfillment here transplanted into reality, with the whole quota of repression which separates his infantile state from his present one. Don't you agree?

Fondly,
Johnny

On the trade paperback table, atop each pile of books, Johnny had put a copy of *The Freud Reader*. One had a bookmark in it. Helen opened it and saw the letter to Fliess. Johnny had quoted from it in his note; he'd quoted the letter announcing Freud's discovery of the Oedipus complex. She laughed. Twelve black-and-white photos of Dr. Freud looked inquisitively up at her.

"Oh, fuck you," she said happily.

13 ✓ ✓ ✓ ✓ ✓ ✓ ✓ ✓ ✓ ✓ ✓ ✓ ✓ ✓ ✓

IT'S AUGUST, HELEN THOUGHT WITH A START, AS she checked her calendar, where she made a list each evening of what she'd have to do the next morning. Johnny stood beside her behind the counter. She felt his presence as a general reassurance. August, she thought again. July has passed, July felt like August — as hot — and now August was here. Would August feel like July? What had June felt like? September? She stood for a moment, forgetting the months and thinking of the days with Johnny. Basking in all the neatly folded bags and filed index cards and shining counters and books, and basking in the shadow of the boy tapping pencils like drumsticks on the counter.

Why can't I take you home with me? she thought. Sleep with you, wake up with you, eat my breakfast with you, watch you step out of the shower? But the truth was she could hardly speak to Johnny on the phone. She could rarely get out of the house without a barrage of questions. It was laborious, having an affair with Johnny while her mother was in the house. Lilian had the sensitivity of the truly self-absorbed — any change in her own routine, in her view, in the air around her, was felt and challenged. She liked to know what was what. Then why not just tell her what was what? Helen pondered this question and thought, Because Lilian would be shocked. Then, immediately, she knew the real reason: because I am shocked.

—

Sometimes she wanted to tell everyone — I have a beautiful, virile boy lover! He loves me! He tells me so! From across the room, I feel his touch. It tears at me. My own desire tears at me like a mourner renting her garments! I think in metaphors like the one above! Music makes me cry now, even bad music! Elton John makes me weep!

Elton John indeed. No — she could tell no one. Not a soul.

—

Helen went home to her mother and grandmother in the sputtering Jaguar thinking of Johnny, the pimple on his chin, his acceptance of Tom Robbins as a serious writer, his politics of ecology. He was born after Woodstock. And she tried to talk herself out of her attachment. But even his faults struck her as fresh and lovely, the dewy fields of youth stretching into the future. Yes! Tell me about you and Nietzsche! Tell me all night long.

But all night long she would lie alone in her bed listening to her grandmother shuffle back and forth, to and from the bathroom; to her mother, an insomniac, rising at four for her coffee.

In his room at home, Johnny looked around. His parents would be back soon, and the house was a mess, a disaster, a cartoon of irresponsibility and neglect. His parents would be home. Then what? He would have no place to see

Helen. He stood up and kicked a pile of dirty laundry out of his way. He had taken to buying new T-shirts rather than washing the old ones.

—

Johnny drove to the beach to swim. He went almost every morning now, for Helen ran not only in the evening to see him at his house, but continued to run before breakfast, usually just in time to meet him as he emerged from the water.

"I'll end up in the marathon for real," she said once as she threw him his towel. She would sit on the sand beside him and share an orange.

Sometimes when I drive I see you, he thought, as he spotted her on the road ahead of him. He pulled up and lowered his window. "Helen," he said, putting his hand out and touching her damp cheek. "You're out so early." She got in beside him and buckled her seat belt, and just those movements made him unaccountably happy.

"Turn up here," she said, and the Lincoln bumped onto a dirt road into a grove of trees.

"A little-known town park," she said.

"Once property of the governor," Johnny said, using a PBS-documentary narrator voice, "what's his name, the one who had his official portrait done in a dress in order to truly represent his entire constituency. His great-grandson fell on hard times, however, and sold the property to a man who made his fortune in frozen vegetables. The mansion was later sold separately and became a country club while most of the grounds . . ."

"You've been here?"

"No," Johnny said. "Read it in the library."

He looked at her, at the space between them, an expanse of cracked leather seat, decades.

"No wonder he wrote you that letter," he said.

"Who?"

"Whoever wrote it."

"It wasn't for me. It was a mistake."

"It was for you. All love letters are for you. There are no mistakes." He unbuckled her seat belt. "Dear Helen," he said, "I am writing to inform you that I want to fuck you from the minute I wake up until I go to bed at night, and then I want to fuck you more. While this is partly a function of postadolescent male hormones, please be advised that they have never functioned quite like this before, for which reason I feel confident in assigning responsibility for this situation to you." He wondered where this facile language came from. Why was it he could speak when he was with her? He couldn't talk when he was with other people. With Helen, although he could barely breathe in her presence, he could speak. "As regards your age," he continued, "this makes you more, not less, responsible for the state of constant physical excitement in which I find myself and about which I expect you to take immediate action as pursuant to our previous conversations on this matter. Sincerely . . ."

"You want to do it in the car?" she asked.

"I don't know what I want, Helen. I thought up that letter last night. That's what I do, think of things to say to you, think of you. All the time."

He stared at her stomach, naked between the line of her black nylon running shorts below and the line of her white jogging bra, wet through with her sweat.

"I love your body," he said. "I've never said that to anyone before. I've never said much of anything to anyone before.

I've never said to some girl, 'I want to fuck you.' They'd probably slug me. And I'd be too embarrassed anyway. I don't tell people I love their bodies. I tell you. I want to tell you. That's all I want to tell you. I want to tell you over and over again."

Helen said nothing.

"Do you mind?"

"No," she said.

He had known she would say no, had known that was all she would say. She gave very little away. A fierce lover, a tender and doting friend, she rarely said anything about how she felt. He knew she wanted him, wanted to have sex with him, wanted to lie beside him, wanted to stand close to him whenever she could. He knew it because she did those things, not because she told him so. He could see now that she wanted him. Her hand had moved to his chest. Her eyes were fixed on his in that hard, terrifying way she had.

"You love me," he said, grabbing her.

"You seem to know a great deal about the residents of Pequot."

"I read it," he said. "In the library."

⌐

As Helen walked through the remaining days of the summer (for that was how she had begun to feel, as if the days were a tunnel she had to pass through; only when she was with Johnny did the tunnel open and the world reappear), as she walked her way dully through the waking hours, she wondered what had happened to her. At the sight of Johnny, she trembled. At his touch, she felt herself lost. She looked at him and wondered at his assertions. You love me, he said. I love you. Confident and pleased, he actually seemed to be enjoying himself.

"Read *Cheri*," she said to him.

"I have. They were together for years."

"Then she got wrinkles."

"You already have wrinkles."

"Fuck you, you callow —"

"Right there, and there." And he kissed her eyes and her neck, oblivious to the future she saw looming hideously before her.

"Arrogant," she said. It's what she'd always been called, and she said it now to Johnny with envy for something lost, although she knew her arrogance had been more like energy and constant vigilance, while his was quite genuine. Now, before the happiness of this beautiful boy who didn't know enough to worry, she felt timid and unsure.

—

Helen didn't formally choose a date, but as she waited with the other parents for the bus carrying the children home from camp, she knew that Emily's return would provide a logical brake, that her love affair with a minor would glide gently to a halt, or skid to a sudden stop — that it would end, at any rate. She knew she had to stop.

When Helen saw Emily get off the bus, she wondered how she had lived without her for even a moment and she wondered who this strange, tall child was. Her daughter's light brown hair was lighter from the sun, longer, pulled back from her face. Emily's arms and legs were lovely arms and legs — girlish now, rather than just belonging to a girl. She had grown and stood almost as tall as Helen, which is not very tall, Helen thought, but is all I've got to go by. Helen hugged her and kissed her forehead and smelled her skin, the familiar Emily smell now mixed with woods and, very probably, dirt.

In the face of this person she had nursed on her breast and to whom she now handed a bag of candy (forbidden by the camp all summer), Helen was speechless. You're awesome in the formal sense of the word, she thought. You're back. You're here. You're you.

"Mommy? I love —"

"Oh, Emily!" Helen said, hugging her.

"— camp."

On the ride back to Pequot, Emily held Helen's hand. I wonder if her father misses her, Helen thought. It was not something she thought about very often. She liked clean breaks, and liked to think she had made one with Dan. But now she considered the possibility that her ex-husband suffered. Well, perhaps, but he was going to see Emily soon for a week or so. Helen's sympathy faded.

"You'll see Daddy soon."

"I know. That'll be fun. We're going to a ranch."

Emily told her about the horse she rode at camp. Smoky. Smoky was fast, Smoky was a good jumper, Smoky liked celery.

"Mommy?"

"Yes, sweetheart?"

"I love you so much."

"I love you, Emily. I love you, too. So much."

❧

Emily cursed under her breath like an adolescent now. She listened to CDs in her room with the door closed. But then, that first night home, she burrowed in beside Helen in bed, asked for a lullaby, and fell asleep. Helen listened to her breathing. You're back, she thought. And she asked God, in whom she did not often believe, to protect Emily and keep her from harm.

Helen took the next day off. She drank her coffee sur-
rounded by female generations. Their voices were familiar.
The sky was blue. In the garden, she picked through her
petunias. She grew petunias in order to deadhead them.
They were a satisfying flower. Emily knelt beside her, and
Helen showed her where to break off the dead blooms.

"Then we'll do the roses," Helen said. "With a *scissors*."

She pinched at the flowers and smiled. Grandma Eleanor was napping in a chair, her hat pulled over her eyes.
This was lovely. She could live like this. She did live like
this. She didn't need anyone else to complicate things. Not
even a nice college student. She would tell Johnny tomorrow.

"Mommy? I like planting better. I like the little shoots
and things."

"And rightly so," Lilian said, coming up behind them.
She dropped cigarette ash on a flower beside Helen.

Helen turned to look at Emily and thought what a luxury
it was to see her in the flesh instead of relying on postcards
and letters. The letters from camp had seemed so exciting when she received them, evocative and precious. Now
Helen realized how little they had to do with the real Emily.
Were all letters like that? Was Ram's letter to Goat so
detached from Ram, the real Ram, whoever that might be?

"Mommy, I'm hungry and bored."

"Me, too," said Lilian.

"Me, too," said Grandma Eleanor from beneath her hat.

Tomorrow I'll see Johnny, Helen thought. And I'll tell
him.

—

Helen and Johnny sat at the counter in the only surviving
luncheonette in Pequot. Helen had come here as a special

treat when she was a child. Nothing had changed, not the diamond pattern in the yellow and gray linoleum, not the food. She ordered a hot dog and a limeade. It was what she always had here.

"Another bit of Pequot history," Helen said.

Johnny didn't want lunch. He ordered a Coke. "Why am I here?" he said.

"We're having lunch."

"We never have lunch."

"I have to talk to you."

"Really?" He gave her an unpleasant, sarcastic look. "Go ahead."

"Well, it's just that —"

"You want to stop, right? I knew it. Emily came home and you figure this is a good place to stop, like the end of a chapter in a book, put in a slip of paper, close it up. Fuck you, Helen."

The waitress brought the hot dog. "Nice breeze," she said, putting it down in front of Helen. "It's like being on the veranda."

Helen nodded.

"I love the word *veranda*," the waitress said. "I use it whenever I can."

Johnny's face had hardened. Helen felt suddenly that what she was doing might actually be happening.

She was saying something: "I'm sorry."

She was saying I'm sorry to Johnny. Did that mean it was over and that was why she was sorry?

Was Johnny saying anything? She couldn't tell. I must have high blood pressure, she thought. The blood is banging in my ears. She had come here to break it off. She reminded herself of this. What an unpleasant sinking sensation, she thought. I wonder if this is a flu-like symptom and I have

Lyme disease. I wonder if I might have done what I set out to do. I'm sorry, she thought. She put her hand across the table to touch Johnny's arm, but he pulled away.

"Fuck you, Helen," he said again. He got up. He was gone.

"I'm sorry," Helen said.

—

Helen left the luncheonette. Was that it? Would the weeks ahead now unwind in no particular pattern or direction, the way they always had before Johnny? Wasn't that what she wanted, to be freed of Johnny's gravitational pull, a gorgeous black hole that sucked up each day as it began and each night as it ended?

She walked to the store, walked past Jennifer and Kelly and went straight upstairs. Johnny had not come back to work, she noticed. Should she fire him? Perhaps she already had. She hadn't even considered his not working in the store anymore. Why have a store at all if there were no Johnny working in it?

Lucy was not coming in today until four o'clock. Helen sat in Lucy's chair and stared out the small square window. This is stupid, she thought. I wanted to end it. I ended it. That's all I need to know. That's all I need to remember. That's all I need.

"Helen?" Kelly called from the bottom of the stairs.

"I'm busy," Helen said. "Take care of it." But even as she said it, she was on her way downstairs to take care of it herself, as she always did. She found the special order Kelly was looking for, then violently rearranged the paperback table, then stormed down to the basement to fold boxes, Johnny's job now left for her to do, on top of everything else.

On the floor, cross-legged, sat Johnny. He was folding the last brown cardboard carton. He stood up.

Helen saw his hands. They disappeared into his pockets. She saw his eyes. They bulged.

"Don't you ever walk away from me like that," she said. She pushed him against the wall. "Don't ever walk away from me," she said. She stood against him. Don't ever leave me, she thought. "Ever," she said. She kissed him. Her hands pulled him closer. She kissed him again and again and felt him against her, felt his hands pull her closer.

"Helen," Johnny said, his voice hoarse in her ear.

"Helen?" Jennifer called down.

"I'm busy," Helen yelled back. "Take care of it."

14 ′ ′ ′ ′ ′ ′ ′ ′ ′ ′ ′ ′ ′ ′

EACH DAY, LILIAN WOKE AT FOUR, HAD HER COF-
fee, smoked, waited for the newspaper to be delivered at
five, stretched out on the couch to read it without refolding
it properly (a daily complaint of Grandma Eleanor's), then
fell back to sleep. When Helen returned from her run to
Johnny at the beach, when her mother had risen from the
couch amid a cloud of floating sheets of newsprint, when
Grandma Eleanor had descended in her paisley silk robe
and Emily staggered in with her hair tangled, the four
females would gather for breakfast. Helen knew the sounds,
the gestures, the shapes around her: her childhood home
and mother; her adult home and child; the smell of her
grandmother's Cream of Wheat, a smell in the way that
white was a color, distinct but not one at all really. Jasper
waited patiently for bits of toast. Or perhaps he was just
there out of habit, as she was, not sure what he was waiting
for anymore.

Opening the refrigerator was climbing the Tower of Ba-
bel. God has sent us so many kinds of milk to keep us
divided and prevent us from becoming too powerful, Helen

thought. Whole milk for Emily, skim for Lilian, Lactaid for Grandma Eleanor, two percent for Helen, and, for Lilian's coffee, half-and-half, which she felt she could afford to drink after limiting herself to skim milk for all other purposes. Once Helen considered making a large cardboard sign: MOMMY GO HOME! She would hang it from her living room window, facing in.

Funny how one longed for one's mother, her attention, undivided, as a child. Now she had her mother, the elusive Lilian. And she ran away to work to escape her. What was Lilian doing here? She seemed to be hanging around, waiting. She daydreamed in the garden. Lilian had never daydreamed. She had napped, yes. Like a cat, quick naps on the arm of a chair, at the drop of a hat. But when awake, she had always been doing something, or ordering someone else to do something.

"I'm off," Helen would say, making her escape from breakfast, half expecting Emily, or even one of the older women, to whine and beg to be taken to the aquarium or to buy a Barbie. But Grandma Eleanor returned to the unpacking of her worldly possessions, Lilian sauntered off to lie down on a lounge chair and sleep, and Emily was deeply committed to her latest best friend, a certain Jessica. Helen could not at first remember exactly which of the four Jessicas this Jessica was, though she did know that this one had a house on the beach. Emily's ardent daily attentions began with morning phone calls, progressed to afternoon bike rides or a swim in the surf, and culminated in joint TV viewing in the evenings, or a poker game with Grandma Eleanor.

"Grandma, you should let us win sometimes," Emily said one night.

"Yes, I suppose I should," Grandma Eleanor said without conviction.

Lilian would sit beside them working on a jigsaw puzzle map of the United States she'd bought for Emily.

Emily was about to be twelve. Helen remembered being that age. She'd wanted a horse. She'd wanted a boyfriend. The horse she would love and cherish and understand better than anyone, taming it, teaching it, guiding it across rolling hills, over tall fences. On a spring day, she would sit, dangling her bare feet in a stream beside her horse's muzzle as it sucked in the cool water. The horse was gray or it was chestnut, a delicate pony or a stamping thoroughbred. These fantasies were detailed and complete. She could feel the warm flank, hear the nicker, gentle and close. As for the boyfriend, her imagination took her no further than her real-life experience: she daydreamed of teasing and throwing pebbles at one.

"Should we get a horse, Emily?" she asked her daughter.

"We don't have room, Mom."

"Oh."

"How about a nice kitten?"

Emily had two of the Jessicas and three other girls spend the night on the weekend before her birthday. Helen could hear them giggling and tiptoeing heavily through the house all night long. Twelve years old seemed so close. When she was twelve, her mother had been on a particularly bizarre diet that included fried pork rinds at every meal.

On Emily's actual birthday, Helen had a party at the store. She did this every year. Emily had always loved her grown-up store party. She sat on the couch and accepted presents and made everyone wear hats. Helen thought this year she might reject the whole idea as too childish, but there she was, taking a Gap box from Lucy, handing her in exchange a pointy cone hat.

Helen never formally invited anyone to this party. She

just mentioned it to whomever she deemed worthy at any given moment. I must have been in an awfully charitable mood this summer, she thought as she looked around her. There were customers, the guy from the coffee bar, a few people she knew from the gym, and of course Barry and Eliot themselves, still in their gym shorts and T-shirts that said TRAINER on the back.

"I dreamt Eliot called me on the phone and said, 'I'm a can maniac,'" Barry said to Helen.

"You did?" Helen said.

"That's an anagram."

"Well," Eliot said, "I dreamt that Spiro Agnew said, 'Grow a penis.'"

"He did?" Helen said.

"Helen, that's an anagram, too. A better one. My dreams are smarter than his."

"You didn't dream that. You heard that on WBAI in 1969," Barry said.

"You did?" Helen asked Eliot.

"Well, I did, anyway," Barry said.

⌒

From across the room, Johnny watched the little girl carefully. A rather officious child, he thought. She stood on the couch, examining Kelly's earrings, adjusting the older girl's party hat. Then Emily jumped down, wandered around with her arms out like wings for a minute, then went behind the counter and rested her chin on a copy of the *Random House Historical Dictionary of American Slang* and let her hands dangle over the edge of the counter like a passenger's fingers in a canoe. She was humming.

She looked nothing like Helen. Slender and pale, she had delicate features. She wasn't a bit shy, which Johnny found unnerving. She instantly asked him what school he went to, whether he liked it, what music he liked, and did he watch *Melrose Place*? Then she skipped off and browsed through a Garfield book as the adults around her interrupted her now and then to hand her a gift or give her a kiss.

This was Helen's daughter. Helen was her mother. He had to say these things to himself over and over. He watched her and repeated the sentences again. Helen's daughter. Helen, mother. And then he saw Emily smile and heard her laugh, and it was Helen's smile and Helen's laugh, and he felt a sudden warmth toward the daughter, pleasure in her. She was Helen's daughter. Helen was her mother.

"When is Jessica coming?" Helen asked Emily.

"Soon. Can I have this Garfield book?"

Helen nodded and kissed her, then hugged her until Emily wriggled out of her grasp.

"We're going to get pizza," Emily said. "Okay? Mom, thanks for doing this. I haven't seen everyone in so long. Mommy? Do you like Lucy's tattoo? Could I get my ears pierced now? I want three in each ear, though. Mom, Grandma's exposing us to secondhand smoke."

"Yes. She says it keeps the mosquitoes away." Helen watched as Emily greeted Jessica. There was a huddle, an exchange of information, then a wave at Helen, some good-byes and thank-yous called out, and the two girls ran out the door.

"So!" Johnny said. "Your daughter."

"My daughter."

"She's great."

Helen saw he was embarrassed. The meeting of Johnny and Emily had filled her with foreboding for reasons so obvious they had begun to seem banal, and she had chosen not to think about them at all. But when the two of them actually stood face-to-face, her little girl and her boy lover, she had been overwhelmed, horrified; and she thought the banal was no less than good common sense, a moral clarity that she had forsaken, a sense of balance and the natural order of our earthly lives. She watched them talking and felt love and excitement and a sickening shame. She wanted them to be friends; she wanted to keep them separate, to protect them from each other, to keep the idea of each of them pure. Emily chatted, Johnny murmured shyly in response. Helen turned away. Lucy walked by and kissed Helen's cheek in a friendly but abstracted way. Helen looked after her gratefully. Lucy had a timeless quality.

"When she laughed, it was just like you," Johnny was saying now. "At first I was, you know . . ." Johnny shrugged. "But then she smiled. So. Now I'm ready to adopt her."

Helen was surprised at how relieved she felt.

"You're wonderful," she said.

"It's no big deal. I did realize you had a kid."

"My child is no big deal?"

"You have a child? Helen, this changes everything."

❧

"Tell me who's here," Lilian said. She flicked her ashes into her party hat, held upside down, then offered Helen a cigarette.

"I don't smoke, Mom. I haven't smoked in twenty years."

"Sorry, dear. I'm nervous."

"You? Why?"

"Empathy. Who's here?"

"I don't know." Helen looked around and wished the store was this crowded with paying customers. "There's

George. There's Lucy. There's Alma Lincoln, and Emily's piano teacher, and the dermatologist's wife whose son joined the Hare Krishnas, but now he's a drug rehabilitation therapist in Milwaukee. Do you remember her? Oh, and here's Miss Skattergoods."

Miss Skattergoods walked toward them and stood with her hands on her hips. Her red party hat was cocked to one side.

"Miss Skattergoods, this is my mother —"

"Oh, we've met," Miss Skattergoods said. "What brings you to Pequot, my dear?"

"Pequot?" Lilian said.

"She's visiting me," Helen said.

"The past," Lilian said. "I suppose."

"The past?" Helen said. "You? Nostalgic for Pequot? You must be kidding."

Lilian said, "You know nothing about it."

Helen shrugged. "Okay," she said. "The past, then."

"And the future," Miss Skattergoods said, raising her paper cup in a toast. "Why not?"

⌐

Helen and Johnny left the store together, Helen in her grandmother's car, Johnny in his grandfather's car. They drove in a convoy of two to Johnny's house. Every visit to the white house on the hill frightened Helen. What if someone found out? she would think. What if there were a fire while they were making love in Johnny's parents' bedroom and they had to run out of the house naked? What if Johnny's parents came home unexpectedly and found them *in flagrante*? Helen even worried about her Jaguar lumbering behind the Lincoln. What if they were seen?

"Seen?" Johnny once said to her when she made her worries known. "I saw Helen and that boy driving on the same road! Scandal."

Anyway, seen by others or not, she knew she had to see Johnny, and like a child afraid of the dark, she reassured herself as best she could and went on her way. After the birthday party, in the chill evening, she drove past meadows of Queen Anne's lace and felt the air against her face, and Helen thought, He's right, this looks innocent enough, and she was grateful for his common sense. As she parked in his driveway, she thought, I have every right to park in his driveway. I am his boss. I have things to discuss with him. And she was proud of her own common sense. After they'd had their discussion in his parents' bedroom for hours, she thought, So I'm late getting home. No one will care. When she kissed him in the driveway as she left, she thought, It's okay, it's dark, no one can see us. Getting into her car, all she thought was, When can I see him again?

Then the car wouldn't start, and she could hardly think at all.

Johnny leaned down to the window. "What's the matter?"

"What do you mean, what's the matter? It won't start! That's the matter." And it's your fault, she wanted to say. For bringing me here. For making me think it was okay. For driving in front of me, for fucking me in your parents' bedroom in your white house on a hill, for kissing me in your driveway. "I'll have to leave it here. What will I say? What the fuck am I supposed to say? Fucking Jaguar. I could have had an accident. What's the *matter*? Everything's the fuck the matter."

"Oh, don't be stupid, Helen," Johnny said. He opened her car door.

Helen looked at him and for that moment hated him.

He had ruined her life. He was an embarrassment. He was dirty laundry.

"You're my dirty laundry," she said.

"I'll drive you home."

"Great. I never should have come today . . ."

"Why don't you belong to AAA like my parents?"

". . . never, never, never."

He dropped her off at the end of her driveway. He was calm. Was that a form of stupidity, she wondered, or just cruelty?

"See you tomorrow," he said. "I'll pick you up. Call a mechanic." He kissed her. "It's just a car in a driveway."

Helen watched him drive off. Just a car in a driveway. No, she thought. It's not.

"I had an accident," she said when she got in the door.

"Are you okay?" Lilian ran over to her.

"The car broke down. I'm fine."

"Thank God."

"In Johnny's driveway."

"Thank God you weren't on the highway."

"Yes," Grandma Lilian said. "Exactly. I *never* drive that car."

—

Helen noticed that her mother had begun taking early morning drives in Helen's station wagon.

"Why don't you take a walk instead?" Helen said. "It's beautiful in the morning. You can go to the cliff, look at the water. Quieter, too."

"I don't want to look at the sea. I don't want quiet. It's too quiet here by half."

While Helen herself could not leave the house without a barrage of questions, her mother came and went as she pleased, without explanation. And why shouldn't she? Helen thought. Late in the afternoon, looking out from the store's front window, Helen often saw her own car cruising through town with her mother at the wheel. Why can't I just go where I please when I please like my mother? she wondered. Because Lilian is innocent, and I am guilty.

Lilian was sometimes out when Helen got home from work, but she always arrived in time for dinner.

"Let's cook out!" she would say.

"It takes an hour to start the fire. It's already eight."

"Perfect." And she would throw briquettes on the grill, douse them with fluid, and light them, watching their progress like an eager witch above her caldron. "I like fire," she said. Then, blowing tobacco smoke from her nostrils, "Don't you?"

Grandma Eleanor still spent a good portion of every day finding space for her furniture in all of Helen's empty rooms. "And those nice Morts are so helpful," she remarked.

"Leave some stuff here when you move on," Helen said. "When are you moving on?"

"Oh, Helen," Grandma Eleanor said. "Don't be silly. And they're such good company."

"Who?"

"Have you noticed an unhealthy emphasis on organized sports in this town?" Grandma continued. "I told him, the older one, the mayor —"

"Ray?"

"Yes. That one. I told him, 'There's more to life than playing fields.' This town is silly with baseball fields, soccer fields, football fields. The town is trying to build a new one as we speak. That's his campaign motto now. 'There's More to Pequot Than Playing Fields!' We're going to save a swamp, I believe."

"You and Ray?" Helen said.

Emily and Jessica called from the living room, where they were watching a frog brought in by the cat. They squealed in a hysterical and most dully, stereotypically girlish way, Helen thought as she captured the terrified frog, at least she assumed it was terrified, and felt its twiggy little fingers scrambling against the cupped palms of her hands. But perhaps it was not frightened at all. Perhaps it was amused at the commotion it had caused. Or perhaps it was moved to frog tears by its rescue. It might simply be enjoying the cheap thrill. She threw it in the bushes and said to the girls, "Don't make such a fuss. You don't have to marry it." And they ate their dinner on the porch by candlelight until the August bees and August flies and two little girls retired for the evening. When Helen blew out the candles, even the mosquitoes withdrew, and she and her mother and grandmother drank their coffee in the dark.

"Ray builds shopping malls," Helen said. "He's a builder. Not a swamp saver."

"People change, dear."

"That they do," said Lilian. "That they do."

❦

Johnny sat at his desk at home. It was covered with pads and note cards and loose sheets of paper. Bits of information that accumulated rather than added up — pointless, haphazard, a pile at the base of a computer. He had stopped working on his research about Pequot. He hadn't been to the library in weeks. He wondered how Miss Skattergoods was. She took pretty good care of herself, he thought. Nice car. What kind of house did she have? Probably had a wonderful old house, part of the family legacy. Why had he never asked her? He wanted to see her, suddenly. Have a drink. See her house. Where did she live? The house must be old, an artifact of the town of Pequot, just like Miss Skattergoods herself. He could drive by the library and see if she were there. Should he tell her? About Helen? The desire to tell someone was sometimes so powerful. He considered writing to his friend Matt in Mexico, but, really, what would he say? How could he describe what had happened? Dear Matt, I have fallen in love. She is bigmouthed, bossy, tough, a breath of sweet air — depends on the day. I get a hard-on if I hear her name. Even if I don't hear her name. See? I have one right now. She likes to fuck. She's very athletic. Cut. Her skin is older, softer. I want to rub against it like a cat. She's very smart — knows everything and knows she knows everything. But she doesn't know she loves me. Yet. She's a great fuck. They really do hit their prime at forty. I'll never see her alone again. Never. As ever, Johnny.

Yes, you go ahead and send that letter, asshole. A boastful yet defensive letter. Horrible, to boast about Helen, whom you love and cherish. Worse to feel defensive. I apologize, Helen, he thought. I won't write a letter. Letters are so easily misunderstood. You can fix them and fuss over them until they're just right. Not like conversation. You can plan a letter, change your mind, make it better, make it more agreeable, make it harsh. But once sent, letters can't change, can't grow or follow a lead or pull back coyly. No intonation, no shift in volume, no alteration of facial expression, can soften the words or clarify a thought. Letters are concrete. They're history.

Yes, but a letter is ephemeral, too, Johnny thought. It changes utterly the moment it slips inside an envelope. It stops being mine. It becomes yours. What I meant is gone.

What you understand is all that remains. Open it — there's nothing there but what you see there. Letters suck.

He waited for the phone to ring. Helen would call. She would say, Meet me at the store. They would clutch each other in the dark and he would feel like weeping.

The phone rang, and he picked it up with trembling excitement, like an aborigine faced with a new machine.

"I can't get there tonight," Helen said.

No hello. Just this bleak message in her deep voice.

"Tomorrow," she added, softly.

"Shit."

"I can't leave my grandmother. She's not feeling too well. My mother's not home yet. God, Johnny . . ."

He heard her voice catch.

"Johnny . . ."

He knew that sound, the sound of desire. For him.

"Shit," he said again. But what he thought was, Darling. An adult word he couldn't pronounce out loud, could say only to himself, for his adult. Darling.

"Darling," she whispered into the phone.

He walked out to his car. He would drive by the library. Maybe Miss Skattergoods was still there. Miss Skattergoods would understand. She knew Helen. She could see what he saw, see Helen in all her womanly power. Telling Miss Skattergoods was not really telling. Maybe he would tell her. Over a gin and lime juice.

The thought of telling someone excited him. To talk about Helen was almost being with Helen. To talk about Helen was to talk about what he thought about. For weeks, everything he said to anyone but Helen was in some way false. "Yes, we have that book right here. No thanks, Kelly, you dust, I'll go to the post office. Hi, Mom! How great that you called. Jennifer, give me a bite of that sandwich." Every word was an evasion, a cover-up, a code secretly spelling out the name Helen.

Now I can speak, he thought. In English. Now the words that I speak will represent the thoughts that I think. If I say Helen's name in a certain tone, I won't be giving myself away, I'll be expressing myself. If I say what I've been doing, I don't have to leave out the part about what I've actually been doing.

He turned onto Pine Street and saw the library at the far corner. The gate was open. Miss Skattergoods must still be there. He parked his car across the street and walked to the door in the warm, noisy August air. Crows and catbirds sang from the trees, crickets from the dry, overgrown grass at the curb. He found the door locked and rang the bell, then banged the large brass knocker.

"Hello? Miss Skattergoods?"

"Johnny?" He heard her voice from inside. She opened the door a little, looking out at him. "What are you doing here, honey? I'm closing up."

He waited for her to open the door wider, to let him in, to give him a drink and lend him an ear.

She stood, barring his way, smiling. "I'm a little busy right now, Johnny. Can you come back tomorrow?"

"Tomorrow?" he said. He didn't move.

"Sorry, honey."

"Tomorrow. I guess so." He backed away from the door. "Sorry," he said. Don't feel sheepish and stupid, he told himself. You didn't do anything wrong. "Sorry," he said again.

Busy? he thought as he walked back to the car. Busy doing what? Dusting? Drinking? Maybe Miss Skattergoods had someone in there. A lover! Or she could have been taking inventory. Just because I'm sneaking around having an affair doesn't mean everyone else is. You have an over-heated imagination, Johnny. He noticed a car farther down the street that was the same model, same color as Helen's station wagon and he thought how lucky he was to have such an overheated imagination so that he could imagine Helen, her neck, her back, the curve of her waist.

—

After she called Johnny, Helen sat with her grandmother on the terrace in the back and pretended she was with him. She closed her eyes and felt his shoulder against hers and heard the mosquitoes and Grandma Eleanor's complaints about the mosquitoes, the catbirds and katydids and the barking of a dog down the road.

"Where's your mother, anyway?" Grandma Eleanor said. "And she's very restless. It's not like her."

"Not like her? She can't stay anywhere for more than two weeks. What is she doing here? I mean, I'm glad she's here. Both of you. But —"

"Your mother is very restless."

"The fruit doesn't fall far from the tree." It was Lilian. She pushed open the screen door and stood in the doorway before them, framed by the light from the kitchen.

"Where have you been?" Grandma Eleanor asked.

"Out for a drive."

"Driving is ridiculous."

"I guess it's too late to go for a run now," Helen said.

"Running is ridiculous," Lilian said.

Her mother and grandmother, the duo, a mother-daugh-ter act, the Bitch Cunts, the B.C.'s. She found them fasci-nating together, too fascinating. Her inner life was florid and perfumed and decadent in riches. She needed her surroundings to be spare and clean, a neutral backdrop, a place of Shaker serenity and order.

But for weeks, even when she got home from Johnny's, at midnight or after, there they would be, comfortably waiting. Her grandmother told her amusing stories of speakeasies and rumble seats. Her mother wondered why Emily was not learning Latin, though Lilian herself had never studied it and had never wanted Helen to. Lilian blew smoke rings, painted her toenails, painted Helen's toenails. Home with her roommates, Helen sat in a pleasant stupor of female inactivity.

"Put on the television, Helen. CNN," said Grandma Eleanor. "Ugh. Turn it off. The killing. I can't watch it."

"What did you expect?"

"The dirty dogs."

"Did you ever notice how much men resemble dogs?" Lilian said. "The way they circle each other when they meet, sniffing."

"Men are pigs," said Grandma Eleanor. "The killing. The violence. The sex."

"The sex?" Helen said.

"On that filthy TV."

"Daddy wasn't a pig. Or a dog."

"No. Daddy wasn't a pig," Lilian said. "Or a dog."

"And my Leonard," Grandma Eleanor said fondly.

Helen would eventually stagger to bed drunk with companionship, her obsessive thoughts about Johnny infused with an almost happy incoherence.

The next morning as Lilian sat at the kitchen table in her sunglasses and Grandma Eleanor tapped her cane absently on the floor, Helen would long for Johnny and remember all she had forgotten the night before — the new books she had to read, the catalogues she had to examine, the orders and letters she had to attend to.

"This is not a dorm," she said one morning. "We're not at summer camp."

"You go about your business, darling," Grandma Eleanor said.

"You're a wonderful daughter, Helen," Lilian said. "We're fine. Go sell your books."

15 ✓ ✓ ✓ ✓ ✓ ✓ ✓ ✓ ✓ ✓ ✓ ✓ ✓ ✓

AT NIGHT, WHEN SHE'D ESCAPED TO HER ROOM, Helen liked to read the love letter. *Is there a precipice, from which you float, over the edge, forever?* She felt herself not so much floating as slipping, skidding down a steep bank, the gravel loose beneath her feet. Down, down, down I go. Where I land, nobody knows. Was this love? At what point do we call passion love?

She lay on her bed with her letter and thought of Johnny's mouth, the way his full lips pulled down in a willful Jeanne Moreau pout. Somewhere, someone who sometimes called himself Ram was lying on his bed without the letter, thinking of Goat's mouth. Did Goat's lips turn down at the corners like Johnny's? Were her lips full like Johnny's? Did Ram feel desperate like Helen? Did Ram reach out knowing the one he wanted was not there? Like Helen?

Helen had spent her life being comfortable, doing what she had to do to maintain her comfort. Like a balancing scale, her life tipped slightly one way — she wanted a family, wanted security, wanted to have a child — and she would pop a weight on to even it out: marriage! Then, when her needs tipped the other way: divorce! Going to graduate school, leaving graduate school, opening the store — Helen was selfish and practical and did what was required. She believed in happiness, or at least removing as many barriers to happiness as possible. "Precipitate and pragmatical" — she remembered the phrase from an Elizabeth Bishop poem. It was how she liked to think of herself. She recalled the next line of the poem: "and look what happens." Look what's happened to you, Helen. You have become impractical. Your life is complicated and silly. This was not the kind of happiness you meant, was it, Helen, this desperate, uneasy bliss? You did not mean to discover pain in the name of joy.

This troubled ecstasy was passion. She understood that. She recognized passion. She'd read about it for so many years. She'd heard it all her life, Mahler or Wagner, sometimes Schubert, Tchaikovsky, Brahms, then Mahler again, then Wagner. Throughout Helen's childhood, her mother had listened compulsively, religiously almost, the music so loud the neighbors complained. Helen heard it and recognized someone else's passion, the composer's, her mother's, recognized without understanding. Now I understand, she thought. She understood passion and, helpless to do otherwise, she clung to it. One night, she came upon her mother listening to Schubert's "Death and the Maiden." Lilian sat with tears in her eyes, and Helen sat down beside her to cry her own tears, and she thought, again, At what point do we call passion love?

—

Johnny and Helen went out to dinner together. Emily was sleeping at Jessica's, Helen and Johnny had been working late, and it seemed reasonable enough, or rather they hoped it would seem reasonable to everyone else. To them, very little seemed reasonable. When they were apart, the distance seemed absurd. When they were together, reason seemed petty, anachronistic, like removing your hat when entering a house. They sat at the table of a small Italian restaurant Helen liked but rarely went to. There were many restaurants in Pequot, all expensive, all mediocre, except this one, which was almost as good as a pretty good restaurant in New York. But just to keep the Pequot quality-to-cost ratio intact, it was also as expensive as the very best restaurants in New York.

"I miss New York," Johnny said. "I think I'll transfer to Columbia. Then I could see you, too."

Helen tried to imagine their affair continuing after the summer. She couldn't. She tried to imagine it ending after the summer. She couldn't.

They drove to the beach after dinner and walked in the balmy darkness. A heavy fog had come in with the tide. They stayed close to each other, cut off from everything but the sound of the waves.

"I once seduced one of my high school teachers," she said. "We were both counselors at a high-minded, interracial day camp. I had a big crush on him and flirted shamelessly on an overnight camping trip, until finally he took me off into the woods. Afterward he told me it was an existential moment, by which I guess he meant it was a one-night stand."

"Is this a parable?"

"You know, when school starts I do drive Emily into the city every weekend to see her father. Unless he comes out to get her, which he usually does." Helen held his hand and looked out toward the water, but she couldn't see it. No moon tonight. No stars. Not even a sky.

Johnny kissed her and said her name. She loved to hear him say her name.

"Sit down with me," he said.

The waves were loud against the shore. There was no other sound. Helen lay back and pulled him against her.

"Say 'Helen,'" she said.

"Helen."

She kissed him.

"Helen."

Helen held him and thought she might cry, then realized she was crying, sobbing, pushing him on his back, kissing him through the ridiculous heaving tears and gasps.

"Emily?" someone whispered in her ear.

Helen sat up straight.

"What?" she said into the fog.

"Shhh," said the voice, a girl's voice. "Emily, is that you? Why are you making so much noise? Where are you?"

"Emily!" Helen said harshly, peering into the dark. "What are you doing here?"

She reached out at a dim figure before her and yanked it closer.

"You're not Emily. You're —"

"Jessica," said Jessica.

"Jessica?" said Emily, crawling into view.

For one ghastly moment Helen wondered if Emily and Jessica had been spying on her.

"Jessica." Emily was whispering. "Come on, what are you doing with my mom?"

"Emily!" said Helen in her stern, loud, obedience-training voice. "*What* are you doing?"

"Shh. Mom! Shhh!" The girls lay flat on the sand. "We're playing capture the flag," Emily whispered. "You'll ruin it.

The other side will find us. Go away. What are you doing here, anyway? Hi, Johnny."

"Come on, Emily," Jessica hissed, and they disappeared into the mist.

Helen and Johnny walked back to the car without speaking. Helen turned on the headlights. Two little girls crawled on the sand before them, illuminated in the sudden circles of light.

———

They lay one night in the master bedroom of Johnny's house and Helen looked around at the private adornments of another family's life. Vivian used the same moisturizer Helen did. Stacks of *New Yorker*s lay beside the bed. The pictures in their charming frames gathered on the dresser were remarkably like the pictures in charming frames on Helen's dresser. There were photographs of Johnny at the beach, some Caribbean beach, as a little boy; of Vivian holding her toddler on her lap; of Johnny between both parents, the three of them posed and smiling.

Here we are on Mark and Vivian's bed, Helen thought. Naked on the parents' bed. Just like high school.

"Helen," Johnny murmured. His head was pressed against her stomach, and she could hardly hear him. She stroked his hair, moving it away from his face, tucking it behind his ears. How beautiful he looks, she thought.

"Helen, my parents are coming home."

High school, high school. Just like high school.

"Next week."

She ran her finger along his cheekbone. She touched his lips.

"Helen, they're coming home. Don't you get it?"

"I get it," she said. She pulled him up to her. His hair

had grown over the summer. It nearly reached his shoulders. She felt strands of it between her face and his. She put her arms around him, held him on top of her. "I get it," she said.

"We'll never see each other. We can't see each other here anymore, that's for sure. Not in this house. Oh God, this house is such a fucking mess. They'll kill me. I'll never get it cleaned up. Helen, can't we just run away?"

"So you don't have to clean the house?"

He burrowed his face into the spot he liked, the curve of her neck. She could feel his breath. His lips were pressed, moist, against her skin.

"Yes," he whispered.

When Helen reached for her running clothes for the trip back home, Johnny was lying on his back with his eyes closed.

"I hate it when you go," he said.

She turned away. You're so beautiful to look at, she thought. Your beauty is overpowering. To leave you is a physical act that has nothing to do with getting up and walking out a door. Tearing, yanking, wrenching. Those are the verbs. The gerunds, rather. Are they gerunds? Sometimes I forget. I don't want to forget. I don't want to leave you. Not for a moment. I don't want to pull this shirt over my head. I don't want to run home and sleep in a bed that you're not in.

"They're coming back just in time for my birthday. My twenty-first birthday."

"That's right — twenty-one. Happy birthday! Should we go and drink legally or something? Does this mean I'm no longer committing statutory rape? I'm afraid the thrill is gone."

"They want to give me a party. Will you come?"

Mark and Vivian Howell were giving their child a birthday party. How sweet. How wholesome. How could she possibly face them? "Do you really want me to come?"

"Yes. Bring your mother and grandmother. The more, the less embarrassing. And Kelly and Jennifer, Lucy, Miss Skattergoods, Barry, Eliot . . ."

She turned to look at him. He was still on his back, his arm over his eyes. She took his hand and kissed it.

"Helen, what will we do?" he said.

"I don't know."

"What do people do whose parents didn't go away in the first place?"

Helen stood up. "I don't know. Go to sleazy motels, I guess."

He rolled over and put his arms around her legs. She felt his words against her thighs. "Can we go to a sleazy motel?"

"Yes, darling," she said. "We can go to a sleazy motel. Of course we can."

⸺

Johnny and Kelly opened up the store the next morning, then sat on the floor behind the counter so that if anyone looked in, they would think no one was there and go away.

"Ugly day," Kelly said. "It's so muggy." She looked up at the ceiling fan. "Twenty-one. You've reached your majority. Very nineteenth century." She kicked his foot with her own. "You'll come into your money."

"I wish." He looked at her, blond and buxom and chewing on her lip. It would be so much easier if he were in love with Kelly. "I can't believe my parents are coming home," he said. "I can't believe they want to have a birthday party. You'll come, right? We'll have hats, just like Emily."

"I told you I'd come. Why are you making such a big deal

about it? I think it's nice of your parents. I'll get you a present and everything."

Johnny drank the coffee he'd gotten next door. He read the note Helen had left for them. Check the pile of white cards, the special orders. Check the green cards, which were removed from the last copy sold and meant they had to reorder. Check this list, make that list, shelve the hardcovers piled on the counter, fold and store the empty boxes so they can be recycled. Wash the windows. Why didn't she computerize the store? he wondered. A computer could do almost everything on this list. Not the windows, it was true; not the boxes or the shelving. But all those lists, surely. Helen had a computer at home, an absurdly powerful and up-to-date machine that she used only to install new software and hardware to make it even more powerful and up-to-date.

"So, what do we do first?" Kelly said, leaning over, trying to read the note upside down.

Written on a sheet of yellow legal paper with a felt-tipped pen, the blue lines of Helen's small, angular penmanship made him smile. There was so little time before his parents came back. So little time together. Every trace of Helen should be gathered and stored. He held the sheet of paper and read the list again. It was Helen's handwriting, true, but the note itself was so neutral. He read it several times, searching for something. For some communication, he thought. That's what letters are for. But here there were only instructions. No joke, no hint, no private word appeared. Nothing for him. He crumpled it in his hand.

"Johnny!"

He shrugged and unfolded it. He looked at the creases and thought of the love letter, the wrinkled letter he'd seen in Helen's bag. This was not a love letter. His name was on top. Helen's was on the bottom. But there was nothing in between.

Kelly took the yellow paper out of his hands. "What is your *issue*?"

"Sorry," he said. He smiled so she wouldn't think he was completely insane.

"Whatever. Let's just get going before the she-hound gets here. You do the boxes, okay?"

Johnny gathered up the cardboard boxes Helen had left strewn around the store. As he started down the steps to the basement with them, he heard a customer come in.

"I'm sorry hello?" she said. "You disturb me."

"Oh, hi, Theresa," Kelly said. "I guess everyone's a little edgy today."

—

Johnny used his day off to clean the house. He started in the kitchen, working his way slowly through the rooms, saving the gray bathtub for last. Helen stopped by to bring him a sandwich, and they had a quick, exciting, uncomfortable fuck against the kitchen counter. But she did not offer to stay and help clean, he noticed. He scrubbed on in lonely determination, hating all adults.

—

Johnny's house stood on a hill. On the evening of the birthday party, the last rich hush of sunlight rested there and the white house glowed. The lawn sloped down to an unmown meadow, stopping suddenly at the taller, wild grasses. Three trees, very old, grew beside the house. A rope swing hung from one, and for a moment Helen allowed herself a pang of tenderness, until she realized it was not Johnny's, had never been Johnny's, that he had moved to this house having already passed the age of swings.

She followed her mother, a flurry of energy surrounded by smoke, and her grandmother, a vision of elegance in a pair of trousers and a jacket of so up-to-date a cut and hue that Helen could not imagine how Eleanor had had time to get them.

"So unusual," Grandma Eleanor was saying. "Such character, such high caliber. When a young man invites an old lady like me to his twenty-first birthday party, well, that tells you something about what kind of a person" — she paused and tilted her hat, a moss green fedora — "what kind of person *I* am."

"Mother, you're disgusting."

"I'm just honest."

Lilian, about to respond, saw Miss Skattergoods approaching and merely shook her head in dismissal before striding off to greet her.

"One down," Helen said. "Come on, Grandma. Let's go drink like the goyim." This was Grandma Eleanor's phrase, to drink like the goyim, and her only conscious affirmation of either Judaism or the Yiddish language. She herself could drink with the best of them, but because she always characterized this activity as drinking like the goyim, a proclivity she as Jew could not share, it didn't really count.

With her grandmother beside her jauntily swinging her cane, Helen made her way across the flagstone terrace to a table serving as the bar. She accepted her gin and tonic from a boy about Johnny's age. He barely noticed her, and without thinking she put her hand gently on his arm so that he looked up, into her eyes. "Thank you," she said. It was all she said, but it was enough. He grinned. A streak of color appeared on each cheek. She was satisfied and moved on.

I'm horrible, she thought, but turned back to glimpse him watching her. I really am horrible, she thought. And proud of it.

While Grandma Eleanor allowed Kelly to try on her hat, Helen chatted with Janet, who related the latest blind dates in her collection. She claimed that one of them was so short and had such little arms that the three buttons on the cuff of his blazer reached his elbow.

"I stared at them all through dinner. I wonder, Helen, can you fix me up with any unsuitable men?"

"*Un*suitable?" Helen said. "Surely you can find more of those on your own." She scanned the crowd for Johnny. "I always have."

"Well, it's just that I read that after you're divorced you have to go out with a hundred men before you find the right one, and I'm only up to forty-one."

Helen saw Johnny's father, Mark, approaching them.

"So," Janet said, "I wouldn't want to go out with Mr. Right right now, would I? It would be a waste. Do you think having dinner with, say, George would count?"

"How about Mark? Shall we ask him?"

"I guess married friends would be cheating," Janet said.

"I guess."

"You're no help, Helen." She moved on in her modest quest.

Tall and bearded, Mark Howell was imposing, bearish, and handsome, with a magnificent voice. He reached Helen with his hand already proffered. His appearance always created an expectation of something grand, and his sonorous greeting furthered that. But he was rather shy, and so often disappointed people. "Well, well, Helen!"

Helen shook his hand, thinking how much he reminded her of a cello, a cello forever tuning up. His hand felt nothing like Johnny's. She thought of Johnny's large, smooth hands, his quick handshake. Do you look like Johnny? A little. Pushed-in nose. Eyes? She'd never noticed Mark's eyes before.

"You have such blue eyes," she said. Oh, Helen, don't start, she thought. But she had instinctively begun doing what came easiest to her. She watched herself as she threw her arms around Mark's neck. She couldn't stop herself. She kissed him. "I never realized," she said.

She recognized her success instantly. All Mark said was, "Well, well." But Helen knew the signs. She had flattered him, she had interested him in himself through her, she had made him aware of her in relation to him. She had flirted.

I'm flirting? she thought. I'm fucking flirting with Johnny's father? It's hideous. A disease. I don't even mean it. I never mean it. But at the same time, she congratulated herself. She enjoyed her little success of the moment. He was surprised, he was flattered. He was another conquest. It was harmless, after all. Warm, friendly. She looked for Johnny and felt unsteady, giddy, as if she needed to hang on to something. She put her hand on Mark's arm, then withdrew it.

"Of course, they're not at all like Johnny's eyes," she said.

See that? That's all it took. Amazing. I've spoiled the whole effect. She watched Mark's reaction with a mixture of amusement, annoyance, and delight in her own expertise. I've broken my own spell. I've awakened my victim.

"Thank you for lending me your son," she added, offering the salve of paternal flattery. And he smiled comfortably in response. They were back where they belonged, two parents talking about kids and summer jobs.

"Oh, you're quite welcome," Mark said.

It was the first she had seen of Mark since his return,

but she had spoken to him on the phone. He had thanked her then, saying Johnny seemed more mature, more responsible. "You've given him quite an education in that store," Mark had said. And Helen had replied, "Oh, yes, well, he's such a fast learner, so enthusiastic, energetic, willing to jump right in." Afterward, shamed, she'd gone to bed with a headache.

"Johnny knows so much about Pequot," Helen said. "I've never paid any attention to the town. Couldn't wait to get out as a teenager. It's a little embarrassing to have a twenty-year-old, well, twenty-*one*-year-old, as a guide."

But Mark's minuscule small talk quotient seemed to have been filled, and he boomed out a mellifluous, "Odd hobby," and shuffled away.

"I gave Johnny his knife," Lucy said, coming up beside her.

"Oh, good. Where is he? I haven't even seen him."

"He liked it, as I knew he would. I think I'll get you one, too. Everyone should have a knife."

Johnny stood beside his mother, whose hand rested on his arm as she gestured with the other.

"It was beautiful there," she said to Barry and Eliot, whose civilian clothes managed to look just like their gym clothes. "Hills, rolling hills covered with wildflowers. Not at all what I expected of Texas."

"What did you expect?" Eliot asked.

"Dust," said Barry. "Cowboys."

"Yes," Vivian said. "Dust."

Johnny looked at her small hands, manicured, polished as they always were, as they always had been. He had caught a glimpse of Helen before and now tried to look for her without actually craning his neck. I'm twenty-one, he thought, and I might as well be twelve.

Helen saw them then, saw Barry giving Johnny a gift, saw Johnny looking for her, saw his mother standing protectively beside him, saw her hand on his arm. You held him when he was small enough to carry on your shoulder, Helen thought. You cradled him in your arms. You smoothed back his damp hair at night. You kissed his soft, child's cheek as he slept. You heard his breath, the murmur as he stirred, as he settled back with a sleepy smack of his lips, a sigh.

"Happy birthday," Helen said.

Johnny grinned the way he had all those weeks ago, that day on the beach. Helen remembered his sandy fingers stretched out toward her, offering a section of an orange. She thought of the orange and then of her letter. She often thought of her letter, bits of it, like snatches of song. When you go to school, Johnny, will you write me a letter? Send it by E-mail. Ram.Boy@College to Nearly.NAMBLA. I'll send you a postcard.

He opened the package from Barry and Eliot. It was a flannel shirt, and Johnny seemed genuinely pleased. How did they think of that? Helen wondered. Every idea for a present had seemed wrong to Helen, insufficient or grandiose.

Johnny thanked the two men, then turned to Helen.

"Whadya get me?" he said.

"A book."

"Whadya get me?" Vivian said.

"A jackknife. Lucy says everyone should carry one."

"*Really* what did you get me?" Johnny said.

"It's a surprise." A surprise to me, too, she thought. "'Happy Birthday, Johnny, live beyond your income, travel for enjoyment, follow your own nose.' That's from an Auden poem."

She wondered whether she was showing off for her lover or trying to establish her distance from him in front of his mother. Auden wrote the poem to a seven-year-old, after all.

"Those are the only lines I remember. Even though the poem rhymes."

"I hope Johnny didn't drive you crazy all summer," Vivian said. "Was he civilized?"

"Oh, he was wonderful. Didn't shave his head or pierce his nose or get a tattoo or any of those things employees feel they have to do these days."

Vivian began to tell her about the wildflowers in Texas, the legacy of Lady Bird Johnson, and Helen thought of what she had to prune in her own garden and watched Johnny watch her. Did he look like his mother? They had the same color hair, dark, dark brown glinting with red in the sunlight. Vivian's mouth turned down, like Johnny's. Helen saw Johnny's mouth, his lips moving, pursing, spreading apart, coming together. Was he speaking? She saw the curve of his neck, his slender shape. He was barefoot. She saw his feet.

"Johnny," she said suddenly.

There was silence. Helen knew she was the one meant to fill it. She had spoken, called out his name. She looked at Johnny. He stared back at her. In the glow of the setting sun, he had gone pale. Vivian waved to someone. Johnny took a step toward Helen. Vivian turned back to them.

"Helen, are you all right?" she said. "You look a little wan."

"Fine," Helen said quickly.

"Wan?" Johnny said.

"No one's ever called me wan before," Helen said. "Sounds so romantic. Like veranda."

"I guess so," Vivian said.

"Well. Johnny — I just remembered something. The store. Can I speak to you for a minute? Just take a second."

"Oh, go ahead," Vivian said. "I've got to mingle now, anyway. Where's your mother, Helen? I want to meet her."

Helen looked around at the figures silhouetted against the pink sky but could not find Lilian. "She went off with Johnny's great friend, the patrician librarian. But I don't see her either. There's my grandmother, though. Grandma, this is Johnny's mother, Vivian Howell. This is my grandmother, Eleanor Lasch."

"Come on," Johnny said. "Come with me while I get some more ice."

But when they got to the kitchen, Johnny put down the ice bucket, grabbed Helen's hand, and pulled her to the back stairs, the same dark, rickety stairs they had gone up that first time when Johnny had been wet and half naked, when he'd kissed her. Now he kissed her on the stairway, pressing her against the wall. His lips are not like his father's, she thought. His lips are not like his mother's.

He whispered, "I love you," and she held him and closed her eyes and felt gentle relief. She buried her face in his neck, in the scent of Neutrogena soap. How sweet that he used Neutrogena. Her first boyfriend had, too. She felt her body relax, though she had not realized it was tense. She let herself be held by him in the dark stairwell and let herself hear him say I love you.

Then it was still. In the stillness, in that moment, Helen heard a noise. She opened her eyes to see someone, no, two people, embracing in the gloom on the steps above them.

She pulled away from Johnny. "Oh, shit."

"Shit!" said one of the shadowy figures, a woman's voice,

and the two stepped away from each other and quickly retreated back up the stairs.

"Shit, shit, shit," Helen said. She pounded her fist against the wall. "I can't stand this," she said. "I have no time with you. Horrible people are everywhere, interrupting. I hate them." She called up the steps, "Fuck off!"

"Hey, Helen —" He took her hands. He held them too tightly.

"I have to see you. Think of some excuse," she said. "We'll get out of here. Just for a few days. A few days together."

———

Johnny told his parents he was taking a little road trip by himself. He'd been working all summer, he said. He needed a break. Yes, they said. You've worked all summer. You *deserve* a break. Helen said she was going to a spa, the kind of trip her mother could readily understand. Emily was spending the week with her father, and Lucy would mind the store, tending the customers with her blue-blooded indiscretion ("Oh, yes, *this* book. Are you an alcoholic, then?"). Helen and Johnny met at a parking garage in a small, gloomy city half an hour east of Pequot. Johnny left his car there and joined Helen, who sat at the wheel of her station wagon, having convinced her grandmother to relinquish it temporarily.

"A door is ajar," the car said.

"A door is not a jar," Helen said, and then they drove, hardly speaking, the silence intimate, the long hours a gentle, welcome pretense, as if they had all the time in the world.

They ended up at a bland motel rather than a squalid one. It was near the shore, and when Helen turned off the motor, they could hear waves crashing on the rocks. She went to the desk herself, leaving Johnny behind in the car. Neither of them discussed this. They just did it that way, both suddenly self-conscious. Helen gave her credit card to a young man not much older than Johnny and wondered what he would have thought if Johnny were standing by her side.

In the room, they clung to each other as if these were their last moments together.

Which they are, Johnny thought. For days they hardly left the motel, taking an occasional walk on the beach, eating at a nearby lobster pound.

Helen woke up during the first night and looked over at him beside her and wondered why he wasn't always beside her. She had imagined him there, just like this, so many times. She touched him, ran her hand across his forehead. He opened his eyes and kissed her and held her in a half-conscious embrace.

"Do you think we'd still like each other if we lived together?" she asked him the next morning.

He hesitated.

"No," she said. "I know. You're right. I'd make you make your bed."

"I never said that."

"I did."

Johnny didn't answer. He didn't want to talk about what they should do, what they could do, about a future so awkward and comic and tragic. He asked her no questions, made no demands, no complaints or entreaties. He had put his watch away in a drawer so he wouldn't feel the time pass. He listened to the sound of her breathing. He inhaled the closeness of her. He felt that here, at least, Helen was his.

"Here, at least, you're mine," he said, and she smiled, and said, "Yes. I am," and they spent most of the next four days in bed, pressed desperately against each other.

Johnny sensed Helen's body even now, as she drove her car south on the highway. The air he breathed was hers, was part of her. There's nothing else, Johnny told himself. Nothing.

They stopped to eat at a dreary "family-style" restaurant, and Johnny looked at Helen across the table. Her face was tired and sad and content. You're lovely, he thought.

"Why won't you let me drive?" he said. "At least a little. It's such a long way."

"Insurance," Helen said. She tried to sound convincing. He was looking at her so tenderly. But he immediately frowned, and said, "Yeah, right," in just the sarcastic tone Emily used.

"I always drive," Helen said.

Later, in the car again, Johnny said, "This is impossible." To go home, he thought, to live separated from Helen, fenced off by his age, his family, fenced off by Helen herself. "It's impossible."

"It's inconvenient," she said.

"Let's tell them." But even as he said it he knew it couldn't happen. Which them? There were so many, all pieces of the puzzle into which he and Helen could not fit.

Helen sighed. She took his hand, held it to her cheek, then kissed it.

"Let me fucking drive," Johnny said.

Helen put her hand back on the wheel.

16 ✓ ✓ ✓ ✓ ✓ ✓ ✓ ✓ ✓ ✓ ✓ ✓

JOHNNY LEFT THE DAY BEFORE LABOR DAY. THEY
gave him a party at the store, just Helen, Lucy, and the girls,
at which they all got drunk. Privately, the next day, Helen
gave Johnny his birthday present — a small gold ring with
a garnet in it. It had been her grandfather's. She didn't know
if he would wear it. It seemed unlikely, actually. She didn't
even know if he would like it. The ring was so old-fash-
ioned. But it was somehow necesssary for her to give it to
him. She had often worn it herself, and he said, "This is
yours," very softly, and put it on his finger.

"I know you really wanted a book," she said.

"A letter."

The next day he was gone.

—

Helen drove to the store, past the curves of her accident,
and hoped Johnny would call her. She would have tele-
phoned him, just to see how he was settling in, but he
hadn't known his new number yet. For two days, each time
the phone rang at home, Helen hoped it was Johnny. At the

store she picked up the first call on the first ring, and said, "Horatio Street Books," with a new, uneasy, eager tone. But it was only a man asking for the Everyman's edition of *The Canterbury Tales*. She recommended and sold a copy of a novel to a woman to whom, she later realized, she had already recommended and sold the same book six months earlier. She wondered if that was an accomplishment or a blunder and hollered at Jennifer for forgetting to sweep the front walk, then went home early with a headache.

The next morning his letter was waiting at the store, buried in a pile of fresh flyers and checks and bills. Johnny is hundreds of miles away, she thought, and held the letter close to her lips, as if that helped. The letter said he knew she loved him. It said he loved her. It said they were fools not to do something about it.

I am transferring to Columbia. I want to anyway. I miss New York. But I also miss you and have to be closer to you. You think I'll drift back to ordinary, college life, and maybe I will. People do drift apart, whatever their ages, don't they? But I'm not ready to drift anywhere right now without you. I'm not ready to give you up. My senior thesis will be on Pequot, of course. I've already warned Miss Skattergoods. Now I'm warning you — I'll be back. I wish I could write a better letter, a proper love letter. I wish that mysterious love letter had come from me. If you tell me one more time to read *Cheri* so that I know what to expect, I'll throw it out the window. You should have let me drive home when we went away that time. I'm a very good driver. I drive all the time here. I take long, long drives and think of you. Sometimes I think I see you, running. "There's only one face, it's all I see, awake or asleep" — Anonymous. When I eat an orange, when I tie my shoes, as ever, etc. Love, Johnny.

—

That night, arriving home from the store, Helen did not go straight into the house. She went around the back and walked through the garden, past the fruit trees, to the cliff and the sea below. It was windy, warm, not quite dark, and a round moon, deep yellow, hovered on the horizon. A bat flew by. She heard a sandpiper. The sea smell, so brisk yet so summery, made autumn seem far off, impossible, irrelevant, but the leaves were already beginning to fade. She had come to the cliffs to be melancholy. She stood for a moment, then got bored, melancholia being too still a pursuit for her, and she strode back to the house.

She could see Emily's window, lit up, Emily at her desk doing her homework, the portable telephone squeezed between her ear and her shoulder, its antenna sparkling in the lamplight. In the nighttime quiet, she heard Emily laugh. Inside, her grandmother was packing boxes. She was moving to Florida to be near her sister, having taken a large house on the same street as her sister's large house.

"I thought Aunt Lila's house was supposed to be big enough for both of you," Lilian said. "I thought that was the point."

"I need room for you to visit, for Helen, for Emily. You will visit, won't you? And what if I require a nurse? I must have room for my nurse."

Lilian shook her head and picked an LP from the pile she had brought with her.

"I'm glad you still have a turntable, Helen."

"Mm-hmm," Helen said. She sat down on the couch and thought about Johnny. She could see him in the shower, his arms lifted to rub shampoo into his hair. Between the muscles in his shoulders, in the slight hollow that formed there, suds gathered, then slid down his chest. From the other end of the tub she watched as he turned toward the water, his eyes closed, his hair streaming behind him.

"Listen," her mother said. And Helen heard the crackling of an old recording, then strings.

"Brahms," said Lilian. "Sextet. Casals."

Helen closed her eyes, the way her mother always did when listening to music. The piece sounded familiar, one of Lilian's favorites, perhaps. No wonder her mother liked this kind of music. Helen felt the sweetness of losing one's way, of being utterly, magnificently lost. No one ever loved me the way Johnny did, she thought. No one ever looked at me like that, up and down, my hands, my face, into my eyes. What rich, weightless, whole music. What will I do without Johnny to look at me like that? Without Johnny to look at? Without Johnny?

"Now listen to the second movement," Lilian said.

"It's so loud," said Eleanor. "I'm going upstairs."

"Louis Malle used this music in *The Lovers*. Do you remember, Helen? I took you to see it. You were about Emily's age. Your first foreign film. God knows what you made of it."

Helen remembered. Jeanne Moreau was in it. Jeanne Moreau picked up a man whose car had broken down. Took him home to her wealthy husband and big country house. Made love to him in the pond. In the dark. Kissed him with her Jeanne Moreau lips.

The music now sounded almost like a march — a solemn, ceremonial march of passion and urgency. When do we call passion love? When it's desperate, exquisite, enormous? When it's delicate and ephemeral? When it's sacred?

The music claimed that passion was sacred. The music demanded it. Helen began to cry.

Lilian, wiping tears from her own eyes, stood up to turn it off. "The rest of the sextet is not very interesting," she said. "But that second movement."

In the Malle movie, Jeanne Moreau leaves with the stranger the next morning; leaves her husband and her whole life behind. Only the French can do that, Helen thought. In their disconnected movies. Why can't I do that? Do I want to do that? Do I want to leave my life? My family, my child? Why do I have to do that? Because I feel passion? Because it's time to call passion love?

"Helen, let's talk for a minute," her mother said, sitting beside her on the couch. "About Grandma leaving. About me. About you, too, cookie."

Helen put her head on her mother's shoulder. She was still crying a little. Her mother put her arms around her and Helen began to sob.

"It's been wonderful to spend all this time with you, darling," her mother said softly, smoothing her hair, kissing her forehead.

"Don't go," Helen said. "Everyone is going."

"Well, that's what we have to talk about. Look, Helen, I know we don't always confide in each other. But I think —"

"Yes. I do, too. Look, Mom —" Helen determined to tell her, right then. She had to. However shocking it would be. She could no longer live like this, secretive, stupefied by passion and by its denial.

"Mommy —"

But her mother continued talking.

"Life does not always take the turn we expect," Lilian was saying.

"No, and —"

"And love hardly ever does, Helen. You can't choose who you fall in love with, you know. I was very lucky with your father, it was all very conventional, but we also truly loved each other. But sometimes, well, conventions get kicked over, knocked over, do you see what I mean? They fall away because . . ."

Because. Because it's preposterous for a middle-aged woman to fall in love with a boy unless you are that middle-aged woman and you have fallen in love with the boy. Then the thing you scorn as unnatural in someone else seems as normal as the sun coming up each morning, and as miraculous.

"Because," Lilian was saying, "because the conventions have to fall away."

Why is she telling me this? Helen wondered. Does she know? Is she trying to make it easy for *me* to tell *her*? Or is it all theoretical in some way, inspired by the music? The memory of the movie?

"Mom, I'm glad you understand, I'm glad you think that way because I do, too, recently, anyway, and now . . ."

"Helen, I'm moving out next week."

"Oh, Mommy, I know you hate Pequot, but I wish you'd stay longer. I never thought I'd say such a thing. I really have gotten used to you, and right now especially I need . . ."

"I'm not leaving Pequot. It is one of the ironies of my otherwise straightforward life that I have fallen in love twice, and each time with someone who insists on living in this town."

"You're —"

"Moving in with Constance."

"Who?"

"Miss Skattergoods, to you. We were together in New York. Well, we never lived together, but, you know."

No, I don't know, Helen thought.

"But then she ran off to Pequot. I still don't understand why. To finish her book, partly."

Book? Miss Skattergoods was finishing a book? Miss Skattergoods's name was Constance? Miss Skattergoods was living with Helen's mother? But not in New York?

"I suppose it was my fault. I'm not very good about these things, settling down, commitment. But when she left, well, I can't actually live without her, you know. So there you are. Mommy's a dyke, Helen."

"Ah."

"She gave me this ring, the one you like so much."

"I don't like it *that* much," Helen said.

"No? I do. Well! That's finished! What was it you wanted to tell me, honey? I can listen to you now. I had to tell the truth finally, though, didn't I?"

"Not really," Helen said. She wondered if her mother and Constance Skattergoods would have one of those embarrassing gay weddings. They could both wear gowns, veils designed by Grandma Eleanor, who could also make an extra-thick, extra-opaque veil for Helen to hide behind.

"Helen?"

"Oh, it was nothing." Nothing compared to this, certainly. All this time she had worried about shocking the world with her affair with a young man while her mother was sleeping with an old woman. Helen was mortified. Her secret was so, so second-rate.

"Oh," Lilian said, kissing her forehead. "I thought you might want to talk about Johnny. I suppose you must miss him, now he's off at college again." She smiled. "Very French, Helen, your affair with him. Constance says he's absolutely besotted. Lovely. I don't suppose anyone else knows about it, do they? But we couldn't really help figuring it out. Will he be back for Thanksgiving? Though I do find it difficult to think that I am the mother of a woman of a certain age. I mean, what does that make me?"

———

My mother is in love.

Helen said this to herself as she unpacked a carton of books at the store. Squatting on the floor, she bent her face into the smell of cardboard, the dim interior of the half-empty box. My mother is in love and listens to Brahms and weeps. The new hardcovers piled up beside her. My mother is in love, enough in love to be in love with a woman. Enough in love to live with a woman. They'll probably join the country club and ride around on one of those golf carts with a sign with their names on it in a couples tournament. LILIAN AND CONSTANCE. Even though they don't play golf. That's how in love my mother is.

The box was empty and Helen sat back on her heels. Jennifer and Kelly were still working for her, even after classes had started up again, and she watched them, one on the phone, the other shelving. She heard Lucy upstairs rolling her chair back and forth. The store was peaceful and orderly and she thought to herself that she might be in love, too, like her mother.

She went upstairs and sat on the desk in front of Lucy, and said, "My mother is in love with a woman."

Lucy looked at her carefully. "Really?"

"Really."

Lucy was silent.

"Miss Skattergoods," Helen said.

"Really!"

"They're going to live together. In Pequot."

"She told you?"

"Mm-hmm."

"She's so open. My mother would never tell me a thing like that."

"Your mother would never *do* a thing like that," Helen said. "I think I'll move to the West Coast. Where no one knows me."

"May I have the store?" Lucy asked.

"Fuck you," Helen said.

"Miss Skattergoods. Well, what do you know."

"More than I want to. Imagine being in love with Miss Skattergoods. Imagine Miss Skattergoods in love with my mother!"

"Imagine being in love," Lucy said wistfully.

I'm in love, Helen thought. I *am* in love.

—

Helen's mother was already packing, getting ready to move in with Constance, as Helen had now been instructed to call her.

"How about Auntie Constance? Isn't that what you call stepmothers?" Helen said. "Or *Maman*? And what should Emily call her? Grandma Skattergoods?"

"Don't be bitter," Lilian said, lighting a cigarette.

"I don't think lesbians are allowed to smoke. Are you a vegetarian now? You'll have to listen to folk music, you know."

—

Miss Skattergoods came by the next day.

"You girls got your PETA memberships in order?" Helen said.

"What's PETA?" Miss Skattergoods said.

"I don't know," Lilian said. "Ignore her."

"People for the Ethical Treatment of Animals," Helen said to Miss Skattergoods. "Shall I call you *Maman*?"

"If you like."

—

Lilian spent that night at Miss Skattergoods's house, and Helen lay in her own bed and thought about how embarrassed she was.

"It's very embarrassing," she told her mother the next day.

"It is, isn't it?" said Lilian, and began humming as she fixed a pot of coffee.

"Sapphists drink tea," Helen said. "Everyone knows that."

—

Miss Skattergoods came to the store that afternoon, and Helen watched her open the door and thought of how many times she had opened the door before, of how Johnny had always run to her assistance, and she thought of Johnny.

"I brought this for you," Miss Skattergoods said.

It was a rather battered copy of Emily Dickinson's *Poems*.

"Isn't this kind of valuable?" Helen said. She looked at the publication date: 1891.

"A little. But it's beat up. Second series. My great-aunt's girlhood copy — the aunt who raised hounds in your store."

"What an unbelievably wonderful gift."

"It's not a gift," Miss Skattergoods said. "It's a bribe."

—

The next day, Miss Skattergoods came to the store again and talked about Johnny, how sweet he was, how smart he was, what a beautiful mouth he had. Helen basked in his name. I always kind of liked Miss Skattergoods, she thought. Her aristocratic plainness, her high New England bearing.

"Johnny is a brick," Miss Skattergoods said. "An excellent drinking companion, you know."

When Miss Skattergoods came by the house that evening to pick up Lilian, Helen went over to her, and said, "Sorry." She held out her hand solemnly. "Okay? *Maman?*"

Miss Skattergoods laughed a rather triumphant laugh.

"*You* never gave me a first edition of Emily Dickinson, Mother," Helen said, carefully leafing through the yellowed pages of her treasure.

"You never called me *Maman*."

———

Yes, yes. All very jolly, Helen thought at the store the next day. Aren't we sophisticated. She had seen her mother pluck a thread off Miss Skattergoods's sleeve, and though her mother had plucked threads off many people's sleeves in the past and it had not been an action remarkable in any way, this time Helen watched and saw that her mother was in love.

And she longed to pluck a thread off Johnny's sleeve. She thought of Johnny's letter and thought of writing Johnny a letter back to tell him he was right, she was in love with him. She would write Johnny a love letter. She went downstairs into the basement, and very softly said, "I love Johnny." She took a pad and pen and sat on the floor beside the folded boxes and the shelves of overstock. "Love's the boy stood on the burning deck trying to recite 'The boy stood on the burning deck.'" Elizabeth Bishop, who labored over a poem for ten years, felt private and free when she wrote letters. Elizabeth Bishop once wrote forty letters in one day, Helen told herself. I'm not even a poet, thousands of whose private letters will be published in a fat volume after my death, so I should feel freer and more private, Helen thought. But no one's letters are private, are they? I saw someone else's love letter. Someone else might read mine. And even if only Johnny reads it, he might find it in his attic one day, twenty-five years from now, and read it again and laugh in embarrassment. And even if Johnny reads it only once, right now, the words would be there, engraved on the paper, no longer just a feeling or a sentiment or even a description, but a record: I love you.

I wonder if that's true, Helen thought. A record. A record of what? Of something slight, perishable, something long gone, a trophy for a local badminton tournament in 1911, the shiny silver cup so forlorn, meaningless. I wonder if I'm afraid of writing it down, *I love you,* so concrete, so eternal. Or if I'm afraid that writing it down won't help, that writing it down will reveal the ephemeral, *I love you,* so fragile.

"I love you," Helen said again in a whisper.

She put back the pad and pen and went upstairs to unpack another carton of new hardcovers. One in particular interested her. It was called *Return to Sender* and might be about letters. It was a mystery by a Violet Shaw Dunston. She was new on the scene, with only one previous book, but that had won an Edgar Award, and Helen hoped to sell a lot of copies of this new one. She looked at the back flap, at a picture of Violet Shaw Dunston. It was Miss Skattergoods.

"Son of a gun." Helen flipped through the book. "That sly fox." It seemed to be about the murder of a mailman, a mailman who knew everybody's business. Miss Violet Shaw Dunston Skattergoods. Auntie Violet Shaw Dunston Skattergoods. And then, toward the end of the book, she saw it. Page 312. A letter, never delivered by the mailman, the clue to the mystery. "Dear Goat," said the letter.

Dear Goat,

How does one fall in love? Do you trip? Do you stumble, lose your balance and drop to the sidewalk, graze your knee, graze your heart? Do you crash to the stony ground? Is there a precipice, from which you float, over the edge, forever?

I know I'm in love when I see you, I know it when I long to see you. Not a muscle has moved. Leaves hang unruffled by any breeze. The air is still.

I have fallen in love without taking a step. When did this happen? I haven't even blinked.

I'm on fire. Is that too banal for you? It's not, you know. You'll see. It's what happens. It's what matters. I'm on fire.

I no longer eat, I forget to eat. Food looks silly to me, irrelevant. If I even notice it. But I notice nothing.

I threw the book out the window last night. I tried to forget. You *are* all wrong for me, I know it, but I no longer care for my thoughts unless they're thoughts of you. When I'm close to you, in your presence, I feel your hair brush my cheek when it does not. I look away from you, sometimes. Then I look back.

When I tie my shoes, when I peel an orange, when I drive my car, when I lie down each night without you, I remain,

As ever,
Ram

Reading the love letter, neatly printed on the novel's page, no creases, no Scotch tape, Helen still thought, This is mine! My love letter. How did Miss Skattergoods find it? Then she realized of course it was she, Helen, who had found it. It had been a page of Miss Skattergoods's manuscript. Miss Skattergoods had sent it accidentally, stuffing it into the envelope with the invitation to the local cookbook writer's reading at the library. The love letter had never been a real letter at all.

Once Johnny had said to her, "You sent me that letter. You left it for me to see. I consider it a letter from you to me, whoever wrote it."

Now thousands of people would read it. Thousands of Goats. Miss Skattergoods was Ram, a writer with a nom de plume (and who could blame her?) who wrote mysteries. She was Helen's mother's girlfriend. They would drive around Pequot in a black Porsche.

Helen stared at the letter, her letter, printed in a book, her letter to Johnny, Johnny's letter to her, Miss Skattergoods's letter, originally a letter to her mother never delivered, perhaps, fallen onto the page of a book. The love letter. She loved Johnny. She loved him when she saw him. She loved him when she longed to see him. She hadn't moved a muscle, taken a step, or blinked. She listened to Brahms and she loved Johnny. She unpacked books and she loved Johnny. It was absurd to love Johnny, impractical and undignified, and she loved Johnny. She read the letter in the book again and realized Miss Skattergoods had not used the entire original. Where was the part about the feuding blood brothers? Where was the dialogue? Helen was outraged. The letter was incomplete. It was not satisfying. Her letter had been altered. Her love letter.

I don't like being dissatisfied, she had always said. It's so dissatisfying. I'll drive, she had always said. A door is ajar, said the car, and of course it was right. I drive all the time here, Johnny wrote, and he was right. I love you, Helen had not written. I don't want to win, Edith Wharton wrote. I want to lose everything to you!

Helen picked up a pen. "Darling," she wrote. It was on a postcard, one with a picture of Pequot's stony beach.

Darling,
Over the edge of the precipice, on fire, forever. I know it, forever.
I see.
I love you.

Forever,
Helen

She didn't read it over, she just sealed the postcard in an envelope, addressed it, and chose a pretty stamp with a painting of bluebells. Then Helen put her love letter beside the other love letter, in the drawer, which she closed and tried to lock. But she seemed to have lost the key.